Bolan committed the landscape to memory

Envisioning the near future with the cold eye of a technician, he calculated the various points of attack and figured out where some of the Cohorts would head when they ran for their lives in the opening moments of the assault. No matter how well-trained these irregular troops were, there were bound to be some who would panic.

A few well-placed shots could boost that panic and spread chaos to the other gunners. Throughout the battle, though, some Cohorts would be able to keep their wits about them and launch a counterattack. The Executioner meant to be ready to shut it down.

The lethal calculations determined the order of battle he would try to follow. But every man in the lodge could affect the outcome. No matter how well Bolan prepared for battle, any bullet could find its mark.

And take him down.

DON PENDLETON's
MACK BOLAN.®

STORM FRONT

A GOLD EAGLE BOOK FROM
W🦅RLDWIDE®

TORONTO • NEW YORK • LONDON
AMSTERDAM • PARIS • SYDNEY • HAMBURG
STOCKHOLM • ATHENS • TOKYO • MILAN
MADRID • WARSAW • BUDAPEST • AUCKLAND

First edition July 2000

ISBN 0-373-61473-X

Special thanks and acknowledgment to
Rich Rainey for his contribution to this work.

STORM FRONT

The history of the world is none other than the progress of the consciousness of freedom.

—Georg Hegel
1770-1831

Some views of freedom are seriously skewed if the notion includes taking up arms against the government. If an attitude adjustment is called for, I'm the man for the job, make no mistake.

—Mack Bolan

PROLOGUE

Sedona, Arizona

Winston Grail's war against the United States government began in a fortresslike jewelry store on Madison Avenue. He was two thousand miles away when it happened, performing a ritual chant with a group of white-robed, blond-haired true seekers who'd come to his Sedona, Arizona, retreat for a week of spiritual and physical enlightenment.

It was two o'clock in the afternoon in Sedona when he led the latest disciples of his Trans Human Evolution Movement through a guided meditation accompanied by music of the spheres. Streams of light prismed through the stained-glass windows of the desert chapel, illuminating the long blond hair that fell to his shoulders, the strong, angular profile and the piercing eyes that looked from face to face, a warrior in monk's clothing taking their measure.

Some looked away. Others locked on to the unyielding gaze of this man who was part Viking, part vicar, hoping to see what he could see. There was a faraway look in his cobalt-blue eyes, but it had nothing to do with spirituality. It was the look of someone about to see a lifelong dream realized.

New York City

IT WAS FOUR O'CLOCK in the afternoon in New York City when followers of another of Winston Grail's movements, a clandestine organization known as Cohort, initiated the assault that had been in the planning stages for years. Now it was time for Cohort to emerge once again and topple the government that tried to exterminate the group more than a decade earlier.

Three men wearing tinted glasses and well-tailored suits that concealed their weapons nodded politely at the armed door guard as he admitted them into the flagship store of the exclusive Etruscan Gem Company chain.

A dark-haired saleswoman in a clinging silk dress smiled at the three men as they strolled past her glass-counter oasis in the center of the store. Her glossy fingernails brushed a thin gold chain that dipped into her neckline like a glittering directional signal for her V-shaped décolletage. She was a perfect model for the men who went to shop there for their mistresses and trophy wives.

At any given time there were millions of dollars' worth of finely cut gems and delicately smithed gold and silver ornaments in the Madison Avenue shop, all watched over by an attractive and professional staff.

These treasures would be the apparent target of the armed squad infiltrating the premises. The real target was the head of security for the Etruscan chain, a former FBI team leader who even now was in the back room surveilling the showroom. With him were the secondary targets, two armed couriers who shepherded Etruscan clients and their valuables.

The Cohorts knew the FBI man's work routine, his home address, the ages of his children and the colleges they attended. More importantly they knew about his sterling record with the Bureau and his heroic firefight with the Cohort organization years earlier.

The trio waited for the signal from the Cohort who had arrived ten minutes before them and now stood at a long L-shaped display case by the door, his tall, lean frame looming over one of the glass counters.

Nicholas Chandler wore a country-squire leather cap with a brim that concealed his face from the motion-activated security cameras that were hidden in the overhead track lighting.

His palms were spread out on the glass counter, and he was looking down into a velvet bed of marquise rings, pear-shaped diamonds, Colombian emeralds and black-sapphire lockets.

But Chandler didn't really see the gems. Instead he saw his own reflection in the glass, and for a moment was startled by the cold, haunted eyes that looked back at him. They were eyes that saw too much sorrow, too little joy and a future red with blood.

Chandler knew this moment had been coming for a long time, and in fact he was one of the old guard who nourished the dream of a reborn Cohort rising from the underground. He was also one of the few insiders who knew that Winston Grail, noted philanthropist and New Age media guru, was the guiding light behind the organization.

He exhaled softly and felt the reassuring weight of the silenced 9 mm SIG-Sauer pistol hidden beneath his light calfskin jacket. The weapon was positioned for quick reach in a tearaway holster sewn into the lining. He felt the eyes of his fellow Cohorts upon him, waiting for the war to begin.

Chandler glanced at the armed door guard, then spotted the fifth Cohort sauntering into the alcove.

Henry Rivers was their spotter. He was dressed in a thousand-dollar suit that almost hid his furtiveness. But Rivers was an agitated sort, always moving, ready for flight or fight no matter how he was dressed.

Rivers gave Chandler a brief nod from the other side of the glass. The split-second motion delivered the message that everything was in place. The mobile evac team was on the street, ready to spirit the strike team away, and a fully equipped surveillance van was monitoring police communications and passing on live situation reports to the flesh-colored receiver that Rivers wore in his ear.

Chandler nodded at the three "businessmen," then reached into his jacket and grabbed his gun.

The movement caught the attention of the saleswoman, who gasped and instinctively drew back. It also caught the peripheral vision of the door guard, who spun to face Chandler. But the man's body was moving a crucial second slower than his mind.

As the guard reached for his piece, his fingers fumbled awkwardly with the flap that closed around the revolver's polished wooden grip.

Chandler casually aimed the SIG-Sauer at the shorter man.

The guard moved his hand away from the holster. "Okay," he said. "You've got no trouble from me." He looked into Chandler's eyes and saw a brief measure of pity there. For a moment he thought that he would only be disarmed and disabled.

But the Cohorts had gone there to make a statement.

Chandler fired once.

The sound suppressor masked the explosion as the 9 mm round crashed into the guard's forehead, giving him a third eye and an instant ticket to the afterlife.

The impact of the bullet rocketed him back against a display case, and he spun, clinging to the counter before slowly collapsing to his knees. His life poured out of him in a long brushstroke of blood that painted the glass.

Chandler had one more soul on his conscience, but years ago he'd learned how to carry the weight.

He turned to face the black-haired saleswoman. She sucked in her breath, thinking it was her turn. "Take it all," she said, almost whispering in her effort to remain calm. "Just don't shoot."

"Not unless I have to," Chandler said, studying the fragile woman's eyes. She was still in shock, and that meant she was still unpredictable. She backed away from him until there was nowhere to go and she was trapped by the glass display cases.

"Please," she said, "don't hurt me. I'm only trying to…to…" She stammered incoherently, just a high-heeled step away from succumbing to an instinctive urge to run screaming from the store.

"Do what I say and you'll come to no harm," Chandler promised her, lowering his voice to keep her in check. He needed her alive. At least for a while longer.

He scanned the rest of the surprised customers to identify any others who might present a problem.

The shock of seeing the 9 mm round drilled through a man's forehead had affected them all. From past experience he knew it was impossible to judge what victims would do in a situation like this.

A man in a trench coat edged toward the exit. He stopped suddenly when he saw Rivers staring at him from the other side of the door. The spotter opened his jacket wide enough to reveal a shoulder holster. The man backed away and pressed himself against a wall.

An elderly man who'd been looking at gold watches slowly raised his frail spotted hands over his head. They wavered slightly as he watched Chandler.

The saleswoman at the far counter had lost all interest in the man she'd been flirting with and was now staring in disbelief at the silenced pistol in Chandler's hand. Employee orientation hadn't prepared her for occasions like this. With so many armed guards on the premises, she'd never expected it to happen.

It was quiet for another few moments, as if everyone were afraid to take a breath. Then the Etruscan security squad made its move.

A hidden door, practically seamless with the cream-colored showroom wall, slid soundlessly open. The two armed couriers sprang out behind Chandler, thinking he was a lone gunman and easy prey.

They barely noticed the three men in business suits

who'd turned slightly, not at all surprised by the "ambush," and leveled Skorpion machine pistols at them.

A steady barrage of 3-round bursts jackhammered into both couriers, dowsing them with a stream of 9 mm lead.

The distinctive coughs of the suppressed machine pistols overlapped one another, making it sound like one continuous burst.

The couriers toppled in bloody synchronization, hands falling lifeless at their sides as their weapons dropped to the carpet.

The Cohorts continued to fire even after they fell. Better to kill them three times over than to risk getting wasted by a desperation shot. The sustained fire punched fountains of blood that gathered in dark pools on the floor.

When quiet returned, the customers stared in horror, holding back tears and choking off screams, anything to keep from attracting attention to themselves. A moment ago there'd been only one madman in the store. Now there were four, and each of them had shown no qualms about killing.

The intruders had sprung up from some dark and unthinkable region, denizens of a nightmare world who'd crossed over into their world of privilege.

The shooters acted as if they were in no hurry to leave, as if they were aware of exactly how much time they had to kill. Nor did they worry about anyone coming in from the street.

The suppressors had muffled the sound of their weapons, so no one outside the shop could hear what was going on. It was almost impossible to see inside the store, thanks to the high walls and thin strip windows that sealed it off like a vault from the outside world, and Rivers was still outside, ready to block the entrance to the store in case anyone tried to stroll in.

Chandler reached behind the counter to grab a handful of jeweler's pouches and tossed them to the brunette. "Fill them," he said, "with the best. Don't try to cheat us."

She clutched the pouches to her chest, then took a half step forward and hesitated.

"Do it right now, and you'll have nothing to worry about," Chandler said. He waved the gun toward her, and like a magic wand it prodded her into action. With a delicate and sure hand she scooped emeralds, pearls, diamonds and sapphires into the soft cloth pouches, which he tucked inside his jacket.

Chandler's three-man backup squad carried out their rehearsed roles. One man stepped over the bodies and walked into the hidden room from where the guards had sprung their trap. He kept vigil at a heavy steel door locked tight at the back of the room.

The other two Cohorts worked their way up and down the display cases, shattering the glass with the butts of their machine pistols, then seizing the prizes within.

Little more than a minute later, they had everything they came for. Almost everything.

"Where is he?" Chandler asked the brunette gem handler.

She tugged at the gold string around her neck. "Who?"

"Stackhouse. I know he's here."

"You mean Walter?"

"I mean the head of Etruscan security. Get him out here."

She looked up at a surveillance camera mounted on the side wall.

Chandler followed her gaze. "That's what I figured. Still watching the show on TV." He waved the gun barrel toward the camera for the silent watcher. "You might as well come out now, Stackhouse. We're not leaving until you do."

Chandler waited fifteen long seconds, then heard the sound at the door. It was Rivers. He was rapping his knuckles on the glass, then urgently tapping the back of his wristwatch.

Chandler hurried to the door and opened it a crack.

"We got no time," Rivers said. "There's a SWAT team not even a mile away. Half of them are heading down here."

Chandler shut the door, then charged back to the brunette. In one fluid move he grabbed the back of her long hair, wrapped it around his hand like a rope and tugged hard. The rapid motion jerked her off her feet and pushed her facedown against a glass countertop. She tried to scream, but it came out muffled.

Chandler looked up at the security camera. "This is on your head, not mine," he shouted to the hidden former Bureau vet. He held the pistol an inch from the woman's face. "Ten seconds and she dies, Stackhouse. Then everyone in the store."

The remaining Cohorts silently trained their weapons on the rest of the customers and staff.

A disembodied voice came from one of the hidden speakers in the wall. "This is Stackhouse. What do you want?"

"Come out here. No weapons. No one else."

"I can't do that."

Chandler nodded and looked at the woman. "Sorry," he said. "He can't do that." He pressed the end of the gun against the woman's temple.

"Wait!" Stackhouse shouted. "I'll be right out."

As good as his word, he walked out through the steel door moments later with his hands up and no weapons. Stackhouse was a heavyset man with thick whitish hair, a veteran warhorse.

"All right," Stackhouse said, spreading his hands out in front of him. "I'm here. You can let her go."

Chandler released the woman.

"Now what?" Stackhouse asked.

"Now we take a trip down memory lane," Chandler said. He looked the other man in the eye, waiting for any sign of recognition. The staring contest unsettled the security man, but for all he knew, Chandler was a stranger to him.

"What's this about?" Stackhouse asked.

"It's about some friends of mine," Chandler said. "Friends who aren't around anymore. Thanks to you."

Chandler raised the SIG-Sauer and pointed the muzzle at Stackhouse, then reached forward, almost touching the gully of his neck with the suppressed barrel before he pulled the trigger and ripped a big hole in his throat.

Chandler triggered the SIG-Sauer once more as Stackhouse stumbled backward, drilling him through the heart for good measure. Then he headed toward the exit, shouting for the others to follow.

But the other Cohorts were ransacking the rooms

beyond the steel door, unable or unwilling to hear, turning their killing spree into a shopping spree.

"Let's move, let's move!" Chandler shouted.

The front door of the shop opened behind him and Rivers stood there with one hand cupped to his ear, listening to the receiver. "Hurry it up. SWAT team's a couple of blocks away and coming fast."

As Chandler backed out of the store, Rivers peered inside and saw the sacks of loot left behind by the other Cohorts. He took a step inside.

"Leave it," Chandler said, backing out onto the sidewalk and weaving through the traffic on the street.

Rivers hesitated, but finally obeyed the order. By then he was a few seconds too late.

By the time Rivers reached the sidewalk, four members of the SWAT team were racing down the street. They were in battle gear, armored vests and antiballistic helmets with protective neck curtains, front and back. Rivers ducked back into the alcove and slammed the door behind him.

Chandler watched from the other side of the street, blending in with the crowd that was stunned into silence by the appearance of the SWAT team. Chandler knew he was safe. His inside pockets were full and his weapon was hidden once again beneath his jacket. From behind him he could hear the choppy rhythm of a motorcycle cruising up the street. His ride out of there.

Other Cohort evac vehicles were also in position for the rest of the team, but the operation was falling apart. The cyclists would go away riderless.

The first man from the SWAT team dived into the alcove of the gem shop, nosing the air before him with a submachine gun as he skidded across the ground. Another man approached the door with a shotgun, then fired a door-knocker load into the lock plate. The echoing blast filled the air with splintered metal and shattered glass.

The shotgunner crouched as the second pair of SWAT operatives stood behind him and tossed flash-bang grenades through the opening. Concussive candlepower illuminated the interior of the store.

Three men charged into the blinding maelstrom caused by the stun grenades, shouting at the top of their lungs, "Down! Down! Everyone get down."

Automatic fire erupted from within as the Cohorts opened up. The SWAT team returned fire.

In the fading shower of incandescence, Chandler saw Rivers's form dancing in a bullet-riddled ballet.

Chandler knew he should leave, but Rivers was down and he deserved a payback.

He sprinted across the street and stepped into the alcove behind the SWAT team lookout, who was peering into the store. The man was seeking targets amid the smoke, but he found death instead when Chandler jerked up the back of his helmet and fired the SIG-Sauer point-blank into his exposed neck. He lunged forward into oblivion, sprawling like a welcome mat on the floor.

The firefight echoed from deep inside the store as it progressed into the back rooms.

Chandler backstepped out of the alcove, swung behind the black-clad biker waiting for him on the street, then rode away, followed by a team of riderless cyclists.

The Cohorts inside the store were on their own.

CHAPTER ONE

Hudson Sanctuary, New York State

Mack Bolan lay flat on the ground, his face pressed close to the earth as he scanned the cabins of the Hudson Sanctuary through the Schmidt & Bender scope.

His Accuracy International PM sniper rifle was painted camouflage green. His face was painted with a more temporary camouflage, streaks of clay, brown mud and crushed leaf he'd dug from the ground.

The Executioner's observation post was shrouded in a tangle of fallen trees and brush less than a hundred yards away from the rustic cabin that currently housed his targets. Only one target was visible now. He was leaning against the edge of a bleached-wood picnic table, reaching into the pocket of his faded denim shirt for a cigarette.

He was in his late thirties or early forties, an outdoors type who seemed to be right at home with the woods surrounding the retreat, basking in the sunlight that peeked through the high interlocking boughs. He tried hard to look relaxed, as if he really were one of the dozen or so guests who'd gone there for an authentic retreat from the city.

But it was definitely the same face that had been caught on one of the Etruscan Gem Company surveillance tapes that Hal Brognola showed to the Executioner during his briefing the previous day. At least, it was the same face minus the well-groomed Vandyke beard the man had worn during the shooting spree. Only a trim mustache remained. Whether it had been a fake beard or the man had simply shaved it off during the night, there was no doubt in Bolan's mind this was the same man.

There was a certain quality in the eyes that couldn't be disguised. Yesterday it had been the face of a hunter. Today it was the face of a fugitive. But the eyes were the same. They were the eyes of a survivor who was used to being on both sides of the hunt. The man was casually but carefully searching the woods and the neighboring buildings, as if he were expecting company.

It would be easy for Bolan to take him out now. One trigger pull and the man was dust. But there was the matter of the second fugitive.

These men had been trained well. Except for the communal meals they took with the rest of the attendees in the fellowship lodge—an open-air shelter with a raised platform and several benches—the men were careful not to be in close proximity to each other.

One Cohort always stayed in the cabin while the other patrolled outside. Now and then one of them went out into the light gray sedan parked behind their cabin to listen to the radio for details of their pursuit.

It was sound operational procedure. If Bolan took

out one of the Cohorts, the other one might have time
to escape. Or worse, the remaining Cohort could take
hostages and create a bloody replay of the Etruscan
hit. Besides, the Executioner was tasked with more
than taking them out. If possible, he was supposed to
bring in at least one of them alive so they could add
to the intelligence pool on the Cohort operation.

The raid on the Etruscan shop had been brought to
Hal Brognola's attention by a friend in NYPD. The
Justice Department's honcho had reviewed all of the
briefing material, especially the video surveillance
tapes from the gem shop.

He was looking for familiar faces.

The big Fed had faced the Cohorts before. Until
the previous day they were ancient history, a bad
memory of the days when self-proclaimed revolutionaries ran wild in the streets, masking their looting and
marauding under the guise of politics. Now that threat
was reborn.

Brognola was in charge of putting together a Justice Department task force at the FBI's Strategic Information and Operations Center in Washington,
D.C., to deal with a potential Cohort uprising. At any
given time the SIOC command center on the fifth
floor of the J. Edgar Hoover FBI Building could handle up to five separate terrorist crises.

Bolan had a feeling that Brognola would soon put
the Cohort crisis at the top of the list. The big Fed's
actions were prompted by the deathbed ravings of a
wounded Cohort who claimed this was just the first
of several shots to be heard around the world. The
wounded man said his name was Rivers, and his fingerprints matched a set in Bureau archives.

Rivers had been rushed from the Etruscan Gem Company to a secure hospital facility where the medical staff did its best to keep him alive, treating him like a chief of state whose continued existence was vital to national security. It was no go.

However, before Rivers died in a state of delirium, he gave up solid leads about the resurrected Cohort movement and the upstate sanctuary that was the first stop on their escape route.

Only two Cohorts had shown up at the sanctuary so far. If others arrived, Bolan would call in for backup.

They still had no idea how many Cohorts were involved in the initial assault on the gem company or involved with the new movement.

There'd been reports of a considerable street presence. Several men on motorcycles were definitely involved. And a van had been seen prowling the area, maybe a roving battle station. They'd obviously fielded a lot of men for the operation. Almost as if they had enough men to fight a pitched battle in the street if they wanted to.

If that had been their real objective, Bolan thought.

The consensus of the intel team was that the hit on the Etruscan shop had two objectives. One was to secure more money for Cohort operations. The other was to get revenge against the FBI agent who knocked out the Cohort network more than a decade earlier.

The image of Agent Walter Stackhouse's murder was still fresh in Bolan's mind. It was caught on one of the security cameras that escaped destruction in the firefight. Stackhouse had been drawn into the open and slain in cold blood, totally unprovoked and unnecessary.

The hit had obviously been planned with murderous precision. If not for the Cohort's greed and bloodlust, they could have gotten away without losing a man. As things stood now, two Cohorts were dead and two more had escaped through the back of the Etruscan shop during the height of the gun battle. The apparent leader of the group had vanished into the street with an undetermined number of backup men.

The Cohorts suffered only minor losses compared to the death toll they exacted from the other side. Counting Agent Stackhouse, four Etruscan security men were dead. Two SWAT team members lost their lives in the firefight, and another was critically wounded.

So far the balance was in the Cohorts' favor.

It was time to start evening the scales.

The Executioner waited in the grass and tracked his scope across the row of cabins on the far ridge. He scoped out every inch of the terrain. In case the men got spooked and made a run for it, he had to know their escape route and any areas that could offer cover along the way.

There was a 12-round box magazine in the Accuracy International PM bolt-action rifle, enough to deal with both men if he had to. The barrel of the sniper rifle rested on a bipod spiked into the ground, allowing Bolan to cover the killing field in a continuous tracking motion without taking his eye from the scope. It was designed to allow continuous observation even during recoil so the shooter wouldn't lose any time or targets in the middle of a hot zone.

Right now the killing field was serene.

A few figures strolled along paths that bordered gardens and stone shrines, kicking through clusters of autumn leaves on the trail. The light fall rain had stopped, and most of the guests were emerging from their cabins and mingling with their neighbors.

The only ones who kept to themselves were the two Cohorts. But they would be on the move soon. From the transmitter darts he'd fired into the eaves of the cabin when the Cohorts joined the others for breakfast fellowship, Bolan heard enough to know they were almost at the breaking point.

The Executioner tracked the rifle back to the man in the denim shirt. The guy finished his cigarette, field-stripped it between his thumb and forefinger, then sprinkled the charred remains into the breeze.

As the man went back inside, Bolan put on the thin headset and eavesdropped once again on the Cohort broadcast.

"SEE ANYTHING?" Crews asked when Buck Lucierre stepped back inside the cabin.

"Not much," Lucierre said, frowning at the spindly armed Cohort who was lying on the ladder-back couch by the window. Crews was doing his best to read a spiritual magazine left behind by a previous guest. It wasn't a good match.

Crews was thin but he wasn't frail. The veins that etched through lean slabs of muscle in his forearms were always pumped with adrenaline, ready to propel him into action at a moment's notice. He wasn't someone to trifle with.

Now that Crews was out of the businessman costume they'd dumped in a trash compactor a few miles outside the city, he looked more like his old self—an agitator who found waiting extremely painful, almost as much as reading.

But the spiritual magazine was the only reading material in the Spartan shack, and Crews had clung to it to get him through the restless hours. The front cover showed an angel hovering above an Earth Mother type who had that glazed look so common to seekers of hidden truths. The magazine featured articles on meditation, fasting, vegetarian pathways to higher spirituality and the power of prayer. Crews studied it as if it were a foreign language he could never hope to master.

Lucierre sat on the wooden rocking chair by the window and glanced out at the bench he'd been sitting on moments earlier. Then he looked beyond the bench into the woods. The tree line was an impenetrable mosaic, and though he couldn't see anything out of order, there was something out there. Or soon would be. He could sense it.

"Well?" Crews asked. "What did you see?"

Lucierre shook his head. "Nothing to see."

"You said 'not much' when you came in," Crews reminded him. "That means you saw something."

Lucierre sighed. "Figure of speech, that's all. There's nothing out there."

"That's a good sign," Crews said.

"I guess."

"So maybe no one else is coming." Crews tossed the magazine on the floor and sat up on the bunk. "What do you think?"

"Maybe no one made it out except us," Lucierre

suggested. "Not much on the radio. Cops aren't giving much out except the usual bullshit. They're pursuing leads."

"Yeah." Crews rapidly nodded his head, pouncing on his next paranoid thought. "What if those leads are pointing right here at God's private acre? And what if some of these religious freaks are watching us, Buck? I swear, they give me the creeps. I don't trust them."

Lucierre shook his head. He didn't feel like hearing another rant from Crews. The man simply couldn't understand anyone who didn't think like he did. His thought process was pretty basic. Hit the other guy first and take what you can. Life was simple for him, deadly for the other guy.

"I mean," Crews continued, "these people are so freaking nice it ain't natural. Everyone smiling at you all the time. Nodding their heads and bowing at you like we're all part of one big happy family. Or else they get that starry-eyed look on their faces. I'm telling you, they're out of their minds. No one can be that peaceful."

"Tell you what," Lucierre said. "I'll pass out a few handguns at the next fellowship gathering. If you pray hard enough, maybe someone will take a shot at you. That make you happy?"

"It just might," Crews said. "Better than sitting around here painting bull's-eyes on our heads." He tossed the magazine aside and swung his feet onto the floor. Then he leaned forward and rested his elbows on his knees, clasping his hands together in a double fist. "I'm telling you, Buck, all this waiting's driving me crazy."

"You want to do something useful?" Lucierre asked. "Go outside and take a hard look around. Beat the bushes and see what you turn up. If you see anything at all moving in the brush—man or beast—shoot the hell out of it and then we'll haul ass out of here."

THE MATTE-BLACK SNOUT of the Beretta 93-R scanned the wooded horizon, following the progress of the Cohort.

Bolan moved almost parallel with the man, hanging back just enough to keep out of the immediate field of view.

The Cohort made no effort to disguise his presence. He moved haphazardly through the forest, tramping through the brush as if he were seeing what he could scare up. He waved the Skorpion machine pistol before him in a constantly moving arc, searching for targets.

The Cohort turned suddenly toward Bolan.

The Executioner froze in the shadows and prepared to take him out. He'd planned on waiting a while longer to see if any others showed up at the sanctuary, but he'd also planned on staying alive.

The Executioner tightened his finger on the trigger.

But then the Cohort won a reprieve. He lowered the Skorpion to his side, turned and walked back toward the cabin.

CREWS RETURNED to the cabin less than a half hour after he went on his patrol. The tight look on his face showed that he wasn't alone. He was dragging ghosts and paranoia with him. "Something's wrong," Crews announced.

"What?" Lucierre asked.

Crews shook his head. "I can't swear it, but it feels like something was shadowing me every minute I was out there. You felt it, too, when you were out there, didn't you?"

"Yeah," Lucierre said. "I did."

"You know, this was just supposed to be the regroup site if there were no hitches," Crews said. "If you ask me, we had about two hundred rounds' worth of hitches, right on Madison freaking Avenue. Talk about snafu."

Lucierre reached inside his pocket for another smoke. "Plans change," he said. "No way we could move south with half of NYC's finest on our ass. We had to come see what's what. The others could be dead, could be still trying to get here. We're lucky we got here."

Once they'd spilled out of the back of the Etruscan shop, they'd stolen one car at gunpoint and abandoned it a mile away. Two stolen cars later, with the last one taken from a long-term parking lot at an Amtrak station, they were sixty miles north of the city. They'd arrived at the retreat just in time for evensong meditation.

"We been here too long with no one showing up," Crews said. "Don't you think?"

It was always this way, Lucierre thought. He led and Crews followed. Before they hooked up with a Cohort cell a year ago, Crews looked to him to make the decisions. Even after carrying out a few Cohort gigs, Crews still took his marching orders from

Lucierre, though they both played along with Chandler as if he were the ultimate lawgiver.

"Time to move," Lucierre said. "If anyone comes now, it might be someone we don't want to see. Maybe the law. Maybe Chandler."

Crews nodded. "He strikes me as a guy who doesn't like to leave any loose ends around. That's you and me, Buck, two loose ends waiting to be tied."

Lucierre picked up his machine pistol, then wrapped it in his khaki jacket. There were more weapons in the trunk of the car, stashed with the gold and diamond pieces from the Etruscan take. "You're right," he said. "Two loose ends with a fortune in stones. Let's go."

THE COHORTS LEFT the cabin separately.

Bolan tracked the man in the denim shirt who strolled to the car as if he didn't have a care in the world. The man climbed into the driver's seat, drummed his fingers on the steering wheel and waited for his partner.

The partner didn't come out until a trio of women walked along the path that ran by the cabin, inhaling the scent of the woods and marveling at the peace that could be found here. The thin man stood in the doorway and watched them pass, paying particular attention to a college-age young woman with long straw blond hair, obviously wanting to commune with her in a most unspiritual way.

Bolan lowered the sniper scope as the women passed the cabin. He wasn't going to move against the two Cohorts now. Especially when it could endanger innocent civilians who'd come to the sanctuary to think about God, not meet him up close.

He folded the bipod and placed the rifle in its camouflage case. Then he tossed the rest of his gear into his carryall, which carried an assortment of weaponry to get him through the mission. He was ready for long-range or up-close combat, whatever was called for.

Keeping low to the ground, Bolan backed away from the edge of the woods, then jogged downhill through leaf-strewn brush and a minefield of slippery rocks.

At the bottom of the hill, a back road followed a tributary of the Hudson River. Hidden beneath a leafy overhang on the side of the road was a pale green four-door sedan he'd driven up from the city.

The Executioner tossed his gear onto the front seat, switched on the ignition, then eased the boxlike car down through the woods toward the access road.

He was a quarter mile from the T-shaped junction when the Cohort car cruised by, well below the speed limit. They were playing it safe. So would he.

Bolan waited until they were almost out of sight before he pulled out after them.

The sanctuary was only a short ride from the thruway. Bolan trailed them from a safe distance until he saw them drive through one of the northbound toll booths. He rolled through the adjacent toll booth, took his ticket, then followed them.

After driving northbound for a few miles, Bolan reached over and tapped the dashboard compartment that hid his encrypted satcom gear. A sleek black tray slid out from the dashboard with a slight whirring sound. He punched a series of numbers on the embedded transceiver keypad that connected him to Hal Brognola.

"This is Striker," Bolan said, when Brognola came on the line. "We've got a situation." He gave the big Fed a quick rundown. The Executioner didn't want to bring in any other agencies unless it was absolutely necessary, but he didn't want to risk losing his prey. They were the only leads to the rest of the Cohorts.

"I'm ahead of you on that, Striker," Brognola said. "I've already made contact with our liaison in the BCI."

Bolan listened to the arrangements Brognola had made with the Bureau of Criminal Investigation, the undercover unit of the New York State Police that frequently worked with federal agencies. They had an aviation unit and a plainclothes task force standing by.

"They're ready if need be," Brognola said. "They just don't know exactly what to be ready for. It's up to you to fill them in, Striker. If you need them."

Bolan knew what Brognola meant. If possible, he was to complete the mission on his own. But if it was necessary, he was to call in the BCI. After all, the operation was going down in their territory. State trooper stations were located all along the thruway, and once the shooting started they had to know who the bad guys were.

The soldier listened to the names and numbers Brognola supplied him, committed them to memory, then broke the connection and concentrated on his driving.

He hung back in the traffic flow and managed to

keep the Cohort vehicle in sight until it made a last-minute swerve that cut across two lanes. The gray sedan roared up a winding road that led to a wooded rest area. No restaurants, no crowds, no witnesses.

They were seeing if anyone was following them.

Bolan had no choice. If he kept going north on the thruway, the two Cohorts could lose him without even trying.

He pulled into the far right lane and drove up the serpentine road that snaked into the rest area. It was flanked on the left by a grassy ravine and a thin strip of woods. On the right was a ribbon of deep forest.

It was a perfect ambush site.

As Bolan took the final turn, he spotted the Cohort car parked at an angle fifty yards ahead, its nose pointing at a few empty picnic tables and a wall of trees.

The vehicle was empty. The Cohorts were out there in the woods somewhere, waiting for him or making a run for it. He dismissed the second alternative. These guys weren't the type to run from a fight.

The Cohorts had either made him, or else their paranoia got the better of them and they were going to take anyone who got a little too close. The shadow game was over, and he was in the line of fire.

Bolan stomped the brake pedal and spun the steering wheel hard to the left. With a screech of burning tires, the car skidded at an angle and fishtailed down the road.

A blizzard of metal rain pounded into the passenger side of the car. Rhythmic 3-round bursts chopped into the reinforced armor and stitched the full length of the vehicle.

Full-auto fire hammered into the windshield as the second gunner joined the ambush. Small pockets of antiballistic glass imploded from the steady fusillade. It wasn't bulletproof, just bullet resistant.

By the time the windshield collapsed under the next burst of fire. Bolan was rolling downhill, holding the Beretta 93-R close to his chest, one hand on the barrel and the other on the grip. He'd jumped through the door and rolled into the ravine just moments after screeching to a stop.

The earth rose up hard, knocking the wind out of him and jarring his teeth together. He stayed perfectly still for a moment to get his breath and check himself to determine whether anything was broken.

Bolan lay flat on his back, wedged into a crevice at the bottom of the gully. Several inches of swamp water and decaying leafy matter seeped into his shoulders.

Without consciously realizing why he was doing it, the soldier arched his neck and held the Beretta 93-R a few inches from his face.

The barrel of the weapon pointed skyward toward the top of the gully. His subconscious mind had taken over during his fall and deciphered the sounds of pursuit. Now his conscious mind picked up the rapidly approaching footsteps scuffling on the pavement.

A gunman's head appeared.

The rail-thin Cohort angled toward the open door of the car, his Skorpion machine pistol leading the way. Then, as if he were aware he was being watched, the gunner suddenly glanced down. He looked right into the Beretta's muzzle, and jerked his head back a split second before Bolan pulled the trigger.

The first round burned a bloody red furrow along the side of his head, the second and third ripping into his checkered plaid shirt.

The Cohort spun in an awkward ballet as the machine pistol dropped from his hand and bounced downhill.

With his last breath he made a final grab for it, but his fingers were lifeless by the time they touched the metal. The weapon slid harmlessly down the hill, staying a few inches beyond the falling man's grasp, as if he were still chasing after it in the afterlife.

"Crews!"

The shout echoed across the ravine. It was hard to tell the distance or the exact location of the second man, but it was obviously the Cohort who broadsided Bolan's car with autofire from the other side of the woods.

"You okay, Crews? Did you get him?"

As quietly as possible, Bolan pushed himself up from the watery crevice. He sidestepped along the bottom of the ravine as the Cohort called out to his dead partner a couple more times.

The Executioner kept one hand on the folding grip in front of his trigger finger to steady the weapon as he tracked the barrel across the top of the incline. He moved toward a patch of cover about thirty yards to his left.

The denim-clad Cohort was also moving stealthily, somewhere above the ravine.

Bolan moved to his left until he reached a chest-high cluster of thorny hedges that climbed up the ravine. He worked his way uphill, moving slowly enough to keep the thorns from clawing into him, then peered through the thorny veil at the edge of the brush.

Nothing was moving. A sudden eerie quiet had settled across the woods after the first shots had been fired. Bolan scanned the car he'd bailed out of, then looked across at the gray sedan the Cohorts had driven.

There was no sign of the second gunman, which came as no surprise. The slain Cohort had been rash. This one was more capable and thorough.

But Bolan had time on his side. The Cohort had to get out of the area before it swarmed with law enforcement. Sooner or later he'd have to move toward his gray car, or make a move against Bolan.

A movement from his peripheral vision brought the soldier's attention back to his bullet-riddled car. There was a bulky shape hidden in the shadows beneath the chassis.

The Cohort had been waiting there for Bolan's head to appear from the ravine, expecting him to pop up like a duck in a shooting gallery. Spooked by the realization that he was alone and facing a serious adversary, the Cohort was shifting under the car, probably looking around in a 360 degree arc.

The Executioner had overlooked the spot in his preliminary recon, but the slight movement was enough to give his adversary away.

The shadow was about to become a distinct target.

Bolan inched forward until he was flat on the ground with the edge of the brush providing a thorny halo of cover. He extended the Beretta's shoulder stock and flicked the selector switch semiautomatic fire to 3-round-burst mode.

With his elbows planted in the dirt, his left hand on the forward grip and right hand on the trigger, Bolan zeroed in on the shadows beneath the car. His view was restricted by the angle of the vehicle and the thick reinforced tires. But there was still a target-acquisition area that could do some damage, even if only with a ricochet. It would either hit him or drive him from cover.

Bolan pulled the trigger.

The 3-round burst chopped into the road just in front of the tires. Bolan adjusted his aim and triggered a second and third burst, sweeping the underside of the car in a left-to-right motion.

The man cried out, from either shock or from being hit, then returned fire. Muzzle-flashes punched the shadows from beneath the sedan and sent a sustained burst scything through the air above Bolan's head. Another volley of rounds shredded the brush to his left.

Then the machine pistol clicked silent.

Bolan dived out of the bushes and landed in a prone position that gave him a better field of fire. He methodically pulled back on the trigger, firing 3-round bursts from right to left.

The 9 mm rounds scythed the air beneath the chassis, making the Cohort jump up and down as if the ground were on fire.

The Executioner rolled back into cover, ejected the magazine and rammed a fresh magazine into the Beretta. The Cohort's position was impossible to defend. He was as good as dead. A few more bursts would make him surrender or send him on his way to eternity.

The solider was about to trigger another burst when a sport utility vehicle rumbled into the rest area at high speed. It was about thirty thousand dollars' worth of chrome, gleaming black finish and outsize tires chewing up the road. Muffled bass lines from a loud stereo system thumped against the closed windows. Even from that distance it was deafening.

The guy inside couldn't hear a bomb going off.

The SUV's telescope antenna whiplashed the air when the driver finally hit his brakes, barely missing the vehicle that was angled across much of the road.

The driver rolled down his window, unaware he was in a war zone until the Cohort slid out from beneath the car and aimed his Skorpion at him. The SUV was his ticket out.

But the driver ducked his head back inside and gunned the engine as a spray of bullets severed his side mirror and poked holes in the front fender. He laid a patch of burning rubber behind him. A cloud of oily smoke enveloped the Cohort as he rolled onto the tar and fired another burst at the fleeing vehicle.

Bolan stepped into the open and angled for a clearer shot at the Cohort, who was now limping across the road. He got off one more burst from the Beretta before the high-performance vehicle got in his way.

In either rage or panic at finding himself running a gauntlet of lead, the driver accelerated toward Bolan. The soldier jumped back and waved the driver past him, catching a glimpse of the man's face as he shouted "Jesus H. Christ," and sped off to safety.

Bolan scanned the area. The Cohort was gone, but a cluster of branches was springing back into place in the woods across the road. He triggered two more bursts to keep the enemy gunner occupied and sprinted across the road, entering the woods near the gray sedan. Off to his right he could hear the man thrashing through the forest, moving with difficulty and looking for a hiding place.

Ten seconds later the Cohort fell silent.

The wounded beast was at bay. Now all Bolan had to do was to take him alive.

The Executioner headed deeper into the shadows, stepping softly through the rain-soaked forest bed to mask his steps. With the Cohort's approximate position in mind, he circled slowly. He forced himself not to hurry, losing track of time as he followed his instincts toward the target.

Then he heard the man's gasps for breath.

Bolan eased forward and parted the branches with the barrel of the Beretta 93-R. He saw the Cohort leaning in the bleached white crutch of a thick oak that had been split by lightning. It gave him both support and cover at the same time.

A loud rasping sound came from his lips. It was hard for the Cohort to breathe, even harder for him to move. There was blood on his leg and his arm. He was holding the Skorpion in his good hand, trying to keep it straight. But his head was nodding forward as he battled unconsciousness.

The Executioner drifted closer a step at a time, thinking if he got close enough he could disarm him.

At first the man didn't hear Bolan's approach because of his own labored breathing, but then he sensed the Executioner's presence. He stiffened and raised his head.

"Don't move," Bolan said. "Don't even look around."

The man froze.

Bolan was behind him and to his right, standing at an angle that would make it difficult for the man to aim at him in the best of conditions.

The Cohort's grip tightened on the Skorpion, his finger twitching. It was an effort for him to stay conscious. Blood loss, shock and the death of his partner had taken their toll.

"You can live," Bolan said. "We can walk out of here together."

"No, thanks," the gunner said. He turned his head and raised the Skorpion at the same time.

Bolan had no choice. He finished him off with a 3-round burst that zipped through his already wounded body and smacked into the tree.

The Cohort was dead.

And for now, so was the trail.

As Bolan stepped toward the slain Cohort, sirens echoed in the distance. They were moving closer with every second, providing a shrill funeral march for the recently departed gunner.

CHAPTER TWO

Sedona, Arizona

Winston Grail sat on the edge of a small stage in a cool dark lecture hall that also served as an occasional screening room.

His hands gripped the edge of the platform as he leaned forward to make eye contact with his third graduating class of the day.

There were nineteen people in the group that had completed the week-long introductory workshops presented by himself and a group of guest lecturers. They were gathered in the first few rows and most of them looked satisfied, though a few were exhausted from the intensive effort they'd put into learning how to relax.

From past experience he knew that approximately fifty percent of them would return for additional retreats or advanced seminars. The monastic life had called to them, and those who could afford it would answer the call.

Grail was still dressed in the style of a casual desert mystic as he spoke to the small group, conscious of the image he had to project—hooded white cotton drawstring shirt, jeans and sandals. His long ash-streaked blond hair was neatly combed back and tied with a leather thong.

"During the past week we've had metaphysical discussions and instruction on chanting, meditation, biosync programming and several other spiritual and mental disciplines," Grail said. "Because there was so much ground to cover, many of those sessions were formal."

Several people in the audience shared looks and nodded at one another. The introductory week had been more regimented than they'd expected.

"That's why tonight's session will be a totally informal dialogue," he continued. "You can share anything you've learned this past week. Or you can ask questions about me, the retreat centers or the other lecturers. The goal is to help you decide whether you want to continue your spiritual journey with us."

A woman in the front row tentatively waved her hand. She was an attractive and recently liberated housewife in her thirties. Grail had spent some time with her in an informal one-on-one counseling session and found her to be charming, open and just a bit skeptical. She had a new haircut, a new diet and now she was looking for a new religion.

Grail searched his mind for her name. Karen? Catherine? No, he thought. Christine? That was it. Christine, who divorced her husband over spiritual leanings. While she leaned more and more toward the heavens, he'd become a fanatic disciple of football and poker and at least a six-pack every night.

Grail bowed his head toward her.

"I have a question," she said.

"Go ahead, Christine."

"It's about belief in a supernatural being."

"Yes," he said.

"That's my question. Do you believe in one?"

"Of course."

She frowned. "What I mean is, does it have a name? Everyone here talks about shamanic guides and ancient entities, but no one ever seems to mention a supreme being by name."

"He—or she—hasn't told me yet," Grail replied.

A few members of the audience laughed. Others seemed a bit uncomfortable.

"If you're asking do I believe in a traditional God," Grail said, "then the answer is no. I really don't know what to believe in. That's why I'm searching so hard. That's why all of us have to search our hearts and minds for the answer. Otherwise, what is the purpose of our time on Earth?"

He glanced around the room and saw that the audience was still a bit apprehensive. Years of training and instruction during their formative years had bound them to the more traditional views of organized religion. They were half expecting a lightning bolt to part the heavens and strike them down for heresy.

"Please don't misunderstand me," Grail said. "At the end of my search, I may be right back where I started from, and realize that God was there all along and I just wasn't smart enough to see him."

He paused for effect and slowly scanned the faces of his small captive audience. There were only two married couples in attendance. The rest were single. The women were looking for a God figure or an alpha male, whichever came first. The men were there to try their hand at soul-searching or just searching for members of the opposite sex. It was impossible to tell at New Age gatherings. Usually it was a bit of both.

It was time for his "All is One" speech, a touch of fire and brimstone and a dash of yearning for a better world.

"The idea behind my workshops is simple," Grail said. "We must evolve beyond the everyday restrictions, the confining rules that limit our ability to think freely."

He looked up to read their expressions and saw that most of them were in agreement. Otherwise, why had they come here?

"It is possible to believe in a certain god one day and deny its existence the next," Grail continued. "We must seek and destroy all of our false beliefs before we ultimately find the one true belief that withstands all of our attacks, answers all of our questions and removes all of our doubts."

He measured the effect his words were having on the group. They were still with him. As he'd learned from his study of political figures and preachers, it was the pacing that truly counted. The hypnotic rise and fall of his voice mattered more than the message.

"That is the goal of the Trans Human Evolution Movement—to find God, to find the source of all things spiritual no matter what name he, she or it goes by."

He looked around once more, raising his hands and gesturing toward the group with open palms. "That's why we're all here," Grail said. "No one way is right or wrong for any man or woman. But if we share the discoveries from our journeys, maybe we can help others find the right path for them.''

He clapped his hands together, breaking the spell of his brief little sermon.

''Any more questions?''

A man in the third row raised his hand. Grail remembered a brief conversation with him. He was a straightforward accountant type, a comptroller who knew the value of the land the retreat was built upon, but not the value of the retreat itself.

''Yes,'' Grail said, nodding toward him.

''My question revolves around a few basic truths,'' the man said as he stood. He wore a smug expression, as if he were setting up a punch line.

Grail nodded. ''Let's hear it.''

''Is it true that you have a private railcar you use to travel around the country? And is it true you have a small fleet of planes? And holdings in media and production companies?''

''Yes,'' Grail said. ''All true.''

The man looked stunned. He'd expected a denial or at least an explanation. ''Then you admit it.''

''Of course. I've never tried to hide it.''

The man took off his glasses and rubbed the lenses with his shirt. He made a show of carefully putting them back on, as if they would help him see right through Grail.

''I guess what I'm saying...'' the man said. He looked uncertainly around the room. ''What I'm asking is how can you reconcile these trappings of wealth with the spiritual message you're selling here?''

''Trappings,'' Grail repeated. ''An appropriate choice of words. Wealth can be a trap if you become enslaved to your material possessions. I can do without them if necessary. But I have them, so I use them."

"Doesn't that conflict with your creed of leading a simple lifestyle?"

"*Simple* doesn't have to mean 'impoverished,'" Grail said. "Remember, this is a foundation. That means it is an economic entity, as well as a spiritual one. And indeed, it is a thriving one."

Grail had faced the same questions and given the answers so many times before that he knew the disarming effect it would have on the audience. Most of them would welcome his candor, but there would always be a few who suspected his motives.

"The planes let me travel across the country on short notice," Grail continued. "The railcar serves as my spiritual center when we tour the country for our seminars. And the media holdings help spread my message. But if all that vanished tomorrow, I'd be saying the same thing as I am today. We're all making the same journey, and we'll get there quicker if we make it together."

His questioner rolled his eyes. But when he looked around the room, he saw that no one else was in his corner.

"The important thing is not the house we live in," Grail stated, "but what is housed inside us. In here." He steepled his fingers inward and pointed at his heart.

The accountant sat down, unwilling to push it any further. The believers believed in Winston Grail and all was right in the world of THEM once more.

A young woman in the second row raised her hand,

but before Grail could answer, a woman appeared in the back of the hall.

It was Jacqueline Spears, his subterranean Joan of Arc, and she was waving urgently at him. The group followed his gaze toward the back of the room to look at the new arrival.

The men spent considerably more time looking her over. Spears's dark hair was cut short except for a few spiky bangs. She had a sharp, upturned nose and high cheekbones that gave her a feline look, a huntress in blue jeans and tight black top.

She walked down the slanted corridor and waited for him.

"Excuse me for a minute," he said to the group, then walked up the carpeted aisle and met her halfway. The serenity and lightness of being faded with every step he took, but he forced himself to remain calm.

"What is it?" he whispered.

"Phone call," Spears said. "It's Chandler. Again." She bit her lower lip and shook her head back and forth in disapproval. "He wasn't even supposed to call here the first time."

Grail nodded. The aftershocks of the operation were still rolling in. "There are a lot of things Chandler's not supposed to do," he said, "but he does them anyway."

"The man needs some reining in," she said. Her gaze let him know that she was willing to do the reining. And she was one of the few Cohorts who could do so.

"I'll keep that in mind," he said.

Spears nodded toward the exit. "I switched his call

to the projection room. He's hanging on the line until you come to him.''

Grail took a few steps back down the aisle toward his small group. ''If you'll excuse me for a moment, a friend of mine is having a bit of a crisis. I'll have to give him some words of encouragement.''

He followed Spears out the exit, then through the door that led into the projection room. He picked up the wall phone mounted just above the spotlight board and spoke softly into the receiver. ''Yes?''

''It's me,'' Chandler said.

''What is it?''

''It's the tour group I brought with me to set up the New York convention,'' Chandler said. ''Remember the two guys who didn't return to the correct location?'' Chandler asked.

''Of course,'' Grail said.

''Like you suggested, we gave them the whole night to show up, then went looking for them, just to make sure that they didn't create a public-relations problem.''

''And?''

''Well,'' Chandler said, ''their membership's been canceled.''

''I don't see a problem,'' Grail said. ''You had to do it. They knew the penalty for not showing up.''

''That's kind of the problem,'' Chandler said. ''I didn't do it.''

''What do you mean?''

''In a way,'' Chandler said, ''they removed themselves from the list.''

Chandler stayed on the line for another minute, speaking in the shorthand that he and Grail had developed over the years, letting him know that the other side was on the move and they were firing back.

"I see," Grail said. "Stay there for a while longer and see if this will have an impact on any future tours."

"Got it," Chandler said, then hung up.

Grail cradled the receiver. Someone was coming after them. Someone who wouldn't be prepared for what he found.

When he returned to his small flock in the lecture hall, Grail told them that a close personal friend was experiencing a dark night of the soul, and asked them to join him in meditation.

"Your prayers, thoughts and affirmations will be appreciated," he said.

He sat on the stage in the meditative pose he'd adapted from years of training in dojos, a half-kneeling position with his back straight, his hands on his knees, and his feet tucked flat beneath him.

While they sank into contemplation, he meditated upon the storm front that was moving in across the country. It was happening now. Just the way he wanted it to happen ever since that night so long ago—1984. He was barely out of his childhood when they came for his parents.

He knew his parents were fugitives. He understood the life they had to lead, and he understood how to use the weapons they carried with them. But he never understood what it was like to see someone die in front of him until that night.

IT WAS A BITTER NIGHT in November, and the wind raged in from Lake Champlain. But it was warm inside the small cottage his father had restored board by board and brick by brick with his strong workman's arms, turning it from a condemned shack into a home. A woodstove filled the air with so much heat that they had to open all of the windows a crack to keep from sweating. They were just another family living in the sparsely populated Vermont township a couple of miles south of the ferry to New York. Their chosen name at the time was Reynolds.

His father was a carpenter and bartender, and his mother was a day-care worker. He was home-schooled, and as far as he could tell he was years ahead of anyone his age.

It was as good a life they could get. Until the phone call came.

It was just past eleven o'clock. They were playing cards on the kitchen table, and his father was pouring a glass of wine for the three of them. They'd treated him as an adult ever since he could remember. That's why he knew to be afraid when the phone rang. No one called at that hour with good news.

His father let it ring twice, then picked up the phone. The caller didn't say a word. Several strange clicks came over the line. It could have been a warning; it could have been a threat.

His father hung up and gave his mother a look that told them everything they needed to know. Suddenly the playing cards, wine glasses and the warm winter home were like relics from another world, a temporary world they had been visiting.

"Someone's given us up," he said.

His mother said, "How do you know?"

"I don't know anything for sure, but I feel it. We've got to go."

His mother hesitated, weary of it all. On the outside she still looked young. But in her eyes you could see the aging of her soul, the yearning to go back in time and live another life.

But their course had been set the day they detonated their first bomb inside an Army recruiting office during the riotous days of the Vietnam War. It was an explosion that echoed for more than a decade as they fought against the war, the world and anyone who came after them. They evolved from radicals to revolutionaries, armed robbers to assassins.

Now it had all come down to this, three fugitives, a father, mother and son, all stricken by the ringing of a telephone. They knew what was ahead of them if they ran and what was coming up behind them if they stayed.

It wasn't the first time they'd moved in the dead of night. He was used to seeing his parents suddenly transform from carpenter and day-care worker to fast-moving fugitives, prying a cash box from the floorboards, grabbing weapons from under the bed and in the closets.

They snatched up the gear they set aside for just such an occasion, then tugged their winter hats and coats from the hooks near the kitchen door. His father turned off the overhead light and the three of them stood in the darkness, adjusting to the light.

When they were about to go out the back door and run for the station wagon, his mother suddenly stopped. Her grip froze around the doorknob.

"Someone's out there," she said.

Heavy footsteps sounded on the grass behind the house, then the footsteps rumbled across the enclosed porch steps. Fingertips drummed on the door in a soft cadence.

"Back me," his mother said.

His father leaned against the door, a Skorpion machine pistol in his hand. The barrel was pressed against a windowpane at chest level. He nodded to his wife, and she opened the door.

It was Chandler, crouching low as he slipped through the half-open door into the kitchen. "They're out there," he said, closing the door behind him. "All over the back roads. Place is turning into a parking lot."

"They see you?" his father said.

"I don't think so," Chandler said. "I hid in the woods and came the back way. Along the lake."

"You didn't call?" the older man asked.

"No," Chandler said.

"It was them."

Chandler nodded.

The older man touched his wife's cheek with his free hand and kissed her on the mouth. Then he gripped his son's shoulder and pulled him tight, embracing him, his lost childhood, his lost parents all at once. "We have to do this," he said. "You don't."

"I'm going with you," he said to his father.

His father released him, exchanged glances with Chandler, then went out the door with his Skorpion hanging at his side. His mother followed.

Then the youth and Chandler went out after them. All four of them were carrying.

A bright spotlight lit up the youth's father as he

reached the door of the station wagon. He darted back behind the wagon, his wife beside him.

There was a shout, and lots of shapes were suddenly moving by the road. A van with dark windows screeched into the driveway, then swerved sideways to block any escape.

His father fired three shots toward the van.

Then the night erupted in a blaze of gunfire and spotlights. Shotgun blasts and automatic fire poured into the station wagon.

His father was hit first. He yelled in surprise, then danced across the driveway like a scarecrow jerking in the wind. The full-auto fusillade riddled his body and removed a good portion of his skull. He went down in pieces.

His mother stood and fired, then was knocked off her feet by a single shotgun blast. She fell on her back, a loud shuddering sigh coming from her lips just before she died.

A strong hand crushed the youth's forearm, pulling him along. He didn't even realize Chandler had been leading him away from the battle until they were in the thick brush near the lake.

Nor did he realize that he'd emptied his Skorpion toward the unseen attackers.

He didn't know if he hit anyone or not. Or if anyone had seen Chandler and him come out of the house. He just knew that he was alone and running for his life from an enemy that someday would run from him.

GRAIL OPENED HIS EYES. He was back in the world he had created, a world that would spawn the rebirth of the Cohorts.

He looked around at the small audience. Some were blinking their eyes as they came out of meditative trances; others were looking up at him expectantly. The comptroller rubbed his eyes, looking as if he'd been sleeping.

Grail clapped his hands softly, relying on the Pavlovian gesture that always seemed to work.

As they looked up at him, he said, ''Now, let's talk about the power of visualization. How to envision the world you want to live in and make that world a reality....''

CHAPTER THREE

New York

The blue-and-yellow New York State Police helicopter skimmed across the treetops that surrounded the thruway rest area, an oasis of concrete in a tangled green wilderness. Downwash from the thirty-five-foot rotor blades carved furrows across the upper branches as it flew a figure-eight pattern over the battleground.

The distinctive mast-mounted sight above the Bell 206's rotor blades scanned the terrain like a giant robotic eye. It zoomed in on the car that blocked the road with its open door pointing to the ravine like an escape hatch and a body sprawled halfway down the hill.

Standing in the middle of the road a good distance from the car was a man in black with a holstered pistol and a canvas carryall by his side. Both hands were raised over his head in field-goal position, signaling them that it was safe to land.

"There's our guy," Captain Robert Kitchener said into the boom mike attached to his headset.

"So that's what God himself looks like," said the copilot, who sat in the observer seat by the open cabin door. He had a Heckler & Koch submachine gun cradled over his lap, and a flak jacket covered his chest.

"Pretty close to it, I guess," Kitchener said. Judging from the traffic that had scorched the airwaves back and forth from the man on the ground to the barracks station at Newburgh, the commandant of the state police, the aviation unit and to a few seldom used numbers in Washington, D.C., this special agent had a lot of pull.

But Kitchener wasn't about to abandon procedure.

He ignored the man on the ground who was now using standard military hand signals to direct him to a landing zone on a stretch of road with a clear approach for his descent. Whoever he was, Kitchener thought, the guy knew his stuff, selecting an LZ far enough from the woods to handle the angle of approach required for the Bell 206. The man was no stranger to dust-offs.

The guy was more like Special Forces than special agent, Kitchener thought. But he kept on flying at treetop level, taking the chopper on another pass over the woods.

The mast-mounted sight that was slaved to the electro-optical visor system provided Kitchener with a magnified look anywhere he turned his eye. He reconned the wooded terrain beyond the fugitives' car until he located the splintered landmark that had been mentioned by the man on the ground in his extremely terse briefing.

Kitchener hovered over the area until he saw the second slain fugitive. His body was anchored near the bottom of the broken tree trunk where a jagged husk of oak rose above him like a private headstone. So far everything was checking out just as the man said.

He made another pass over the area. To be on the safe side, before landing the Bell 206, he had to make sure there were no fugitives in the area the special agent didn't know about. During his years with the aviation unit, Kitchener had worked with more than a dozen special agents from almost as many different agencies. Some of them knew what they were doing. Others could get a man killed.

Kitchener never put himself or his men into a potentially lethal position like this without knowing who and where all of the players were.

As he made his final approach, he radioed the pilot in the backup helicopter to let him know he was going in. The Sikorsky H-76 helicopter was hovering about three-quarters of a mile back above a drop area that masked its presence. There was just enough room on the sparsely wooded shelf for the heliborne troopers to drop onto a hilltop.

"How many are we dealing with?" the Sikorsky pilot radioed back.

"One man standing," Kitchener replied.

"You think we got enough to handle him?"

Kitchener laughed. The Sikorsky carried a dozen specially trained troopers and paramedics who were ready to evacuate or infiltrate the area as necessary. "With these guys, you can never tell. Bring everyone in."

He landed the helicopter at the LZ designated by the man in black, settling the skids gently onto the hard-surfaced road. Kitchener kept the rotors spinning to cover any sound the Sikorsky made as it dropped its heliborne troops.

THE EXECUTIONER WATCHED the state police pilot duck his head from the rotor wash that was kicking up a whirling cloud of debris around him. As the man continued moving in a half crouch, Bolan recognized the gait he'd seen in countless combat situations. This was someone who knew how to get in and out of a hot zone fast and still get the lay of the land. The pilot used his peripheral vision to scan both sides of the road while still managing to keep his attention on Bolan. He was trim and solid, a fast mover who maintained his fighting weight. The only hint of his age was a silver-streaked mustache.

From the helicopter cabin the copilot looked on matter-of-factly, Heckler & Koch submachine gun in a ready position.

In the background Bolan saw a host of trooper vehicles and unmarked cars sealing off every possible access and exit from the rest area. Several uniformed and plainclothes officers were moving around.

It was a tense situation. On one side there was a veritably army looking to secure the site. On the other side was Mack Bolan, who, through Hal Brognola, had given them orders to cool their heels until the FBI's forensic unit arrived. Any minute now bureaucratic warfare could break out.

The pilot stopped several feet away, folded his arms in front of his chest and appraised Bolan with a neutral gaze. "You're Special Agent *Striker*," he said, emphasizing the obvious code name.

"That's the name," Bolan replied. At least for the duration, he thought. "And you're Kitchener."

"Right," the pilot said. "You called for a taxi?"

"If you're on duty, yeah."

The pilot gave him a thumbs-up and jerked his head toward the helicopter.

"Great," Bolan said. "Just a few things before we go."

"Maybe you could start with the national-security blanket that's been thrown over your operation here," Kitchener said.

Bolan gave him a quick rundown of the Cohort connection to the Etruscan Gem Company shoot-out, his surveillance of the two men at the retreat and the ensuing battle, as well as the inventory he found in the trunk of the gray sedan.

He gestured toward the vehicle and said, "Along with the gems, that trunk's got a rack of Skorpion machine pistols, authentic period pieces from the days when the cold war was running hot."

"What's their provenance got to do with it?" Kitchener asked.

"Not many people use them," Bolan said. "Cohorts used them a lot. These weapons probably came direct from an STB armory in Prague, manufactured back when Czechoslovakia was still behind the iron curtain. Does that tell you anything?"

"Not till you tell me what STB is," Kitchener said. He glanced back at the impatient wall of troopers. Though they'd been given orders to stand down until federal units arrived, it was in their nature to take control of the scene. Especially on their own turf.

"STB was the Czechoslovakian version of the CIA

and KGB,'' Bolan said. ''They were the main conduit to the radical underground in the West. Provided weapons, training and refuge to the Red Brigades, ETA, Cohorts. All the hardcore revolutionary groups.''

Bolan hefted his carryall, which was heavier by one East European machine pistol he'd taken from the trunk. ''These Czech-made Skorpions are in mint condition, which means they were part of a cache somewhere or were recently introduced to the market.''

''And that's good news?'' Kitchener asked.

''Could be,'' Bolan said. ''Now that the Czech Republic is a part of the West, their spook shops cooperate with ours.''

''You seem to know a lot about them,'' Kitchener observed. ''Then and now.''

''I used to travel a lot in Europe,'' Bolan said, remembering the flash fires he put out on both sides of the iron curtain. ''The thing is, the FBI unit can probably trace these arms to the source, STB or their middleman. Ultimately that could lead us to this alleged army of Cohorts.''

''Our forensic crew knows what it's doing,'' Kitchener said. ''They won't step all over the set.''

Bolan nodded. ''No argument. But the weapons in that trunk left a trail that could take your people months to sort out. We don't have that kind of time. But we do have the unlimited resources and manpower to shorten that process. That's why I want your copilot to secure the area for the FBI when you and I take off to Washington.''

"Washington?" Kitchener shook his head. "That's not going to happen."

"Trust me, it is," Bolan said. "And while we're on our way, your guy has to make sure no one else touches anything—weapons, gems, bodies—until the FBI teams from Albany and Manhattan arrive."

"You're not serious," Kitchener said.

The Executioner glanced toward the ravine where the nearer of the Cohorts had fallen. "Dead serious," he said.

Kitchener shrugged. "Look, I can see your position, but you're not hearing me at all."

"Give it a shot, guy," Bolan said. The outcome wouldn't change, but it was better to listen to him than to steamroll him.

"Fair enough," Kitchener said. "First off, we got an SOS from some guy whose fancy Jeep got shot up—while he was still in it. Then we got calls from motorists who caught a glimpse of what's going down here. Add two dead gunmen who may or may not be Cohorts. Just because the government says they are, or thinks they are, doesn't make it so."

Bolan nodded. The guy had been burned before by government white hats. So had he.

"And then we got some fire-breathing calls from you and the head honcho in the Justice Department," Kitchener continued. "Meanwhile every barracks in the region is rolling, and there's a special response team nearby that you don't know about—"

"You mean the ones that came in the Sikorsky transport?" Bolan asked.

"You heard it?"

"It's a sound you don't forget," Bolan said. "This special response unit follow your orders?"

"They do."

"Maybe they can help your man secure the site," Bolan suggested.

"It's a thought." Kitchener took another look toward the contingent of troopers waiting to descend. "But I can't just walk away. I have to hand off to the lead investigative unit. A flight to D.C. is out of the question. Unless…"

"Unless what?" Bolan asked.

"Unless the word comes from on high again," he said.

"Follow me."

The soldier walked back to his vehicle. The passenger side was raked with gunfire and the windows were imploded, but the communications gear was still intact. The high-tech unit was protected by a hard armored shell that could withstand a lot more than a strafing from 7.65 mm weapons.

Under watchful eyes, he picked up the transceiver that he'd already used to bring in Kitchener and the army of troopers. He raised Brognola once again to obtain necessary clearance.

"Striker," came Brognola's voice from the com unit, "this was supposed to be low profile. You trying to create an international incident out of this?"

"I think it already is, Hal," Bolan said. "I'll tell you more when I get there. In the meantime, see what you can do about extending the aviation unit's cooperation. I want to be airborne and heading for D.C. before the media descends on the place. Meanwhile, Kitchener's got a copilot who can hold the fort until the FBI teams get here. And there's one more thing you might want to start working on.'' He tipped Brognola to the possible Czech connection, then let the big Fed do his bell ringing.

Less than five minutes later the Executioner was the sole passenger in the Bell 206 helicopter that Captain Kitchener lifted off the ground in a steady autumn rain. Bolan sat in the copilot's seat, wearing a headset and watching the pilot work the controls— just in case. It was force of habit, the kind of thing that Bolan couldn't turn off when he was on an operation.

The next stop was Washington, D.C. Once more, thanks to Brognola's intervention, Kitchener's commandant had given him the green light to go to the capital.

"One request," Kitchener said as they cleared the treetops.

"What's that?" Bolan asked.

"Can you do anything about this rain?"

"I used up my favors for the day," he said, grinning.

As they headed south, Bolan looked down at the small army of troopers who'd sealed off the site. A lot of firepower had been concentrated in a short time, ready to go into action if they had to put the hammer down. They didn't need it this time. But Bolan had a feeling it wouldn't be long before they were called in again. And next time it would be the real thing.

Though they spoke sparingly on the way to Washington, it was enough for Bolan to realize that the pilot was the real deal. They'd covered a lot of common ground. Kitchener had been in combat and he'd been in law enforcement. And he wasn't the kind of guy who let himself get distracted. Once he was airborne he didn't gripe about the orders or the change in plan. He just set his course and got it done.

A half hour out of D.C., Bolan broke the easy silence they'd fallen into. "You planning on taking any vacation time soon?" he asked.

Kitchener cocked his head at him. "Why? You trying to sell me a time share?"

"The guy who usually flies us is otherwise engaged at the moment," Bolan said. Grimaldi was in the middle of another operation Brognola was coordinating.

"That's why you gave me the heavy briefing, huh," Kitchener said. "You were interviewing me? My calendar's clear. Got a few fires burning, but nothing my people can't put out."

Bolan nodded. "Good. If this thing leads to your neck of the woods again, we'll need someone with your background. It'll be official this time. You'll be seconded to an FBI advance team or the Marshals Service. The cover story will be something like—"

"I know how it works," Kitchener said, halting him with a wave of his hand. "I've been on a few 'training' tours with the Feds before."

Washington, D.C.

THREE HOURS after they lifted off from the war zone, Mack Bolan was in full bureaucrat camouflage, taking an elevator to the fifth floor of the block-long complex where Hal Brognola was temporarily stationed.

Bolan wore the kind of dark blue suit that passed as a uniform at the FBI's Strategic Information and

Operations Center headquarters in the J. Edgar Hoover Building on Pennsylvania Avenue. As far as anyone but Brognola and a very few insiders would know, the Executioner was just one more field agent.

The muck, sweat and scrapes from his twenty-four-hour war had been washed off, and his weapons were locked away in the E Street safehouse Brognola had snagged for him. It was one of several apartments in a well-fortified building the Justice Department kept available for short-term ''guests'' like Mack Bolan.

When he stepped out onto the fifth floor, Bolan was toting an official-looking briefcase. Unlike most of the other suits who carried minilaptops, lab reports and cyber-sleuthing gear in their briefcases, Bolan carried a change of clothes and a Skorpion M-61 machine pistol in his.

The sleek weapon could be one of the keys to tracking the Cohorts, Bolan thought, a psychological and physical connection to the old-guard revolutionaries. But the real key was probably the unlimited manpower and mindpower that had been collected here in the forty-thousand-square-foot Strategic Information and Operations Center.

Bolan followed standard SIOC security procedures for admission to the compartmentalized areas of the fifth-floor command center, using his Belasko nom de guerre and magnetic identification cards required at several entry points along the way. Out in the field he was code-named Striker, but here in the charcoal-gray confines of the windowless center, he was Michael Belasko, just another high-ranking fact chaser.

As he walked toward the conference room that

Brognola had set up for this aspect of the Cohort crisis, Bolan kept in mind that there were probably a good number of other special operatives gathered in SIOC with equally deceptive covers.

Every single person on the fifth floor was geographically accounted for, thanks to the magnetic strips on the ID cards they all carried. The strips were tracked on a large screen in a spaceship-like control room that could communicate with every room in the building. The human radar screen could locate anyone at a moment's notice.

Bolan got himself located once more by swiping his magnetic card through another door slot and stepping into the appointed conference room. Half a dozen men and one woman were positioned around a long executive-gray conference table flanked by screens on two walls. The screens were blank now, like dark electronic windows.

The teak-colored captain's chairs around the table were designed for comfort. Upon the table was a water pitcher and a nearly empty coffee decanter, indicating that the group had been there quite awhile. Staggered between coffee cups and water glasses were stacks of computer printouts, videotapes, discs and folders full of dossiers on the Cohort movement. The information gathering was well under way.

Hal Brognola stood at the head of the large conference table, shirt sleeves rolled up and eyes red from lack of sleep. He nodded a brief welcome when the Executioner entered the room, but continued to talk to the group.

Several enhanced photographic images of suspected Cohorts were spread out like a hand of cards before him. Brognola was getting the group up to speed on the potential enemy they faced. When the stocky Fed came to a stopping point, he waved Bolan over and introduced him briefly around the table as counterterrorism expert Michael Belasko.

Bolan committed the names and faces to memory. He knew one name from past experience, a warhorse from the U.S. Marshals. William Freeling had an extremely short buzz cut that made his silver-specked-tinted hair look like a sprinkling of gun powder.

The only woman at the table got his full attention from the moment she shook his hand and looked into his eyes. Her name was Doreen McKenna, late twenties or early thirties, with dark red hair and calculating green eyes that measured everything about him. It was hard to tell from her speculative gaze whether she was interested in him or thought she'd seen him on a wanted poster.

Brognola had mentioned that he was bringing in an agent with a psy-ops background, who created profiles of homegrown terror groups like the Cohorts and then devised methods to tear them apart.

She was younger than Bolan expected and probably a lot tougher than she looked at first glance. Her blue blazer and white blouse subtly emphasized her figure and painted a portrait of a professional woman. But something in those eyes convinced Bolan that she had more than a scholar's knowledge of counterterrorism.

The other men positioned around the table were unknown to Bolan, but he knew the type—veteran officers and upper-management types who assembled the manpower and logistics for large-scale covert ops. At first warning, the SIOC teams prepared thorough contingency plans for a major operation. If it turned out to be a false alarm, everyone could stand down. But if it turned out to be the real thing, the apparatus would be in place. They couldn't afford to run any more of the misguided cowboy operations that plagued the Justice Department in recent years.

That was why Hal Brognola was handling the intraagency coordination. They needed a smooth-running machine this time. A war machine.

After the introductions, Brognola waved toward the connecting door that led to his temporary office. "A lot of this is familiar territory to you, Mike," Brognola said. "Make yourself at home in my office and prepare your report. I'll be in shortly."

Bolan nodded and headed toward the door. It was a standard Brognola tactic. He wanted the others to see that Bolan was a trusted associate who would come and go and get full cooperation from anyone in the task force.

When he closed the door behind him, Bolan started "preparing his report" by dropping his briefcase on the floor, taking off his tie and suit jacket and lying down on the full-length sofa across from Brognola's desk.

He needed the downtime. He'd had little sleep in the past two days and was wrung out from crawling through the woods, surveilling and tracking the Cohorts and ultimately putting them away.

There was always a chance that on very short notice he could be sent out into the field again, where being dead tired was pretty close to dead. He closed his eyes, and within one minute, drifted off into dreamless sleep.

Douglas County, Oregon

THE FROTHING STRETCH of white water came to a sudden end, dropping Arnold Ashcroft's dark green canoe through a pair of slick boulders that stood like gates on both sides of the creek.

The nose of the canoe rode down the chute and slapped hard on the water. With a practiced thrust of his thick veined forearms, Ashcroft swept the paddle through the water one more time. Then he rested it across the wooden slats and glided across the smooth and glassy pool of water. He leaned back and propped his elbows on both sides of the light aluminum alloy canoe as he leisurely floated downstream. After shooting the rapids, he knew exactly how long he could glide before he'd have to pick up the paddle again.

For about a year now, ever since he'd retired from the Bureau, Ashcroft had traveled the same white water and fly-fishing circuit. He'd always start out moving east along the North Umpqua River, then veer off onto the wide creek that led down toward Crater Lake. Weather permitting, he spent all of his free time on the water.

One full year and he hadn't grown tired of it. Yet.

Maybe he'd eventually go back to the working world, perhaps get a job with a security company or even work as a river guide. But so far he didn't really feel the desire or the need to work. Unlike the horror stories he'd heard from fellow agents who'd gone before him, Ashcroft found that retirement more than agreed with him. He still had a lot of good years ahead of him. His hair and his health were still holding out, and in his mind he was just entering middle age.

Ashcroft had put in his time over the years and had made some cautious but reasonably profitable investments, enough to buy an A-frame just outside the town of New Herrick. And since his ex-wife had remarried, he had no real debts anymore. Except to himself. All he had to do these days was glide across the water and feel the autumn breeze that rushed in from the pines.

As the mild current swept the canoe along, Ashcroft occasionally stroked the paddle lightly through the water and steered a course right down the middle.

His thoughts drifted along as placidly and aimlessly as the creek.

Until something hit the canoe.

It made a loud thunking sound that shook him from his reverie. He'd been through this stretch of creek so many times before that he knew there were no dangerous rocks to watch out for, especially when the creek was this high.

While he was still trying to discern the source of the noise, there was another loud thunk. This time it punched a jagged hole in the bow of the canoe and sent a piece of aluminum flying through the air.

The hole was too high up on the left side of the hull to take in water, but that provided little comfort to Ashcroft now that he recognized the sound of a muted automatic weapon coming from the left bank.

When a 3-round burst of silenced rounds punched holes in the other side of the hull, Ashcroft jerked his head toward the right bank. A second gunman was hidden on that side of the creek.

The second shooter opened up with another burst that zipped across the bow and smacked into the water. Muzzle-flashes gave away the location of the shooter, who was enshrouded in a string of tall and narrow trees that ran along a ledge on the right bank.

Bastards, he thought. They were toying with him, taking potshots at him from both sides while they made him run the gauntlet. At this range it was impossible to miss unless they wanted to. He wasn't too surprised. He'd gone up against all kinds of freaks in his years in the Bureau. Some killed out of need. Some killed for the fun of it.

Maybe they didn't want to kill him, he thought. Maybe they just wanted him to realize how desperate his position was so they could take him prisoner. But for what? He'd been away from active operations for a year and figured he had little information to offer anybody.

Still, there was always a chance.

A flash of movement drew his attention back to the left bank where a man stepped out onto a grassy overhang. The trees behind him covered the gunner's upper body with shade, but the machine pistol in his right hand was gleaming in the afternoon sun. It had a sound suppressor, and it was pointed right at Ashcroft.

At the same time there was another movement on the right bank. Almost as if these guys had choreographed their every move, the second man stepped out into the open and walked down to the edge of the creek.

He stood perfectly still, a guy with short brown hair in a military cut and sun-weathered skin. Maybe in his late twenties or early thirties, Ashcroft thought. Probably too young to have had anything to do with him during his Bureau days. This one also had a sound-suppressed machine pistol.

Ashcroft was just about close enough to make out the face of the man on the right bank. He didn't look familiar, nor did he look forgiving. The game they were playing would soon come to an end.

He thought of jumping overboard, but pictured himself flailing about in the water. Weaponless. Easy pickings. No, he thought. His only chance was to cut sharply toward the shore, push aside the camping gear stored beneath the seat and grab the revolver that was packed in the tackle box. It wasn't much of a chance, but it was the only one he had. If he reached the shore and got out his weapon, he might be able to make a go of it.

Ashcroft was tempted to reach for the weapon now, but he knew they'd take him out the instant he posed a real threat to them.

It was strictly a one-sided game.

His mind raced as the canoe drifted slowly along with the current and took him closer to the gunmen. They'd chosen a spot where the creek was the narrowest and had been waiting for him. That meant they'd thoroughly cased him. They knew his habits and knew where they could take him where no one could see it go down.

Fight or flight? He'd done both before and managed to survive with his pride and his body intact. It was always a tactical situation. Sometimes you pulled back, and sometimes you charged ahead.

After several seconds passed without any more

rounds buzzing the air around him, another alternative came to mind. Maybe he could just keep floating along and keep his hands where they could see them. Hopefully he could get them talking and find out what they wanted. The rational part of his mind was seeking a way to defuse the situation and stay alive.

But a few moments later, when he got close enough to read the eyes of the gunner on the right bank, he knew that negotiation wasn't an option. Ashcroft had seen that same kind of look too many times to mistake the man's intentions.

It was a hit, and it was just seconds from going down. They'd just been waiting until he was in the best position for them to take him out. He was delivering himself to the firing squad.

Ashcroft flicked the broad blade of the paddle through the water and pushed the canoe toward the right bank.

The maneuver was exactly what they expected.

A burst of metal rain struck the bow of the aluminum canoe, making loud thunking sounds as the full-auto rounds bored through the metal.

A follow-up burst raked the sides as he paddled furiously toward the shore. Spouts of water fountained in the air when several more rounds chopped into the water from the other side of the creek, zeroing in on the canoe.

Ashcroft let go of the paddle and made a grab for the revolver, managing to raise it almost to a firing position before the first rounds stitched him in the right bicep, shoulder and chest.

At first it seemed as if his arm had disintegrated. But then came a band of pain that pulsed up his arm and across his chest. Other rounds whipped through the air around him, but it no longer mattered if they hit him or not. The main damage was done.

The .357 Magnum revolver was too heavy to hold on to anymore, and his fingers were no longer working properly. The heavy weapon slipped from his hand and fell into the water with a loud splash, sinking to the bottom of the clear creek bed. As he keeled forward, his shocked gaze locked on to the gun as it was covered in a swirl of sand.

And then he saw the reflection of a dead man floating on the water and looking back at him. He knew he didn't have much time left.

His torn right arm sloshed through the water as the momentum of the canoe carried him toward the shore. His left hand clutched ineffectually at his wounds, unable to stop the bright red flow seeping down his shirt.

The water beside the canoe was turning red, a billowing cloud of dark rich dye pouring into the creek. But at least the pain was dimming now, washing away with his blood.

William Ashcroft was aware of only a very few things now. His mind had a hard time accepting what had happened and was trying to plot a course out of there. But there were no more paths to follow.

The bullet-riddled bow of the canoe plowed through reeds at the water's edge, then scraped across the rocky creek bed.

The gunman stepped into the water up to his knees, grabbed the rope hooked through the bow ring and dragged the canoe halfway out of the water.

Ashcroft teetered backward from the sudden motion, groaning loudly as his shattered and useless arm flailed against the side of the canoe. While the life-blood poured out of him, the forest began to take on a paler hue. The rushing sound of the creek started to fade, and a cushion of silence was enveloping him like a sweet fog.

The man suddenly released the rope, and the aluminum hull thudded hard against the ground.

It should have hurt, but Ashcroft barely felt it. A growing sense of numbness swept through him like ice crystals.

His life didn't flash before him. None of that seemed important now. What was really important was the life that came after. Ashcroft had never been a religious man, not in the traditional sense, but he had a feeling that he wouldn't be alone when he crossed over. He heard voices and saw shapes, saw that bright tunnel everyone had talked about.

Through the haze Ashcroft realized one of the voices belonged to the gunman who'd dragged him out of the water. He looked up at the man who was now only a few feet away. There was no hatred in the man's face. No joy. Just a man doing his job.

Ashcroft searched his memory but he couldn't recognize the face. He'd earned a good many enemies during his time with the Bureau—put a lot of them behind bars, put some of them underground.

But he was pretty sure this man was a stranger. Probably a hired gun. Ashcroft would never know who killed him. Neither would his ex-wife. Hell, he thought, maybe no one would even know he died out here.

Then Ashcroft noticed the details of the machine

pistol and the sound suppressor. It was a wicked little gun that he'd seen before.

Skorpion, he thought. There used to be so many of those things floating around in the old days. He'd gone up against a group that particularly fancied that deadly weapon. Ashcroft had escaped its sting back then, but now it had finally caught up to him. Now that he was no longer in the game.

As the blood continued to pour out of him, Ashcroft had a hard time focusing his eyes and deciphering what the man was saying.

"Snap out of it," the shooter said. He propped one foot on the canoe and rocked it back and forth until the jarring motion temporarily brought him back into the world.

Ashcroft managed to fix his gaze on the shooter. He had a haughty expression on his face, as if he were something special because he took out a man in a canoe. But at that point no one was special anymore.

The man wanted something from Ashcroft, he realized. Fear maybe. But Ashcroft had none to give.

"You're wondering why we chose you," the man said.

Ashcroft nodded. If the man was giving out answers, he'd take them with him. His head felt heavy and his soul felt light. This conversation was a mere formality, a vestige of the world he had visited for nearly six decades.

"Remember a group called the Cohorts?" the gunman asked.

Cohorts. It came back to him then. The underground cells. The bombings and robberies and shootings. The final pursuit.

"Yes," he said. "I remember. But the Cohorts are dead."

"Not anymore," the man said. "They're alive and well and back in action."

Ashcroft laughed for the very last time and said, "Not for long."

The man raised the suppressed snout of the machine pistol toward Ashcroft's chest and triggered a 3-round burst.

But William Ashcroft was gone before the first round hit him.

WITHIN MINUTES OF THE KILL, Roger Hale transported the canoe and the body through the woods. The aluminum coffin slid easily over the leafy matting on the forest floor. It snagged only a few times before he brought it to the deep depression in the woods that he'd previously scouted.

Hale scattered the camping gear around the brush, then overturned the canoe so its green color wouldn't be visible from the air if there ever was a search for Ashcroft.

Next he fished through the former FBI agent's pockets and removed every trace of Ashcroft's ID. License, credit cards, library card. A family portrait of him with his arm around his wife and kids. Photographs of those same kids grown up years later.

Hale put the salvaged IDs and photos in his jeans pocket to destroy later. No sense in making it too easy for anyone who chanced across the body.

He left the slain former FBI agent faceup in his final resting place, an uncovered pocket of earth. The guy looked almost serene, as if he enjoyed his new digs. Maybe he was, Hale thought. The guy had gone out well. No pleading or curses of eternal damnation. He just did what he could until he could do no more.

The animals would soon erase the rest of the agent's identity. First the birds would peck away at him, then the larger predators would come for their share. Maybe even fight over him.

It didn't matter to Hale. Nor would it matter to the guy who checked out. William Ashcroft was beyond all that kind of worry.

Hale felt nothing except satisfaction for a job well done. The hunt was over. They'd bagged their man.

He and his partner, a hardcase who'd drifted in and out of jail before finding his true calling with the Cohorts, had stalked Ashcroft through all of his haunts.

They shadowed his car from a distance and called off the surveillance whenever he seemed to be looking around. They tracked him to his favorite fishing holes. They drank in the same backwoods bar he frequented, with its ancient pinball machines, pickled eggs and the long dulled mirror that had been worn down to a dull murky sheen from eighty years' worth of backcountry reflections.

And then they followed him on his final trek into the wilderness. Except for the actual hit, it was almost like going on a long camping trip.

But that part was over now. The war had begun, and there would be more operations to conduct. Hale had a feeling that none of them would be as easy as this one.

He made his way back through the forest, angling toward the creek where his partner waited on the other side. About a half mile south there was a section of the creek that was only waist high. He'd strip down just like before, wade across the frigid water with his gear resting across his shoulders, then head for the car.

The heater would be blasting and so would the radio as they raced across a few state lines, driving night and day to their home base.

After all, they had a bounty to collect.

Washington, D.C.

AN HOUR PASSED before the clicking sound of a magnetic card sliding through a slot intruded into the Executioner's sleep. He came awake immediately by force of habit, looked around at the office and remembered he was at SIOC headquarters.

By the time Brognola stepped into the room with Doreen McKenna in tow, Bolan was standing up and shaking off the lingering effects of sleep.

"Here," Brognola said as he handed him a cup of black coffee. "Thought you could use some fuel."

"Thanks," Bolan said. "I'm running on empty." He sipped the coffee, savoring the jolt of caffeine as he moved over to one of the chairs that flanked Brognola's desk.

McKenna took the other chair.

The big Fed sat behind his empty desk and smoothed his hands across the smooth gleaming surface. The rest of his office was packed with position papers, tapes, electronic chalkboards and computer gadgetry, but except for the phone bank, the desk itself was clear. Compared to the clutter in the room it seemed like an airstrip.

"All right, Mike," Brognola said, "fill us in. Everything."

The Executioner nodded and reached for his briefcase. "I'll start with this," he said, opening it up and taking out the M-61 Skorpion machine pistol. He placed it gently on top of Brognola's desk.

For the benefit of McKenna, Bolan said, "Skorpion M-61 machine pistol. Czech made, easily concealed. Relatively effective in close quarters, but it has a reputation as a spray gun that can be hard to control. That made it attractive to a lot of revolutionary groups because indiscriminate killing was their modus operandi. The early Cohorts used it extensively. Four out of five of the current version of the Cohorts also used them."

"I'm familiar with the weapon," McKenna said. "East Bloc instrument of terror. It spread through the European underground like wildfire." At seeing Bolan's look of surprise, she smiled and added, "Hal gave me a crash course."

"She's been looking into it ever since you called," Brognola said. "I've also got some of our old State Department hands looking into the possible Czech connection."

"You're right about the appeal of a specific weapon," McKenna continued. "It's an icon, a totem. A passing of the sword to the next generation that shows a continuity or allegiance to the cause. And that may be exactly what we're facing here."

Bolan considered her response. "Second generation," he said. "Is that an educated guess?"

"More than that," she said. "It's fifteen years of experience tracking and infiltrating underground groups, cults and militias. I'd call it a strong probability rather than a guess.''

"Why is that?" Bolan asked.

"For this group to reemerge, it has to be stronger than ever. That means a new leader is in place. Someone with fanatic dedication who can drive a cause that by rights should no longer exist. The old leadership was killed off, died in prison, got religion or faded away. Who else would keep that dream alive except someone who was indoctrinated to the group at an early age?''

"The guy who was caught on the video didn't look so young," Bolan said, thinking of the man in the leather cap who'd obviously commanded the squad.

"He's not," Brognola said. "A forensics unit has been working around the clock to identify him, morphing in the years. Several reconstructions match up with a guy named Chandler. And he's a known associate of Rivers, the guy who caught it in the store.''

"He got a history?" Bolan asked.

"The guy's a real hardcase," Brognola said. "A strong-arm guy, but a lieutenant rather than a headman.''

"He's not the leader," McKenna stated. "They wouldn't risk losing their top man on their first strike.''

Bolan nodded, then finished briefing them on his surveillance of the retreat and his gun battle at the rest area. He also mentioned the possibility of bringing in Captain Kitchener for airborne operations if they needed someone familiar with the territory.

"Kitchener's good," Brognola agreed. "We'll use

him if Jack's still tied up and we have to go back up north."

"I got a feeling we will," Bolan said. "Especially with that retreat angle to look into."

Brognola shook his head doubtfully. "We're already looking into that. Not much there. The retreat, or 'sanctuary,' is privately run. The guy who owns it is a former pastor in his sixties, and his foundation got several grants and trusts over the years. All look like reputable sources."

"Look a little deeper," Bolan suggested. "There's something there."

"Is that a guess?" McKenna asked.

"No," he said. "It's a probability."

"Based on what?" she asked, leaning toward him.

"That," Bolan replied, pointing at the Skorpion. "They only had two Skorpions when they escaped from the store. That means they got a trunk load more somewhere else, probably planted at the retreat for them."

"Maybe," Brognola said. "But we don't know where or when. And that doesn't mean the retreat's involved. The reservations for their cabin were made three weeks ago. They used a ten-dollar calling card from a phone booth on Broadway."

"It's just a hunch that bears looking into," Bolan said. "Same as the Czech angle."

"Will do," Brognola told him. "Now, let me fill you in on what SIOC's been doing."

The big Fed briefed them on SIOC progress to date. The desktop commandos were sifting through their databases, resurrecting names, faces and fingerprints of known Cohorts, and uncovering every possible connection, including families, associates, places of employment, prison sentences and burial plots.

But the army of SIOC field operatives Brognola was in charge of wasn't going to wait around for the results of the data gathering before going into action. SIOC had compiled a likely-enemies list for the Cohorts that included active and retired FBI agents who pursued the group in their glory days. Though the agents would be given discreet around-the-clock protection, they would also be working as decoys.

"It's a calculated risk," Brognola explained. "The agents *will* be targets, but the Cohorts do considerable recon before striking. At first sign of activity, Mike will be sent into the area."

McKenna glanced sideways at Bolan. "Why him?" she asked, impartially studying the man beside her. "I'm sure he's good at what he does, but the department must have equally competent men they can count on."

"We do," Brognola said. "But they'll all be playing by the rules."

"And he won't?"

"He'll be playing to win," Brognola said. "Just like you. His mission will be to intercept the Cohorts before they're taken into custody and turn them."

"Into what?" she asked.

"Collaborators," Bolan said. "Prisoners. Ghosts. Whatever the moment or the method requires."

She nodded. "Befriend them or behead them, is that it?"

"If they have knowledge that can stop an atrocity from happening, I'll acquire that knowledge any way necessary. I got a feeling that doesn't offend your sensibilities."

"Not likely," she said.

"That's why I've paired you for this operation," Brognola said, nodding toward McKenna. "She's planned covert ops, as well as executed them. She'll sift through our Cohort intel and develop a strategy to force their hand."

"The Cohorts have dreams of glory," McKenna said, "but they're forced to operate in the shadows. This is a paradox we can exploit, since they want the world to know their glorious deeds. Counterpropaganda will provoke responses from them. The more they respond, the more we'll know about them and how we can take them down in the field."

"We?" Bolan asked.

"I'll be going inside," McKenna said. She spoke as if it were preordained.

"That's only one of the scenarios," Brognola cautioned. "We'll be fighting them on several fronts. And that includes infiltrating their organization if the chance comes up."

"That's a hard sell even in the best of times," Bolan said. "Especially hard when they're at war."

"That's just it," Brognola replied. "If the Cohorts are fighting a war, they're bound to suffer casualties. That means they'll need new blood."

McKenna nodded. "These organizations all have a similar structure. Logistics group, front organizations, a network of sympathizers and supporters, and a recruiting arm to winnow the hard core from the poseurs."

"And you plan on going in as hard core?" Bolan asked.

"Whatever fits their pattern and expectations," she said. "They'll have their own profile of the best fit for their group. Disenfranchised radicals, fanatics, borderline terrorist. Fugitives. Whatever it is, that's what I'll be. I'll go in alone. Or maybe with a partner."

Bolan cocked an eyebrow. Brognola nodded.

"You mean if the pattern fits, we go in as a couple?" Bolan asked.

"Like man and wife," she said.

"Or like shrink and patient," Bolan said. He looked at Brognola. "Your call, Hal," he said. "If it plays that way, I'll go under. Until then, point me in the right direction and let me do it my way."

CHAPTER FOUR

Karlovy Vary, Czech Republic

The cobblestoned streets of Karlovy Vary attracted an international clientele who came for the hot-spring spas that were scattered throughout the town and the surrounding countryside.

Mack Bolan was more interested in the terrorist clientele that had frequented the region years ago, as well as their lethal descendants who apparently spent some time in the area recently.

And now he and Doreen McKenna were doing the same, trying to pick up their trail. Ever since they took the nonstop flight from New York to Prague, she'd been playing the part of his wife. Their joint cover was a recently married couple on a tour of Europe.

After picking up the specially equipped Skoda sedan that Brognola had arranged to have waiting for them at Prague's international airport, they'd driven straight to Karlovy Vary to check in to their hotel.

The short trek from Prague brought them deep into the heart of Bohemia, the ancient forested region that was so well known for its resorts and spas. It was also known, to those who had fought in the trenches, for the hidden training camps that formerly catered to East Bloc special-forces units and deep-cover operatives.

Bolan knew the hidden heritage of the region well, which was why he found it so unusual to be relaxing in the small town, just a few miles from the former secret bases.

They were sitting on a terraced café close by the long stone bridge across the Tepla River, lingering over a rich breakfast of pastries and coffee.

At the moment McKenna was playing her role to the hilt, acting as if she'd left her regular diet behind her in the States. To help wash down the thick fresh pastry, she had a tall ceramic flute of steamed parfait coffee.

Sitting at the tables next to them were a charter group of British tourists, some college students and a trio of hikers who'd obviously come to explore the trails that led from the town up into the mountains.

The nearby hills were dotted with medieval monasteries and modern bed-and-breakfasts. Castles in varying states of repair, ranging from ruins to regal palatial estates, cast their spired shadows across ski restaurants and secluded taverns. While the town itself tried its best to maintain a medieval atmosphere, several modern theaters, galleries and casinos had sprung up alongside the hot springs and healing centers that were the main attraction.

The spas of Karlovy Vary and nearby Marienbad had long been the haunting ground for well-to-do tourists and the upper class. But during the cold war, it was also the spiritual center of the East Bloc intelligence services. Chief among them was the STB, the elite Czechoslovakian security corps that rivaled, and in many cases surpassed, the KGB. In addition to Karlovy Vary's strategic location, the STB operatives appreciated the luxurious lifestyle that could be found there between missions.

Bolan glanced around the small square, casually watching a middle-aged man and a woman break off from a group of tourists who were walking past a row of quaint old-world shops. The expensively dressed couple stopped in front of a china shop directly across from the café. From where he sat, Bolan could see their reflections, just as they could see his. The man, with the carriage and build of a professional athlete, didn't seem to be very impressed by the display window. Perhaps he was just humoring his wife. Or perhaps he was angling for a better look at Bolan.

They could be window-shoppers or they could be part of a team keeping tabs on his movements, Bolan thought. The Executioner automatically calculated how long it would take him to get to their car if they needed serious weaponry in a hurry. If they were cut off from the vehicle, he would just have to rely on the one-and-a-half pounds of steel and polymer resting comfortably in the underarm holster beneath his windbreaker.

The Heckler & Koch Universal Self-loading Pistol was chambered for 9 mm rounds. It could handle seventeen rounds in all, one in the chamber and sixteen in the quick-change magazine. The USP was becoming pretty popular with embassy personnel and had been part of the travel kit stocked in the Skoda along with satcom gear, maps, currency, grenades, automatic weapons and the latest in mountain climbing gear.

McKenna was also carrying a weapon with her. Nestled inside her leather purse was a Walther TPH, a small .22-caliber weapon designed for ease of concealment and up-close precision work. It was a hitter's weapon, and she was obviously familiar with it.

The Executioner shook his head. The sun was shining, and he was sitting next to a beautiful woman in one of the most romantic spots in Europe. And here he was figuring out whom to take down first and which was the best evac route.

Maybe he was being just a bit too cautious, he thought. On the drive down here earlier, he had a feeling that he was being followed, and that put him in a defensive mode. But that could have been his combat instincts kicking in from the old days, when Karlovy Vary hadn't been such a friendly place. At least it hadn't been friendly to him.

"Is something wrong?" McKenna asked.

"No. Nothing's wrong."

The Executioner looked past her at the china shop. The man and woman were walking away without giving him a second look. He watched them head toward a narrow alley lined with boutiques, trying to see if they shared signals with anyone passing by, a sign that they were handing off the surveillance to a new team.

But when the couple vanished down the alley, no one took their place. At least no one who seemed to be watching him and McKenna.

"I'm losing you again," she said.

He turned back toward her. "I'm still here," he said.

The woman shrugged. "Maybe now you are. But a moment ago you looked a world away from here."

"Probably because I was," Bolan said. "Last time I traveled close to these parts, it was quite a different atmosphere. It was another world back then. Another war. It's hard to get used to moving so freely here. Hard to get rid of old memories."

On one of his previous blitzes through the region, he and Phoenix Force had skirmished with a group of Czech special forces who were supplying West German "revolutionaries" with Semtex plastic explosives. They also had been supplying the terror groups with the expertise to use them against live targets.

At the time, many of the Soviet satellites were using Western terrorist groups as proxies to attack American and European forces. While some of the groups operated on their own, many of them were provided with the kind of intelligence that could only be acquired by military or covert agencies.

The West suffered through several political kidnappings and terrorist attacks on police and army units before striking back with assets like Bolan, sending them across the border to attack the source. Except for the men who actually fought those cross-border actions, very few people realized how many live-fire incidents had occurred between Western and East Bloc forces.

And many of them had been fought around Karlovy Vary. Or were launched from there.

The town was in the westernmost province of the Czech Republic. It was a short drive from the capital

city of Prague and an even shorter drive to the
German border. In the days before the Berlin Wall
fell, it was an ideal staging area for cross-border covert ops. Since the Bohemian provinces were sand-
wiched between the formerly separate states of East
and West Germany, the Czech-based agents had hundreds of miles of forested regions they could slip
across and find sanctuary.

Karlovy Vary had been the home of Radio Prague.
It had also been the main stopover point for Italian,
French and German revolutionary assault units who
trained at the camps before moving on to Prague.
Once they reached Prague, they would receive additional funding, unlimited fake documentation and
weapons of any caliber they desired from the STB
arms factory. And then they would bring the instruments of terror back into their own countries.

Like a tourist pointing out the sights, the Executioner gestured south toward the distant layers of hills,
plateaus and roadways that surrounded the valley
town.

"That's where the monks operated from," Bolan
said, using the term that the STB special units were
known by. Part of it was due to the fact that their
actual headquarters was based in a monastery, but it
also reflected the almost religious zeal they brought
to their work. "For a while there, the monastery was
one of the busiest armories in the East. Men and ma-
tériel were constantly on the move through there."

Judging from the intel that Brognola had put together with his Czech counterparts, the Karlovy Vary
operation was still intact. Many of the same people
who ran the armory back when they were STB op-

eratives now ran it as private entrepreneurs. With their connections and contacts in the government, they knew when to lay low and when it was safe to go active. Preliminary intelligence passed on from the Czechs revealed that the group had recently moved another cache of Skorpions from the monastery. The end users were one of their long-standing customers. In exchange for the latest shipment of weapons, a small fortune in money and gems had been delivered into the collection boxes of the underground church.

"You know," McKenna said, "it may seem strange at first, but a monastery isn't such an unusual place to plan a war from. When you think about the Soviet philosophy, it makes a lot of sense. Since part of the Russian master plan was to stamp out religion and replace it with the state, why not convert a sacred site to profane use?"

"Are you giving me a history lesson?" Bolan asked.

"Do you want one?"

He looked at his watch. They had an informal meeting scheduled later in the day with a former high-ranking STB official in Prague. Their contact was a monk who may or may not have been defrocked. He'd cooperated with Brognola on several occasions in the past and apparently had sufficient reasons of his own for cooperating with him this time around.

But before the meeting with the monk, they had to conduct a quick recon early in the afternoon. That gave them some time to kill and some kick-back time to recharge their batteries before they went into action. And he could use a bit more time to shake off the jet lag. He signaled the waiter for another mug of black coffee. "Go ahead, Professor," Bolan said. "We've got some time."

McKenna pushed her coffee flute and plate to one side, giving herself a clear desk for her lecture. "It's basic psychology. Conquering armies have a choice. They can either raze everything to the ground and rule over a pile of rubble, or they can convert the old symbols of power into symbols of the new regime. That provides a physical and psychological continuity. Supposedly the occupied people will transfer their loyalty, or at least the appearance of loyalty, to the new lords of the castle."

"You mean like all those churches that were built on top of pagan sites," Bolan said. "Out with the old, in with the new. But just in case the transfer didn't take place, many of the churches were also built like fortresses. What once was hallowed ground could easily turn into a hellground."

"I see you paid attention in history class," she observed.

"You know what they say," Bolan said. "Either learn from it or be condemned to live through it again. That's why we're here now. We learned what the groups were capable of in their glory days. The Italian government nearly fell. West Germany, too. We've got to stop them before they get to that point again and do it in the States."

"Shall we start now?" She leaned over and picked up her purse, which had been sitting on the chair next to her. It had been within reach throughout their breakfast. Apparently she, too, had been feeling wary.

Bolan glanced at his watch and nodded. "Yeah. Say your prayers and let's check it out."

He finished his coffee and paid the bill. Then they walked across the square to where the Skoda was parked in the hotel lot.

THE SPIRE of the former monastery was visible from the winding backcountry road that the Skoda cruised along at a leisurely pace, moving in a southwesterly direction toward the German border.

When they drove around the next bend, they saw the full view of the gray stone monument to the glory days of the monks. It was perched upon a bare hill that rolled down to the road in a series of slopes, then continued on a slant toward the fast-flowing mountain stream.

The hill had such a steep slant that it almost looked like a ski run carved out of the Bohemian forest.

"Is that the place?" McKenna asked as she drove slowly around the bend in the road.

"Yeah," Bolan said, staring up at the imposing structure. Until now he had only seen it in satellite photos back in the SIOC command post. "That's the target." He studied the landscaped hill closely, searching for potential avenues of escape in case they had to leave suddenly.

A circular driveway that looped in front of the gabled portal was flanked by long white stone benches. Two late-model cars, a utility truck and an oversize van were parked on the edge of the driveway.

Like many ancient buildings, the monastery was in more need of repair than the sat photos could possibly show, but it still looked as if it were livable and reasonably well kept.

"Want me to turn around so you can get another

look?'' McKenna asked when the monastery was no longer in sight.

"No," Bolan said. He didn't want to risk driving past it again so soon. No sense in attracting attention when they had more than enough time to do it right. "I need to get a closer look at the monastery anyway."

They continued on for just short of a mile before Bolan instructed her to pull onto the side of the road and park under a cluster of shade trees. She moved the car across the solid earth, inching forward until it was fairly well covered by the leafy boughs overhead.

Still continuing in their "newlywed," mode, they carried a picnic lunch toward the stream and spread out a blanket close to the bank. Along with a light lunch, the contents of the basket included a pocket scope about the size of a small flashlight. It had enough magnification for him to see the walls he meant to scale later on.

After lingering by the water for a while, Bolan went for a quick stroll. He crossed the road and moved uphill into the woods. He covered the forested ground quickly, then found a good observation post in a small incline not far from the road.

Bolan swept the facade of the building with the scope, scanning past the rose windows and the stone images carved into the wall beside them, stone archangels and guardians protecting the building from interlopers.

He spent a good deal of time studying the cornice that traversed the upper level of the monastery. The sill of the cornice slanted upward and was just wide enough for a man to stand upon. It was designed for practical matters such as repairing the outside of the building, as well as for the medieval esthetic it bestowed on the structure.

After the Executioner scoped the site for another ten minutes, he heard a heavy thumping and grating sound coming from inside the monastery. A few moments later the thick wooden double doors of the portal opened. Two men stood in the shadowed portal, talking with a third man that Bolan couldn't see very well.

The Executioner rolled his thumb lightly across the pocket scope's magnification wheel and zoomed in on the portal.

With the increased magnification he could make out the faces of the two men standing just outside the doors. The two men were thirtyish and thuggish, despite their expensive suits. He could make out the pieces that were holstered beneath their jackets, ready to administer penance to any uninvited guests who crossed the threshold.

The third man stayed just out of range. He was obviously someone who was careful not to make himself a target. Bolan had seen that kind of caution in some covert operators who'd managed to survive for decades in an extremely lethal trade. They'd stayed in the game so long that sooner or later the odds turned against them. Sometimes that very same caution got them killed, when they were no longer willing to take the kind of risks that could keep them alive. Whoever he was, Bolan thought, his number just came up.

When the inside man closed the doors, Bolan once again heard the grating sound of heavy locks shuttering against a thick wooden crossbar. The only way through that portal was by invitation, divine intervention or a high explosive knock on the door.

The two men got into one of the cars, a cream-colored Mercedes that looked a bit bulkier than usual. Probably one of the armored versions, he thought, with a reinforced engine block, bullet-resistant tires and antiballistic glass.

Bolan watched the Mercedes roll down the circular driveway, wondering which direction they'd take. The road toward the Skoda and Doreen McKenna? Or the road toward Karlovy Vary?

If they went toward Doreen McKenna, she would be on her own, he thought. But she could take care of herself.

The two gunmen drove toward Karlovy Vary, which meant they were still undetected.

THE CAR SLOWED as it passed the long flat stretch of road that ran parallel to the stream. The driver shifted into lower gear, almost as if he were pacing Bolan as the Executioner walked back across the field to resume his picnic.

Without being too obvious about it, the Executioner glanced toward the road. It wasn't the white Mercedes. It was an older model, a blunt-nose red coupe with a high-performance engine. Two people were inside.

It slowed even more, then pulled off the road just past the spot where the Skoda was parked.

Bolan glanced back toward McKenna. She was still sitting there, apparently enjoying the bright fall afternoon in Bohemia. But her hand was in her purse, ready to pull out her backup piece.

"Did they make you at the monastery?" she asked when he reached the blanket.

"No," Bolan said, jerking his head toward the car. "Not them. That car wasn't even there. Is this the first time it's gone by?"

McKenna shook her head. "No. Twice before. Both times it was going slow as if they were looking for somebody."

Bolan sat beside her, unzipping his windbreaker a bit more so he could get at the Heckler & Koch USP in a hurry.

While both of them watched the car without seeming to watch it, they saw a man and a woman get out. The man was carrying a fishing rod and a bait bucket. The woman had a rolled-up magazine stuffed into her purse.

"This is getting to be a popular spot today," Bolan stated.

"Actually it is. While you were gone, a couple of other cars stopped. One was a family with small kids. Another was a young couple, just barely out of their teens."

"Did you notice anything about them?"

She shook her head. "Nothing unusual."

"Notice anything about these two?" he asked, indicating the two newcomers.

Again she shook her head. "No. Should I? Do you know them?"

"Not by name," Bolan said.

She raised her eyebrows. "You're watching them like they're familiar to you."

"They are," Bolan said. "Remember earlier when you asked me if something was wrong?"

"Yes," she said. "Back in the café."

"Right." The Executioner nodded toward the man, who was now standing at the edge of the bank and casting his line into the fast-moving water. After looking around for a spot that wouldn't ruin her crisp new jeans, the woman daintily sat on a bare patch of ground about thirty yards farther down the bank. She lit a cigarette, then leafed through her magazine. She appeared to be totally separate from the middle-aged man, almost as if she were window dressing for him. *They* were what was wrong."

"They look harmless enough."

"Look closer," Bolan said. "Those two were standing in the square across from us, looking in a shop window. I thought they were watching us at first, but then I wrote it off to paranoia."

"And now?" she prompted him.

"Now I know they're watching us," Bolan said. He got to his feet and unzipped his jacket all the way. The holster rig with the Heckler & Koch 9 mm automatic was showing. "We drove for about a half hour to get to this spot. Then after we scout out the monastery, our Bohemian Hemingway shows up at the same spot."

"How do you want to handle it?" she asked.

"I'm going over to have a talk with him. Stroll along the river after me. And bring your purse."

Bolan walked slowly toward the angler, who was playing it like he didn't see him.

The middle-aged man had a thick head of hair that once had been blond but now was rust. He was clean shaven and had the thick neck and the stocky arms of someone who trained religiously. He almost looked middle class, except for the single earring in his left ear and a slight scar over his right eye.

He suddenly glanced up at Bolan as if he were seeing him for the first time. He pulled in his line and said something unintelligible, speaking in the soft staccato tones of a native Czech.

"You were at Karlovy Vary," Bolan said.

"Yes, I was," the man said. This time he spoke perfect English. "I noticed that you were there with your—" he nodded toward McKenna, who stood behind him "—wife?"

"Right," Bolan said. "Hell of a coincidence that we were all visiting the town at the same time and now we're all out here at the same time."

"It is," the man agreed.

"I don't believe much in coincidences," Bolan said.

The man seemed unperturbed. "How was your ride down here?" he asked, changing the subject.

"Forget all that," Bolan said, stepping closer. He was within striking distance, and the other man knew it.

The man's smile vanished, knowing that it was quite possible that one of them could end up in the river unless they clarified the situation.

"I was inquiring about the car, *Striker*," the man said. When he used the code name, he made a point of looking at Bolan's eyes to see his reaction.

The Executioner let it ride, acting as if he hadn't heard it. "You mean the Skoda," Bolan replied.

"Yes. Extremely well equipped, if I recall." The

man looked back toward the Skoda where it was parked beneath the trees. "That kind of vehicle will see you through a lot of rough traveling. The travel kit should see you through any number of emergencies."

"What do you know about the car?" Bolan asked.

"Our mutual friends on Trziste Street asked for it," he said.

Bolan considered the man's response. Trziste Street was the address for the American Embassy. Obviously this man was well plugged into the covert operation. But what side was he plugged into?

"Do you work out of the embassy?" Bolan asked.

"Not directly," the man said. "I work with them on occasion. When they received the request for a vehicle, they passed it on to me."

"You're a car salesman, then," Bolan said.

He laughed. "I dabble in many things. And I assume many roles."

"What about her?" Bolan asked, looking past him toward the woman who was still calmly reading her magazine, totally absorbed in it as if the rest of them didn't exist.

"Ah," he said. "The lovely Violetta. She is usually someone else's wife. She is mine just for the day."

"A nice name, Violetta," Bolan replied. "Even if it's just for a day. How about you?"

"My name is Alexander Lux," he said. "But I also have another name that is applied to me from time to time, just like Striker is applied to you."

"What is it?" Bolan asked.

"Summer Visitor," he said. "Pass that by Mr.

Brognola the next time you talk to him. He'll tell you what it means. And that should also establish my bona fides to your satisfaction. Apparently my use of the Striker code name hasn't done so.''

''It's a name,'' Bolan said. ''It's not proof of anything.''

Lux nodded. ''Call Brognola.''

''That won't be for a while,'' Bolan said. ''We're maintaining silence for the rest of the tour.''

''Things have changed,'' Lux told him. ''That's why I made sure you noticed me in Karlovy Vary.''

''How'd they change?''

The big man exhaled. ''I'm sure you'll like to hear it from his mouth rather than mine. But here's the gist of it. Originally this was going to be a sanctioned operation. The highest levels of the Czech government were going to be in our corner and help us flush out this rat's nest.''

''And now?'' Bolan asked.

''And now—for political reasons, I'm told—a much smaller force will be involved. Initially.''

''How many?''

''Let's see.'' He pointed a finger at Bolan and said, ''One.'' Then he looked past Bolan toward McKenna. ''Two.'' Finally he tapped himself on the chest. ''Three.''

Bolan was prepared to go in by himself if he had to. That was why he'd come out here to do the recon before he even met with Brognola's contact. It was standard procedure to assume that something would go wrong.

''Do you have a plan worked out?'' Bolan asked.

''Yes,'' Lux said. ''I plan to go in right after you.''

He gestured toward the Skoda. "Before we get into that, use the dedicated satellite link to call the man with the cigar."

"I guess you do know him," Bolan said.

CHAPTER FIVE

Washington, D.C., SIOC

Hal Brognola looked at the triple-sectioned computer image displayed on the wall-length screen in the SIOC conference room. The multimedia projection was one of the more useful tools in the center's space-age computer network.

With a flick of a button he could transfer the image from the small computer screen to the oversize wall screen and view the entire scope of the operation at a glance. He could also transmit that same screen throughout the SIOC facility, as well as to any other secure-linked FBI sites. The real-time network ensured that all of the key players would be reading from the same page.

Voice-activated commands gave him the ability to zoom in on any section of the screen. He could call out for blowups of any of the maps, addresses and names on the screen, while also summoning any of the additional background information that was embedded in the program: photographs, fingerprints, records, aliases, date of birth and of death.

The system was like a high-tech seer that could

brief him on all known information about the Cohorts. Unfortunately it couldn't tell him where the Cohorts were located. Not yet anyway. But the databases and image banks were constantly being updated, and eventually it would pay off.

Until then they had to work this operation the old-fashioned way, pouring their blood, sweat and tears into the pursuit of the Cohorts until the investigations bore fruit. Brognola had been doing an awful lot of that lately, spending more time on the fifth floor of the FBI building than he was at home.

He had to coordinate all aspects of the joint task force and keep the lines of communication open for all of the players. To keep himself going through the long nights, he often took brief catnaps on the lounge in his office and fueled himself mainly on coffee and mineral water.

Brognola sat on the edge of the conference table and scanned the screen, which was tasked to the Cohort mission. The screen was divided into three segments. Each had a subtly different shade of background color to indicate the separate focus of the three-pronged operation.

The left column mapped out the current location of every FBI agent, both active and retired, who'd been involved in taking down the Cohorts back when the homegrown terrorist group posed a constant threat to the government. Right now these agents were deemed the most vulnerable, although Brognola knew that the Cohorts could shift their attack at any moment to any FBI targets.

Color-coded triangular icons were positioned next to the names of the agents to indicate the presence of a security unit from the U.S. Marshals or from an FBI Hostage and Rescue Team. Though the HRT groups were officially tasked with handling siege situations and negotiations, they were also trained to carry out one-sided negotiations if that was the only course left open. Along with the rescue personnel, the HRT groups included highly trained sniper-observer teams that usually had extensive military backgrounds.

Brognola had the HRT and Marshal teams sharing the bodyguard tasks because the manpower was getting stretched thin. For several days now the security teams had been shadowing the potential FBI charges whenever possible. Some of the "vulnerable" agents had been traveling and were hard to locate. Several other agents were extremely resistant to the idea of having bodyguards around the clock, especially since the Cohorts hadn't made another move. At least no moves that they were certain of, Brognola thought.

There had been the incident in Oregon where an agent named Ashcroft had turned up missing. So far the teams hadn't been able to determine if Ashcroft met with an accident, suffered foul play or had simply taken off for an extended wilderness trek around Crater Lake, one of his favorite haunts.

Brognola had sent additional teams into the area to join in the search. Part of him hoped they didn't turn up anything. He'd worked with Ashcroft at one time and remembered him as a dedicated agent who took no nonsense from anyone, and played down his accomplishments in the Cohort campaign. He didn't seek glory, just results. Those results may have got him killed.

Other than the possible move against Ashcroft,

there had been no officially confirmed Cohort action since the initial assault on the Etruscan Gem Company. Whether or not the Cohorts were intentionally biding their time just to waste the FBI's resources, they were benefiting from the massive deployment of manpower. Tempers were growing short, expenses were mounting and other Justice Department operations were being hampered by the loss of available manpower.

Already the second-guessing was setting in and the higher-ups were wondering if the manpower was justified. Some of them were wondering if Brognola had overreacted, that maybe the Cohort involvement was just a cover for everyday criminal activity.

It was always like that, Brognola thought. The cover-your-ass mentality sank in from the moment an operation was launched. The higher-echelon advisers and the cabinet honchos all wanted instant results. Or else they wanted someone they could hang. Someone like Hal Brognola.

Though he'd seen his share of actual combat, these days most of Brognola's wars were fought in airconditioned rooms just like this one. Whether it was at Stony Man Farm, SIOC headquarters or his usual office in the Justice Building, the big Fed was usually the covert-ops guy who called all the shots and took all the hits.

Brognola had been measured for the noose several times before but so far he had managed to survive. His previous record brought him some extra juice with the bureaucratic brigade. And it didn't hurt that he had the ear of the man in the Oval Office.

He moved his attention to the second section of the

screen. It showed the location where, at this very moment, he was fielding the operatives who had the most potential of bringing in results: Mack Bolan and Doreen McKenna.

The second section of the screen showed a map of the Czech Republic, highlighting the area around Prague and Karlovy Vary where the lead to the Cohort cache of Skorpions was delivering some promising results. When Brognola got in touch with one of his clandestine counterparts in Prague, a former top-ranking STB officer named Jaromir Zizka, the Czech grand master quickly got his people in motion.

Zizka owed Brognola some heavy-duty favors for the help he'd received in crushing a branch of the Russian *mafiya* that tried to set up shop in the Czech Republic shortly after the Russians officially pulled out in 1993. Overtures the *mafiya* had made to certain criminal elements in the States had resulted in a gun pipeline being shut down by agents of the Justice Department. The leaders of the *mafiya* cell had been put out of business. Since that time Zizka had called on Brognola for assistance in other matters. Brognola had always complied.

Now it was payback time, and Jaromir Zizka proved to be very cooperative. At least he had been in the beginning, Brognola thought.

Zizka not only knew that the Karlovy Vary monastery was functioning, but he also knew that the people behind it were former members of his own STB unit. Along with their gunrunning activities, the STB rogues were also involved in the flow of illegal synthetics flooding the European drug markets.

A discreet investigation by Zizka's people turned

up the fact that Skorpions had been moved from the monastery quite recently. He also confirmed that the Cohorts once had been regular clients of the Czech secret service. These days the Cohorts worked through underworld intermediaries, but with Zizka's help the links could be unraveled.

It was supposed to be a fairly straightforward operation. Bolan and McKenna would meet with Zizka in Prague. Zizka would have a covert unit ready to go in. Any intelligence captured at the site would be shared between the clandestine services of both countries, and Zizka would be able to bank on a considerable number of favors from the West. And as a personal incentive, Zizka would have an opportunity to remove a former protégé who had become a dangerous rival.

That was the original plan. But now Zizka was having second thoughts about the operation.

The STB man who currently ran underworld operations from the monastery had benefited from a couple of behind-the-scenes shake-ups in the Czech government. Now he was even more protected and connected than before. To move openly against him could cause chaos in the Czech intelligence service. It could also cause the ruin of Jaromir Zizka, an asset Brognola wanted to keep.

An alternative plan was in the works, and one of the linchpins of that plan had been waiting in the wings for more than a decade. The Summer Visitor. While he waited to hear from the Czech team, Brognola scanned the third section of the screen.

It showed a map of all known Cohort hideouts from the early days of the movement. Many of them were in heavily populated areas of the northeastern United States, close to major cities such as New York and Boston. Others were located in the uppermost regions of New York and Vermont near the Canadian border. There had also been a few known sites in Los Angeles and San Francisco.

Along with the houses, the wall screen showed drop-down lists for all of the known vehicles ever driven by the Cohorts, the dead drops they used, and the noms de guerre they adopted.

A family tree showed the hierarchy of the Cohort organization as far as it was known. Much of it was guesswork due to the fact that the philosophy of the group changed just as often as the leadership. At times they proclaimed themselves to be members of an international terrorist network. Other times the Cohorts saw themselves as misunderstood patriots or egalitarian resistance fighters with no designated leader. Toward the end they regarded their outfit as an underground commando unit taking orders from a military chieftain.

Brognola studied the computerized map, focusing on the Vermont area where the last known leadership of the Cohorts had been taken out. It was on the Vermont side of Lake Champlain, south of Burlington.

From a pair of Cohort captives turned informants, the FBI located the hideout of Garett Provost and Regina Lind, who'd been living as man and wife under the name of Reynolds. Someone else had also been staying with them at the time, either a teenager or a young man in his twenties, but no one seemed to know much about him. The family kept pretty much to themselves except for the time they put in on the small jobs they did in the community.

By most accounts, when the FBI field units made their move against the Vermont hideout, the Cohort leaders fired first. But it had been a confusing night with a lot of lead flying in the air. There was still no way to know exactly what happened in the opening minutes of the firefight.

Some agents believed that the Cohorts had been tipped off by a phone call from one of the informants who originally turned them in, and were prepared to shoot their way out of it when they burst out the door. Another report mentioned a rumor that someone from the local law-enforcement group working with the FBI made an unsanctioned or accidental phone call to the residence.

No one knew minute by minute what happened. They just knew the outcome. The Cohort leaders had been shot and killed, and that was the death knell for the entire organization. One or possibly two fugitives escaped minutes before the firefight, but there had been no sign of them. Until now.

The third man, Brognola thought.

He remembered Doreen McKenna's comment that the new Cohorts constituted a second-generation movement. Was the leader of the reborn terror group actually the son of the man and woman who were killed in the Vermont house? A literal child of the revolution who was carrying on the fight in their name?

If so, who was he now? And what was the apparatus that he was hiding behind?

Brognola was trying to summon the phantomlike

image of the Cohort leader when the secure phone unit on the center of the table rang.

For a moment Brognola thought about clicking on the speakerphone. But even though he knew the SIOC room was totally secure from eavesdropping, he maintained his habits of old and picked up the receiver.

It was the Executioner, calling from the unit in the Skoda.

"I've been expecting your call," Brognola said.

"I hope so," Bolan replied. "There's a few things going on here that you should be aware of."

"I take it you've been contacted by someone."

"Yeah."

"Did he give you a name?"

"Two of them," the Executioner said.

"He has several that I know about," Brognola said. "He should have given you one name that stands out."

"Yeah, he did," Bolan said. "The Summer Visitor."

"That's it." Brognola explained the play on words behind the code name. Alexander Lux was an American citizen who penetrated Czechoslovakia long before the fall of the iron curtain, a deep-cover operative planted behind enemy lines to be activated in time of war. He'd been infiltrated into the country shortly after the failed Czech rebellion against the Soviet overlords known as Prague Spring. Hence the code name.

Lux was a Special Forces vet who had been recruited by the agency for his military skills, as well as his abilities as a linguist. They needed someone who could not only pass as a native but also stand up to the psychological pressure of living a secret life in an occupied land. Someone willing to save his country by living in another.

When the cold war finally ended for real and the Czech Republic struggled toward democracy, Lux maintained his cover as a Czech national. Now that it was easier to move back and forth across borders, he made several trips back to the States and to embassies across Europe. He became a go-between for U.S. operatives and their East Europe counterparts, including Jaromir Zizka.

"You never mentioned him before," Bolan said.

"He was an asset I never thought we would have to use," Brognola replied. "But the time has come. You'll need his help to get out of there once this goes down."

He spoke with the Executioner a while longer, providing more background on Zizka, the Czech spymaster who had become an uneasy ally.

Prague, Czech Republic

THE MAN WHO HAD ONCE BEEN a monk for the notorious STB terror training camps now looked as if he were doing his best to atone for those years.

His hands were clasped together beneath his chin in an almost prayerlike fashion, and his elbows were resting on the wooden table. His head was bowed, partially because of his penchant for secrecy, but also due to his need to see the eyes of the two American operatives who faced him from across the table. He was an old soldier with a bit of vanity about him, and that was why he squinted rather than wore glasses.

Other than the eyes and the weathered skin that showed the signs of age, he still radiated a formidable presence.

This was a man who was used to deciding the fates of others. He saw that same look reflected in the Executioner's eyes and had come well prepared to deal with such a man if need be. The booths on both sides of them were occupied by rugged-looking men who were obviously more than the monk's spiritual advisers. He had brought his action arm with him.

Jaromir Zizka studied Doreen McKenna with a somewhat warmer gaze, but he didn't make the mistake of underestimating her abilities. The Czech operative knew that she, too, could pose a serious threat. The fact that she was here with Belasko spoke volumes about her capacity.

They were sitting in the back booth of a small tavern in an out-of-the-way district of the area known as Lessor Town, the ancient part of the capital. It was far removed from the baroque palaces, stately museums and baronial beer halls that filled many of the squares they passed through on their way to the rendezvous.

Introductions had been made quickly. After the false names had been exchanged and their bona fides established, Zizka quickly warmed up to the subject that had brought them together.

"The Cohorts were a special breed," Zizka said. "They stood out from all of the others. Red Brigades, the Japanese Red Army, Direct Action, Baader-Meinhof." He listed several other revolutionary groups that at one time had been under his covert jurisdiction, practically shaking his head in dismissal at the mention of their names.

"All of them passed through our facilities at one time or another," he continued. "But none were quite so zealous as the Cohorts. Everyone they encountered they tried to win over to their side—even those of us who were schooling them in the finer arts. In their minds there was only one course to follow. They had to convert you or condemn you. There was a fire burning inside them, and they wanted to spread it."

"And you helped them," Bolan said.

Zizka's warm eyes suddenly went cold as his memory scanned the years, recalling the bombings and the wreckages of buildings and human beings, the killings on the street, the kidnappings of innocents.

"Yes, I did," he said. "When it was unavoidable. It was a different time back then. A different dominion. Soviet tanks rolled through our streets whenever we tried to pilot our own course. The more unreasonable of my people—those who wouldn't listen to reason according to the Soviets, that is—were invited to Moscow for discussions that often ended with fatal cases of lead poisoning. When you were summoned there, you never knew if you were going to come back. And if you were lucky enough to come back, you looked at the world through different eyes."

Zizka stopped speaking. His troubled gaze made it clear that he had been invited to Moscow and had left part of his soul there. He struck a wooden match to light another filterless cigarette and take a sip of the dark thick beer in front of him.

"They infested our police," he said. "And they monitored our citizens, turning one against the other.

The only way to work against them was to work with them. To become as strong as they were. In order to know what they were doing and to whom, we had to play the good soldier.''

Bolan tried to remain impartial. The man across from him had obviously suffered, just as others had suffered because of him. It was hard to judge what any man would do in that situation. Maybe Zizka had prevented more evils than he caused.

The Executioner remembered what it had been like when the Czechs were at the peak of their powers. Czech ''diplomats'' were routinely declared persona non grata by their host countries. Italy, France and Germany expelled scores of STB agents year after year when their support for terror groups became too overt.

At times some of the terrorist groups claimed up to five hundred members. The Czechs funneled millions of dollars of support to them. Their rents were paid, safehouses and communication networks were set up for them and vehicles were provided. Weapons, advanced training and unlimited documentation were theirs for the asking.

Despite many of the terror groups' supposed security measures, they were well known for their repeated failure to cover their tracks, almost as if they wanted the world to know the caliber of their covert sponsors. Many times, when members of the radical gangs were killed or captured in shoot-outs, the evidence gathered in their safehouses and vehicles provided links to international sponsors. More often than not, the operations were bankrolled through STB benefactors.

"Make no mistake," Zizka said. "I am not asking forgiveness for anything I have done under the Russian thumb. Because of my position in those days, I was able to stop some of the atrocities the groups had planned."

"How was that?" Bolan asked. It seemed odd that a man in charge of training saboteurs and assassins would then turn around and sabotage the people he set loose on the world.

"Whatever way I could," Zizka said. "Sometimes it was a matter of sending a letter to the proper authorities. Other times I arranged for anonymous calls to the Italian and German police. The callers would give them names of terrorists and the locations where they could be found. If it was safe to do so, I would pass along intelligence to my brethren in the West. Of course, I would do nothing that ever hurt my country. I am offering that same help once again with the Cohorts."

As Bolan listened to the Czech controller, he realized the man was caught in a modern-day Frankenstein situation. Originally the revolutionary groups had become secret armies for a secret war. But their military targets quickly gave way to innocent civilians. Their armed offensives turned into kidnappings, bank and armored-car robberies, drug and gun trafficking. They worked alongside the underworld gangs, planning operations together and sharing expertise. They split the profits and cemented relationships that blurred the distinction between terrorist and gangster.

And now Zizka's own Czech Republic was threatened by some of the very monsters he had helped to create. Cohorts in America and STB rogues in Karlovy Vary. Countless other revolutionaries that passed through the training camps had become terrorists, murderers and criminals. Like a plague, many of them were plying their trade in former East Bloc territories.

Though Zizka held the key to destroy them, he couldn't use it himself because of the change in his personal situation. But he was willing to hand it over to them under certain conditions.

"It is not going to be as easy as we thought," Zizka said. "Our mutual friend in Washington has explained that to you by now."

Bolan nodded.

The veteran Czech monk made a gesture that took in the men who had filled the booths around them. They watched Bolan and McKenna with neutral eyes. At a word from Zizka they could turn on them as enemies or embrace them as allies. Their loyalty went to no special cause. It belonged to Jaromir Zizka.

"If my people went in directly and stormed the monastery, there would be an outcry heard all across the country," Zizka said. "The men who operate from there—my old comrades—have insulated themselves well with their friends in the ministry. An open attack could lead to civil war in our intelligence and police ranks. Nothing but chaos would come of it. All of the freedoms we worked so hard for would be lost."

The Executioner leaned forward. "So far you told me a lot about what you can't do. How about telling me what you can do?"

Zizka smiled thinly. "Very well. What we can do is respond to any incident that legitimately requires our presence. For example, if war were to break out between underworld factions at the monastery, a war sufficient to reveal that former government agents were smuggling former government weapons to terrorist groups...then of course we would be obliged to come in."

"You need someone to light the fuse," Bolan concluded.

Zizka nodded. "I understand that is one of your areas of expertise."

"I'll make it happen," Bolan said. "Provided we get additional help in tracking the shipments to the Cohorts."

"My people are already working on that," Zizka said. "They are looking at a chartered tour group that happened to be across the border in Germany at the same time the shipment of Skorpions was taken from the monastery. The group traveled across Germany and France, then back to a place in England where the tour originated."

"Where was that?" Bolan asked.

"Glastonbury," Zizka said. "From there, who knows how the weapons made their journey?"

From McKenna's reaction, the mention of the location obviously struck a chord with her.

"You recognize the name?" Bolan said, turning toward her.

"Yes. It's a small town in the southwest of England. There's a mystical site very close to the town. Thousands of pilgrims go there every year."

"Sort of like a retreat?" Bolan asked.

They shared a look. It was a pattern that would bear looking into. First there was the retreat in New York that the Cohort gunmen fled to, then there was the monastery in Karlovy Vary. And now a religious site in Glastonbury. It was almost as if the Cohorts deliberately chose sacred sites to cloak their activities.

"The intelligence on Glastonbury and the Cohort connection is preliminary at this point," Zizka said. "We'll have more when we open up the monastery to the light of day."

"Let's see what we can do about that," Bolan stated.

THE EXECUTIONER CLIMBED uphill toward the monastery, retracing the path he'd taken earlier in the day. The siege had begun. Flickering streams of moonlight pierced the canopy of the forest, but there was no reflection on the man in black. His face was streaked with camouflage paint, and his black combat suit merged with the shadows.

He continued moving uphill, keeping parallel to the monastery until he reached the midpoint of the stone edifice. From his previous recon and his conversation with Alexander Lux, the deep-cover operative accompanying him on the night mission, the Executioner had decided upon the best way to breach the walls.

The double doors in the portal were too secure for an initial charge, and the small side door at the back of the monastery was too risky.

Bolan was going to drop in on them. If he failed to gain entry, then Lux would try the same maneuver from the other side of the monastery. Once he was inside and engaged the monks, McKenna would drift out of the woods and start knocking on the front door.

Bolan paused in the darkness and listened. The

wind had picked up a bit and was hissing through the overhead branches, kicking up some of the leaves at his feet. But the night was still relatively quiet. Much too quiet for what the Executioner had in mind.

The only way he could make his move was under cover of sound. Otherwise the ''monks'' who were cloistered within the walls of the monastery were bound to hear his approach.

Maybe Jaromir Zizka had a change of heart, he thought. Maybe he was withdrawing even the minor support that Bolan and Lux got him to commit to back in the restaurant.

But then he heard the welcome sound of a plane droning in the distance. The whine grew louder as the aircraft flew closer.

Zizka had come through for them.

Since Prague was only a short distance from the Karlovy Vary region, it wasn't too much of a coincidence for planes to circle over the Bohemian forest while they waited to make their descent into the busy hub airport. But tonight Bolan couldn't afford to count on coincidence. He needed considerable sound to mask his approach.

That was why Zizka called upon some of his behind-the-scenes contacts to arrange for a few flights to be stacked up over Prague. For a short time the aircraft would fly in ever wider circles that took them over the Czech countryside, long enough to become unwitting allies to the covert action.

The Executioner waited out the first plane to get the rhythm of the sound, see when it was loudest and how much time it gave him to make his move.

When he heard the first faint sounds of another

plane approaching from the distance, he stepped out into the open. He timed his movements with the overhead sound as he made his way toward the monastery. He crept close to the strip of grass along the outside wall and was careful to avoid the thin walkway that ran along the full length of the ancient structure. Even with his rubber-soled boots, the loose stone surface of the walkway could tip the enemy to his presence.

By the time the droning sound was just at its loudest, Bolan was standing at the front corner of the monastery. He uncoiled the loop of black nylon rope that was tied to the rubber-tined grappling hook. It had three curved prongs, three wishes to use all at once in the hopes that the hook would catch on the upper-level cornice.

Bolan stepped back to give himself enough of an angle. He gripped the rope with his left hand and played out enough length so his right hand could swing the hook back and forth. He continued testing the weight and balance of the metal until he could sense the necessary amount of force to use to cast it overhead.

With a final swing he released the grappling hook and watched it sail in a gentle arc above the cornice. Then it came down with a soft thunk.

He pulled gently on the rope until he could feel the tines claw into the slanted stone. He kept a steady pressure on the rope, aware that a sudden release in tension could spring the tines free, then he put one foot flat on the wall and tested half of his weight on the rope.

It held.

After he tried his full weight with the same success,

Bolan gripped the rope with his fingerless leather gloves and pulled himself up hand over hand, scaling the monastery wall.

The soldier was halfway to the cornice when a creaking sound echoed from below. The side door opened and a strip of light fell onto the walkway. He flattened and shifted his body toward the front of the building to reduce his silhouette.

The man at the door warily looked out into the darkness, as if he'd been alerted by some suspicious sound. Maybe the tines on the stone gave him away, Bolan thought, or maybe it was the sound his feet made when they dug into the wall.

Whatever the cause, someone had sent the man outside.

He closed the door behind him and stood there listening. His hand was on his holstered pistol, clutching the butt like a security blanket.

The monk spent almost half a minute just looking around and letting his eyes adjust to the darkness. After several more seconds passed, the monk's hand finally fell away from his side arm. Now that his fear level had ratcheted down a few notches, he began moving along the walkway.

The rope, Bolan thought. He looked down at the thin black cord and saw it dangling a few inches from the stone. It was drifting back and forth in the breeze.

A hard wind could push it against the building and maybe make enough noise to attract the gunner's attention. Or he might pick up the snakelike silhouette.

Bolan held on to the rope with his left hand and swayed it gently with his right hand, trying to bring it closer to the building.

The man started walking toward him.

The soldier stayed flat against the building, measuring the man's location by the soft scratching sounds his feet made on the gravel.

The man stopped below him, right at the corner. He looked left and right and was about to look up when Bolan pushed off from the building.

The rope whipped through his hand as he rapidly descended toward the target. The friction of the nylon spent itself against the thick leather guard and kept his hand from being sliced in two. Just before he hit, Bolan planted one foot against the stone. Before the hardman even knew what was happening, the soldier looped the free length of rope in his right hand around the man's neck.

Bolan's other foot touched the ground like an anchor, which dragged the monk forward and snapped his neck with a sudden jerk.

The man's knees thumped hard against the ground, then he bounced back against the rigid stone corner. His head dropped down to his breastbone and he sat there, as still as the stone images carved into the gray stone walls.

The monastery was minus one defrocked monk.

The Executioner glanced back toward the side door. No one else was coming, but it wouldn't be long before they checked on him.

He quickly made his way back up toward the cornice, thanking Jaromir Zizka for the frequent flights that were droning in the distance.

When he was about a foot below his objective, Bolan reached up with his fingertips, clenched them tight on the sill and pulled himself up over the edge. He gripped the tines of the grappling hook and quietly tugged them free from the cornice.

Maintaining a crouch so he could keep his balance, he moved slowly across the stone platform toward the double lancet rose window in the middle of the facade. His immediate target was directly below the rose window.

As he neared the multicolored glass, he could hear snatches of conversation and music coming from the window directly below. He moved one foot at a time, painstakingly setting each one down before lifting the other, careful not to make a sound.

Bolan crouched lower, then wedged the tines into the sill once again. It was almost time to go over the edge and let them know of his presence. He had the USP pistol in a side holster, and in his underarm rig was the familiar weight of the Beretta 93-R that Lux had obtained for him.

In a close-quarters battle like this one, the Executioner wanted to go in with something he knew he could count on. The USP would be a good backup, but for the initial assault, he wanted some fast firepower.

The soldier scanned the ground below him. From this height he could see the road and the stream beyond. He could also see Doreen McKenna at the edge of the wood looking up at him and waiting for his signal. Lux was also ready to do his part as soon as Bolan breached the monastery.

The Executioner chopped the air with his hand, letting them both know that he was going in.

He gripped the cornice on both sides of the grappling hook, then eased himself over the side, using his upper-body strength to keep his feet from scraping against the stone.

When his lean frame was fully extended, Bolan tugged on the nylon rope until it was taut. He abseiled down the facade, dropping several feet until he was hanging just to the left of the target window. He glanced inside the room and gave it a quick recon. Two monks were sitting at a wooden table with a half-empty bottle of wine. They were playing cards and talking softly to someone on the other side of the table.

In the background, maybe in another room, someone was turning a radio dial left and right and trying to tune in a Prague station.

Bolan lightly planted his feet against the stone. He bent his legs and then pushed off into space. Anchored by the nylon rope, he swept out into the nothingness, then swiftly came back toward the half-open window, knowing that there was just enough space for him to slip inside—as long as he came in hard enough.

His feet speared through the air with only his heels touching lightly on the sill as he rocketed into the room.

Three shocked men looked at him as if he'd just fallen from the heavens. They were turned to stone for a critical few moments, long enough for Bolan to get his balance and come up with the Beretta 93-R in his hand.

ADRIAN GREGOR PUSHED away from the table.

The Czech underworld soldier was unaware of exactly what was going on, other than it was something that he had to react to quickly. One moment he'd been reaching for another glass of red wine while he casually scanned the hand of cards he'd been dealt, the next a wraithlike creature crashed into their midst. The first thing that came to mind was that it was some kind of bat fluttering through the open window. But then the black shape on the edge of his vision took on form.

On another night, Gregor would have responded in a much more efficient manner. The gun in his holster would have been in his hand before the intruder touched the floor. Or at the very least he would have flung the heavy glass wine bottle at the man's head and put him out, just like throwing rocks at a rodent.

But tonight the world around him was moving in alcohol-fueled tableaus, quick glimpses of slow-motion clarity followed by blurry images that moved too fast for his mind to decipher in real time.

Though he was slower than usual, Gregor wasn't totally defenseless. His instinct for preservation caused his meaty left hand to grab the edge of the thick wooden table and pull upward. The table upended with a loud crash that sent bottles smashing to the floor and cards and coins spinning in the air.

The table balanced itself on its end, giving Gregor a temporary shield as he staggered backward. From his drunken vantage point, the stocky Czech hardman could see just over the upturned table. He caught a glimpse of the deathly black shape who was crouching on the floor with a Beretta in his outstretched hand. The barrel followed the panicky movement on Josef, the man Gregor had been playing cards with, who had a winning streak until now.

Just as Josef managed to pull his automatic pistol free from his holster, the man triggered a 3-round burst from the Beretta. The trio of slugs knocked the card player back against the wall.

Josef's weapon clattered to the floor, unfired, and his arms flailed uselessly at his sides, fingers clutching as if he were trying to hold on to life.

"Gregor!" the man shouted with his last breath. It sounded like an accusation, that Gregor had failed to protect him as he'd done so many other times. Or maybe it was a cry for vengeance.

Whatever it was, the cry ended in blood as a streak of red poured from the man's lips and he keeled over.

Gregor heard the sound of splintering wood and felt tiny shards digging into the back of his wrist. His mind caught up with his body a second later when he realized the splinters chewing into his flesh were coming from the table he was firing his Skorpion into. He'd triggered a couple of short bursts that drilled through the wood and chewed into the floor near the man in black. Or where he had been a moment ago.

And then Adrian Gregor heard the buzzing whine of three metal hornets cutting the air just above his head. The return fire jolted him another step closer toward sobriety. The man in black wasn't going to go away that easily. Not from a blind-fired round through a tabletop.

He stepped closer to get a better look, but the intruder was moving too fast for Gregor to follow. For a brief instant he caught a flash in the man's eyes, a gaze that was calculating who he could put away next—Gregor or the third man in the room.

Gregor voted for the third man.

He backstepped several paces and squeezed off a burst from the Skorpion. At last his system was fully responding to the shock of the attack, to the near miss that almost took off his head and to the sobering sight of Josef checking out once and for all.

Gregor made it to the door, reached behind him for the handle and flung it open hard enough so it banged on the wall in a loud reverberating shudder. He fired one last burst of rounds as he stepped out into the hall.

As soon as Adrian Gregor stepped from the room, he shouted out a warning to Matthias. His voice echoed through the cavernous hallways, sounding like a wounded creature, a member of the flock calling for the shepherd.

Gregor felt guilty at his momentary cowardice, but the guilt was more than compensated for by the sweet sensation of his feet pounding on the floor as he retreated from the room where death waited.

Whoever the man was, Gregor knew he couldn't handle him alone. Not in his present state.

"Matthias! Matthias!" he shouted again and again, calling out the name as if it were some kind of chant.

The guiding light of the monastery crew probably had heard the sound of the firefight by now, although with the stone walls and the drinking habits of nearly everyone in the group, it was hard to tell. As he ran down the hallway he heard more shouting coming from behind him.

Some of the others had joined the fray…or had been sent on their way by the intruder. He didn't stop to find out.

BOLAN HAD KEPT MOVING from the moment he touched the floor in the midst of the hardmen. With split-second judgment he'd taken in the scene before him, noted the position of the hardmen and quickly went about the task of identifying the monk who presented the most danger.

It was a split-second decision, but he went about it with the computer-like precision of a man who'd been in this position countless times before.

The Executioner recognized two of the monks from his earlier recon, the hardmen who'd driven off in the Mercedes. The man who was sitting on the side of the table farthest from him, a tall and top-heavy bruiser, looked drunk and startled and not an immediate threat. The man next to him was also temporarily dazed by the Executioner's sudden entrance.

But it was the man on the side of the table closest to Bolan who had the best chance of responding. Of the three, he was the one who'd kept his wits about him. There'd been no wineglass parked in front of him, and there was no glazed look in his eyes.

The gunner jumped back from the table with the kind of speed that came from athletic grace or from stark raving panic. Whatever the cause, the man had his weapon in hand by the time he reached the wall behind him.

Bolan drilled him with a 3-round burst from the Beretta, then kept his eyes on him just long enough to make sure the guy was down for good.

Then he rolled across the floor a split second before the huge wooden table flipped into the air as if it were made out of cardboard. It came down with a loud crash just inches from Bolan's foot and nearly trapped him. It would have clipped him if he stayed put and made him an easy mark for the other two monks to finish off.

By yielding to the subconscious commands that had kept him alive for years, Bolan found himself rolling back toward the window he'd come through. Just as he braced himself against the wall, he saw the bloodshot eyes of the bigger monk glaring at him from over the edge of the table.

The guy still looked groggy but had somehow managed to steady himself. The teetering monk was following Bolan with the eyes of a wine-muddled marksman who was readying himself to fire.

The Executioner tapped a burst toward the big man's head, then dropped flat on the floor, anticipating the other man's move an instant before a volley of rounds bored through the wood and chopped into the wall behind him.

That left the Executioner face-to-face, or face to foot, with the other monk, who was springing up from his chair, shocked by the bullets ripping through the wood and by the man at his feet. The stunned hardman was looking down at the floor as if it were suddenly full of real scorpions instead of the metal kindred favored by the monks.

The monk went on automatic pilot and aimed a snap kick toward Bolan's face with his pointed boot. The soldier moved slightly and took the sharp thrust on his shoulder. A spike of pain shot all the way down through his neck and arm, nearly short circuiting all of his nerve endings. But he managed to keep his grip on the Beretta 93-R.

At the same time, he curled his left hand around

the man's ankle and twisted hard, tugging the gunner off his feet and toppling him backward at an awkward angle.

Even as he fell, the monk realized he only had a scant few fractions of a second to alter the course of his suddenly endangered life. He overcame his body's natural urge to protect itself during a fall and instead reached for his weapon. It was a SIG-Hammerli pistol with a walnut grip molded for an exact fit with his hand.

Bolan spun halfway around and got to a half-sitting position. He closed his left hand around his right wrist to steady his still weakened gun hand as his opponent's pistol swung in a rapid arc toward him.

The monk fired but not before Bolan squeezed off a 3-round burst that caught him in the face.

The hardman's gun went off as he fell backward, but the round sailed harmlessly past the Executioner's head. The report from the SIG-Hammerli echoed loudly in the room and left a ringing in his ear.

Bolan shook it off and scrambled to his feet. He flattened against the wall and edged toward the door the monk had fled through.

CHAPTER SIX

When the sounds of bedlam first began to echo throughout the monastery, Vaclav Matthias turned down the radio. The station was broadcasting Stenhammer's *Excelsior!* and the symphonic overture had barely begun.

He turned off the lights in the chancellery, where he'd been sitting behind his desk, sipping cognac and listening to a classical music station from Prague.

For most of the evening, while the monks who worked for him were engaging in their favorite pursuits of wine, women and cards, Matthias had been attending to his own favorite pursuit. Solitude. He enjoyed the quiet isolation so much that he probably would have fit in well with the monks who lived here so long ago. But instead of chants, he liked opera and the grand symphonies.

And there was also the matter of his current occupation, one that would definitely banish him from the order. The only faith he had was in the faith of the gun. Wielding it or selling it.

Matthias had been a weapons master for decades. His country had trained him to work with the underworld of terrorists and zealots of all stripes. When peace broke out, he had no desire to change his occupation. So now he continued to ply his trade. If that hurt his country from time to time, there was nothing he could do about it. It was just the way of the world he lived in.

For years he'd reaped the rewards of that philosophy. And only now, he thought, was he reaping the punishments. As he listened to the shouts and the gunfire, both silenced and unsilenced, he wondered who had come for him.

Matthias had made many enemies over the years. Though he'd done his best to send them to their just rewards, there were still a few of them determined to outlive him.

He listened to the shouts and the sounds of gunfire, then calmly opened his desk drawer and removed a blue-steel automatic pistol. It was loaded with a full clip. It always was. That was one of the few rituals Matthias followed in his monastery. Whenever he entered his office, he checked to make sure the weapon was ready for work.

Matthias sidled closer to the door. He opened it a crack, just enough to hear the sound of distant voices and the rapid burst of a machine pistol. He was about to open the door all the way and slip outside, when he heard running footsteps pounding on the floor at the end of the hallway.

He stepped back several feet into the room and leveled the automatic at the open door. His finger tightened on the trigger, ready to take out the first man who came through.

Adrian Gregor lurched through the door, stepping into the splinter of light that followed him in from the hallway. He came to a dead stop when he noticed the silence.

"Vaclav?" he said.

"I'm here," Matthias said. He stepped out of the shadows and lowered the gun. "What is happening out there?"

"Upstairs," Gregor said. "In the card room. Through the window. A man attacked us—"

"Just one man?"

"This one is enough," Gregor said. "So far we already lost two of our own. Maybe more. The others are trying to hold him off. They have him contained on the second level."

Matthias looked at the tall Czech gunner. The man was one of his best, he thought. Or he used to be. Now the big man was fighting a war against the bottle and he was losing it. Even though adrenaline was pumping through Gregor, it was easy enough to see the drunkenness in his eyes. He was trembling. Was it fear or was it simply that he was reaching the end of the line?

"One more question," Matthias said. "If the invader is up there, what are you doing down here?"

"I came down here to warn you," Gregor said, "as soon as I could."

Matthias nodded. It was possibly true. It was just as possible that whoever the invader was, he had unsettled Gregor so much that the big man had to run away from him. It was hard to judge the merits of anything he said. But from the familiar sound of rapid-firing Skorpions on the upper level, his men indeed had this man contained. One of the chief methods his men used during close-quarters engagements was to lay down a thick wave of suppressing fire. There was no shortage of machine pistols or ammunition in the monastery.

Rather than berate Gregor, who had done well by him in the past, Matthias simply acknowledged the information that the intruder obviously knew what he was about. One lapse wouldn't automatically condemn Gregor to the trash heap, provided that he seized the next opportunity to redeem himself.

"Who is this man who attacks us here?" Matthias asked. "What kind of man would dare to go against me in the sanctity of my home?"

Gregor shrugged. "I've never seen him before. He didn't say a word. He just came in shooting."

Though he didn't know who the shooter was, Matthias could guess who sent him. "One of Jaromir Zizka's people."

Gregor shook his head. "No. We know all of his men by now. This one is new."

"Maybe he imported some foreign help." Matthias gripped the larger man by a shoulder and guided him out into the hallway. "That is about all that's left to the old man," he said. "He's growing too weak and he cannot even trust his own people for this kind of work."

Gregor nodded. The weaknesses of Jaromir Zizka were remote to him at the moment. The man who'd stormed in from the darkness was the more immediate threat. "It is not one of Zizka's people," Gregor said. "It is someone worse."

"He will bleed just like everyone else," Matthias replied. "Let's go and find out who he is."

Matthias led the way down the corridor that ran

past the altar. He moved slowly and cautiously as he took in every inch of his surroundings. He was in no immediate hurry to directly confront his enemy. That was what his men were for.

Matthias exited the corridor and stepped out into the high-ceilinged nave. It echoed with gunfire from above.

He looked up on the balcony at the front of the monastery. One of his men was dead. His hands were gripping the railing, and his head was bloodied and bowed. Four others were scattered on the floor. They were aiming their weapons at the door that was the second from the right, squeezing off chattering bursts.

Matthias shook his head in disgust. It looked as if his men were fighting a defensive battle. Rather than storm the room and finish him off, they were willing to wait him out.

On the other side of the altar, two more of his men were slowly stepping out into the open. With their weapons at the ready they drifted past the few remaining pews. Since there was no more worship to be done here, Matthias had cleared out the rest of the pews and used them for firewood.

The room was like a great baronial hall with thick carpets covering the cold stone floors and long regal tapestries hanging on the walls. Several clusters of long couches, tables and chairs were positioned in the four corners of the room. And they, too, were filling up as more of his men came from the sleeping quarters at the back of the monastery.

Matthias glanced back to the room where the invader was pinned down, thinking that there was no way the man could ever leave here alive, and that it was time for him to say his prayers.

That's when an explosion rocked the front of the monastery and a spout of flame chased across the carpet.

FROM THE TIME Bolan approached the corner of the monastery, Doreen McKenna had been ready to back him up. She was standing at the edge of the woods when the monk had stepped out of the side door and meandered below the figure in black who was scaling the wall.

The barrel of the Heckler & Koch MP-5 SD-3 that was nestled in her hand moved slightly with every step he took. She tracked him through the night scope mounted on her suppressed subgun.

The monk was about to fall into that killing range when he stopped right beneath Bolan. She got him in the crosshairs of the green screen and was ready to take him out when Bolan dropped down the rope and hung him sideways.

She covered him as he scaled up the wall again. And then, when he gave the signal, she moved toward the front of the monastery. She lay prone on a small incline that gave her enough cover, but also gave her a clear field of fire.

Right after Bolan went through the window, McKenna hurried forward and took up her position. She crouched on the ground and aimed the submachine gun toward the windows on the second floor, tracking the barrel left and right.

She also kept an eye on Alexander Lux when he

made his way toward the thick doors and affixed several strips of explosives.

Lux positioned the shaped charges along the hinges, near the top and bottom of the doors, and then made a final "crossbar" over the thick iron handles.

Bolan was buying them crucial time on the upper level of the monastery, engaging the monks in a room-to-room firefight and drawing their attention toward him.

Midway during the shooting, McKenna saw a shape creeping through the window of one of the darkened rooms next to the one Bolan had breached. The monk stepped out onto the cornice and began to make his way toward the room.

McKenna allowed him to make it all the way to the edge of the window, waiting to see if any other monks were following him, before she raised the barrel of the H&K and pulled the trigger. The volley of suppressed 9 mm rounds stitched him from foot to face, exterminating him in a split-second spray.

The man crumpled to the cornice and lay there with his hand dangling over into space and his machine pistol falling to the ground.

A flash of movement to her right caught her attention.

It was Alexander Lux, signaling her to take cover. He was ready to announce their presence in a big way.

McKenna dropped back down to the incline while the deep-cover op scrambled for shelter on the opposite side of the circular driveway. She could see him raising his head above ground level and aiming the remote triggering device toward the door like a high-tech magic wand.

With a click of the button, he sent a storm of fire and brimstone through the portal and into the monastery.

The middle sections of the doors disintegrated in a cloud of smoke and fire. The upper sections shot straight up into the stonework like rockets, burrowing into the ancient facade. Chunks of stone and metal reinforcement bars dropped like a guillotine to the floor or flew into the monastery like catapulted stones. Tongues of flame scorched the ground, and clouds of suffocating smoke billowed from the sundered entrance. It was a blast of hellfire that had long been overdue.

From inside the monastery they could hear screams of wounded men and the confused shouting of orders.

"Now!" Lux shouted. "Set it up."

"I'm with you," McKenna yelled, pushing herself up from the ground. She sprinted toward the left side of the portal, knelt and triggered a full-autoburst from the suppressed Heckler & Koch. The muffled burst swept from left to right, spitting out a 9 mm clothesline of lead that cut down anything that moved.

Lux fired his submachine gun from the right side of the portal, sweeping from right to left. Together the 9 mm X crisscrossed the interior of the monastery and shut down any possible escape or immediate counterattack.

McKenna changed magazines, rolled across the ground toward the center position and laid down covering fire as Lux raced toward the side of the crumbling stone opening.

He tossed two multiple-bang stun grenades through the shattered opening. Bright flashes and concussive blasts erupted inside the building, concentrating violent halos of illumination on the surprised hardmen. The flashes measured more than two million candlepower and carried a concussive punch greater than two hundred decibels. It was more than enough force to deafen and dim the senses of even the best trained operatives.

As the rolling echo of destruction poured out of the shattered stone mouth, Lux tossed in another stun grenade.

This one was a "blinder," designed to create an unearthly flash that imprinted itself on the victims' eyes for days to come. While it didn't cause permanent damage, McKenna and Lux weren't all that concerned. They had come to put a permanent end to the unholy order of monks. If any of them had managed to recover from the first round of flash-bangs, this one put out their lights for the near future.

Lux went in first, darting toward the left side, followed by McKenna, who moved to the right.

They stood there in the midst of a group of armed monks who were looking for targets but couldn't see a thing.

The duo triggered selective blasts, taking down the enemy gunners one at a time, then moving on to acquire a fresh target.

Some of them fired back, blindly sweeping the area with their Skorpions. Sometimes they hit their own comrades who stood just a few feet away from them. Other times they came close to hitting the intruders.

But the steady thumping sound of Doreen Mc-

Kenna's Heckler & Koch subgun continued punching away until the Skorpion fire gradually fell off.

THE EXECUTIONER MOVED fast as soon as he heard the explosives going off. He rolled out of the doorway and started to fire before he even hit the floor. The Heckler & Koch USP bucked in his left hand and sent two quick shots toward the nearest monk.

The first shot caught the hardman in the forehead and knocked him off his feet as if he'd been hit with a sledgehammer. The second shot sailed overhead and struck the wall next to another monk who'd been looking down at the source of the explosion. Chips of stone from the bullet pierced his skin and brought his attention back to the Executioner. He was looking eye to eye at Bolan when the Beretta 93-R dropped him with two bursts.

The soldier continued to sweep the Beretta to his right and fired off three more bursts.

And two more monks went to their rewards.

Bolan stood by the railing and looked at the carnage below. Someone was shouting orders to his men, but they were too busy trying to stay alive to carry them out. The monks who were still on their feet had to deal with the aftereffects of the stun grenades while trying to avoid the chattering submachine guns that had drastically reduced their ranks.

MATTHIAS HURRIED from man to man, trying to marshal some kind of defense from the stunned men. He waved his automatic around but was still suffering from the effects of the flash-bangs himself.

He turned suddenly, sweeping his gun hand in a

rapid arc, the barrel of his automatic coming to rest on Doreen McKenna.

Lux stopped him with a short burst that nailed him from hand to shoulder, spinning him in the process. Blood sprayed from his suddenly loose fingers as the automatic skidded across the floor.

When Matthias went down, the will of his men went with him. There was no resistance left. Just a lot of wounded and dazed men who gradually realized they had only two alternatives: give up or die.

Lux shouted at them in their native tongue, using quick commands that left no doubt in their minds about how they could go on living. Almost like a choreographed line, the Czech hardmen dropped to their knees, then spread out on the floor and put their hands behind their backs.

Lux and McKenna collected their discarded weapons, then roped their hands together.

Bolan made a quick survey of the interior of the monastery, holding the Heckler & Koch USP and the Beretta 93-R at an angle slanted toward the floor. He moved up and down the remaining pews, then scanned the area behind the altar. Before they did anything else they had to make sure that none of the rogue monks were lying on the floor and playing dead.

While McKenna covered the bound survivors, Bolan and Lux made a quick recon of the chancellery office. Matthias had kept a bank of filing cabinets and a set of books. The entries made little sense to Bolan, but after scanning the characters Lux shook his head.

"Something wrong?" Bolan asked.

"You could say that," Lux replied. "These books

all seem perfectly balanced, which means they're probably fake. The transactions and the inventory have nothing to do with the kind of goods they shipped from here. Unless, of course, it is a code that someone else will have to figure out.''

''What about the caches of weapons?'' Bolan asked.

''From what our friends tell us, they're still in the basement vaults. That's where any real intelligence will be found.''

In the distance they could hear sirens approaching. The sound had been growing gradually. The raid had made enough noise to alert the proper authorities. Right on schedule, Zizka's people were responding to the open warfare that inexplicably broke out between two underworld gangs.

''It could take days to search this place,'' Bolan said. ''Under the circumstances I don't plan on spending another minute here. Just in case they feel like they have to take someone in.''

Lux nodded. ''We'll have to leave it for Zizka and his people to sort out.''

''Can we trust the guy to follow through?''

''I'm sure of it,'' the deep-cover agent said.

''Why's that?'' Bolan asked.

''After he sees what's been done here, I don't think he'll want to spend the rest of his life looking over his shoulder for you.''

CHAPTER SEVEN

Sedona, Arizona

Linda Norris tried hard not to stare at the face of the security guard who blocked the door to Winston Grail's inner sanctum, a futuristic glass-and-steel ark perched on a desert plateau a few miles outside of Sedona.

After all, it was what was inside a person that counted, wasn't it? Burne Taggart couldn't help it if his face had been tragically rearranged. Her eyes drifted as she spoke with him, scanning the broken terrain of his face so she wouldn't focus on one particular area.

A circular scar ran from the underside of his chin, up behind his cheekbone and across the top of his forehead. Then it ran back down behind his other cheekbone to complete the unbroken circuit of scar tissue. The translucent furrow of skin was the thickness of broken glass or the blade of a hunting knife.

It was a handsome face. Or it had been until the almost symmetrical scar permanently altered his appearance, making his face look like a piece of a jigsaw puzzle that was forced into place. The whitish

scar line stood in marked contrast to his tanned and
weathered face. Maybe he'd gone through a windshield or suffered some other kind of private hell, she
thought. The important thing was that he had sur-
vived.

And he wasn't an easy man to get by.

"But I *must* see him, Mr. Taggart," she insisted
again. "It's a spiritual matter. An urgent one."

"I'm sure it is," he said. He glanced over his
shoulder at the double glass doors that led into the
pyramid-shaped entrance. "Otherwise, you wouldn't
have pounded on the door hard enough to trigger the
alarm."

A tinted luminaire above the entrance cast a dif-
fused cone of light around them. Under other circumstances the intimate, warm lighting would almost be
romantic. "I'm sorry," she said. "I didn't know if
there was any other staff on-site."

"Just me," Taggart replied. "It's usually enough."
He stood before her, totally undisturbed by her plight.
One hand was clasped over the other, and his thick
wrists were just about even with the cuffs of the long-
sleeved shirt that he always wore, a sand-colored
shade of brown.

In many respects he looked just like one of several
casually dressed professionals she'd seen at the complex. Except perhaps for the prominent knuckles on
his hands, she thought. They had obviously been seriously bruised or broken at one time. Between the
knuckles there were spiderweb scars that ran across
his skin. He looked like someone who'd come up
through hard times and thrived on it.

"Look, I really need to see Mr. Grail tonight," she said.

"I've told you several times now, miss. Mr. Grail sees no one at this time of night."

She let the "miss" go. When she was on a story, she didn't mind if they called her a miss, Ms. or even mistress. But in her everyday life she was Linda or, in some of the newsrooms where she'd worked, she was just Norris. She was as down-to-earth as any New Age reporter could possibly be and still be receptive to the etheric vibrations attuning the planet for those who could hear them.

But the guard wasn't receptive at all, even when she flicked her long black hair over her shoulder, shifted her body to emphasize the tight beige halter top and gave him her best like-to-get-to-know-you gaze.

Taggart was immune. Or maybe worse. For a moment she caught a glimpse of the real man behind the mask, and it chilled her.

His empty gaze had suddenly looked through her as if she were some kind of windblown spiritual debris that drifted across the desert and ended up here with all the other "kindred" spirits visiting the resort. She was barely registering on the guard's radar, just part of the scenery.

The faraway gaze passed when he caught the look of worry on her face. Then he smiled at her for the first time. It probably had been her imagination, she thought, or a trick of the light. No man was capable of such a cold and soulless gaze. Especially here.

"Please, Mr. Taggart," she said. "I'm speaking as

a friend. If you could just call him and let him know I'm here, I'm sure he wouldn't mind.''

"That's something we'll never know," he told her. "Even if you were a friend, it's still against the rules.'' He spoke evenly, and his face remained placid and unbothered, almost as if he'd discovered the lasting inner peace that supposedly could be found in Sedona.

Okay, she thought, it was true that she really wasn't a friend of his. Yet. But that was only because she was a relative newcomer to the Trans Human Evolution Movement and its ways. She'd spent her first few days getting the lay of the land and figuring out how to cozy up to the key players. But now the land was getting crowded, and the players were rarely seen. Nearly two hundred others like her had gathered there in the high-priced, high-desert resort to realize their inner potentialities and commune with their peers. That, or maybe just get a good sun tan.

She was open to either possibility. But to offset her considerable outlay for her expenses, including reservations, seminar fees, workshops, plane fare and rental car, Norris needed some face-to-face time with Winston Grail. As the materials for THEM so often quoted him, Grail's earthly mission was to provide his guests with the materials they needed for their spiritual journey, sort of an astral outfitter. But it was up to them to dream and shape their future.

Unfortunately, Burne Taggart was barring the door to that future.

"Listen," she said, leaning forward as if she were sharing a confidence, "I'm doing a series of articles for all the major magazines and some of the newspaper syndicates. That kind of exposure can do him a lot of good.''

"He's doing good enough," Taggart replied. "Take a look around." He gestured at the modern haciendas that artfully blended in with the landscape, using the ancient red rock canyons as a backdrop. Then he nodded back at the observatory-like building behind him. The price tag for the headquarters of Winston Grail's various New Age enterprises was definitely in the stratospheric range, more than most mortals could even contemplate.

"I get the picture," she said. "But a little extra publicity never hurt anyone, even someone like Winston Grail.''

"Contact the public-relations office tomorrow," Taggart said. "I'm sure they'll be able to help you.''

"I'll do that," she promised. "But I really do need the personal touch for the story. Some behind-the-scenes material. Maybe you could help—''

"Tomorrow you can go through channels and make an appointment," he said firmly. "Tonight you'll go back to your room, or maybe walk around the grounds and look at the stars. And I'll go back inside to do my job. How's that for a story?''

"I like everything but the lead, the body and the tag line," Norris stated, forcing herself to smile. Right now his patience was wearing thin, and as the keeper of the gate, Taggart was definitely someone she wanted on her side. Any further attempt was useless. Tonight, anyway. She wished him good-night, then walked away.

As she headed down the redbrick walkway that led toward the residential areas of the complex, she looked over her shoulder. With a bit of jealousy she watched him disappear into the building where Grail was rumored to spend most of his free time. The communications and broadcast center, or as the skeptics called it, the ''Broadcast Center on the Mount,'' was the most sacred spot in the entire complex. It was the heart, soul and chief revenue producer for Grail's entire THEM organization.

BURNE TAGGART SAVORED the air-conditioned hush that enveloped him when he walked back inside the building. He also savored the opportunity to escape the chattering of that woman. She was just like so many of the others, he thought, children who had to be handled and guided. Coddled, really. What planet did they come from?

They were all so wide-eyed and innocent when they first came here, so eager to be led down the garden path. He thought of the women in their neo-hippy clothes, the robes, shawls and vests, designer sandals, moccasins and jeans. And some of the men were just as bad. Many of them had monkish razor cuts and half beards and wore absurdly expensive walking boots that helped them cover the rugged territory from their Hummers to their penthouse elevators.

Out here in the desert they would ''center'' themselves and look off into invisible horizons, go on vision quests that would bring them face-to-face with the eternal hereafter. Taggart could never picture himself sitting still long enough to contact whatever it was so many of them believed was just waiting for their call on some interdimensional plane. He cared only for the here and now. Everything else was guess-work, and he would deal with the afterlife when it came for him, not before.

Taggart took a quick walk around the lower floor of the building. He stopped now and then to peer out the wall-length windows at the small groups of men and women walking the landscaped grounds of their luxurious pilgrimage. Clutching their beads, rubbing their lucky stones.

They all carried so much junk with them, he thought. Crystals. Pendants. Rune stones. Whether they were hanging from chains, mounted on rings or nestled in their pockets, men and women alike carted around their trinkets everywhere they went, as if they were mystical marbles for grown-ups.

And they practiced such a casual and contradictory mixture of beliefs. Gnosticism, paganism, Zen Bud-dhism, shamanism. There were wiccans and Templars and channelers rubbing shoulders with ascended mas-ters, alchemists and adepts from every conceivable and inconceivable order.

The followers of Winston Grail had come here to see the light, but they were all in the dark, Taggart thought as he reset the alarms that turned the building into a fortress. They were a deluded but basically harmless group, and that made life a lot simpler be-tween missions.

The day-to-day operations of the Sedona site didn't require such a large security force to handle Winston Grail's followers, but it provided a perfect cover for Taggart and the men under his command. They were like sleepwalkers, making the rounds of the resort while waiting for the signal from above. It would come from Chandler, sometimes from Grail himself.

Grail, he thought. Now, there was a man with vision, a man who really knew how to put on a show. Sometimes Grail himself seemed to believe the truisms and half-baked mythologies he shilled to the public.

But Taggart was one of the chosen few who knew Grail's real identity. He knew that the leader of this holy sanctuary was the leader of a group that soon would offer sanctuary to no one. That was the real reason Taggart was attached to Grail's Arizona operation. He wasn't as gifted in helping others contemplate the hereafter as he was in sending them there.

As he walked up the zigzag staircase that led to the upper floors, Taggart ran the tip of his index finger along the groove beneath his chin. He idly traced the path of the scar that traversed his face. It was a habit, one that caused him to constantly relive the memory that had been carved into his consciousness deeper than any blade could ever reach.

It was a memory of blood and murder in steaming jungle sunlight, of endless pain, of near death and resurrection.

It was a memory of a man with a gentle voice that seemed totally disconnected from the depravity of his actions.

The man who sculpted such a lasting look on Taggart's face had been one of those cultured Company spooks who was never short on cash or contacts. His name was Preston Montgomery, and he was a tall, well-mannered and well-spoken country-club type whose clothes never seemed to wrinkle, even in the jungle. He was also something of an amateur vivisectionist.

Montgomery ran a Contra guns-and-drugs operation back in the days when a fortune could be made on a single flight into any of the Central American countries dragooned into the war. Cartel pilots on loan to the Contras flew weapons in and cocaine out, and everybody got a cut along the way.

Especially Taggart. He worked both sides of the conflict, depending upon where he could make the best dollar. On Tuesdays he could be a drug warrior, burning fields of high-grade smoke or bombing drug labs buried deep in the jungle. On Wednesdays he could be a drug dealer. Whether he was running coke and smoke, stolen weapons, or staging raids against the cartel du jour, Taggart had been making a good living in the clandestine world.

Until he took out the wrong bunch of renegades.

He'd smoked a small band of Contras, two brothers and a Sandinista double agent, shortly after they unloaded a plane full of automatic weapons and reloaded it with a return cargo of high-quality coke. It happened on a makeshift airstrip in the middle of a Costa Rican plantation where not another soul could be seen.

Temptation and the laws of probability got the best of Burne Taggart when he realized all that stood between him and a quick score were three Contras and one cartel pilot. It took only one clip from his AR-15 and a few rounds from a .357 Magnum pistol to put them all down.

They hadn't suspected it was coming simply because Taggart had dealt with them so many times before, and he'd always been fair. That was what made it such a beautiful opportunity, a dream come true. For about thirty seconds after he clipped them, Taggart was figuring out how to spend the unexpected windfall.

Unfortunately the Company spook had been watching over his flock from the sidelines. Montgomery dented the back of Taggart's head with a pistol butt, then dragged him into a chemical-laced processing lab.

There the spook tied him to a cold steel surgical table and began to take Burne Taggart apart, uncovering his life story with every cut of the knife. By the time the spook knew all there was to know about Burne Taggart, there were cuts all over his body. They glistened like bloodred tattoos, newly flowing veins that ran on the surface of his body, mapping out the sharp trail etched by the spook's sure hand.

Taggart had passed over into the region beyond pain, looking into the face of death and seeking its dark embrace. The screaming thing on the table had to be someone else, had to be someone who was no longer alive. How could a man survive all that and hold on to his sanity?

Montgomery had been about to finish the debriefing by lifting off Taggart's face, one more exotic death mask to add to his collection, when Taggart's crew arrived on the scene. Leading the crew was the man who would become known to the world as Winston Grail.

At the time Grail was a Special Forces veteran with a background in unconventional warfare. He acted like just another one of the mercs on the scene. But even back then he was planning for his future, building a war chest, honing his skills and spotting likely recruits for his movement.

The spook had been so engrossed in his operation that he didn't notice the arrival of Grail and the other mercs until it was too late. They broke into the lab and rushed the amateur surgeon before he could complete his task.

Grail clutched the Company op by the back of the neck, ran him across the floor and smashed his head against the wall. As the man doubled over, Grail hit him in the sternum with a bone-cracking knee thrust. He followed up with a hammer fist to the back of the neck. Then he dropped Montgomery onto the floor for Taggart to finish off. "All yours," Grail had said. "U.S. government prime."

Taggart could barely walk when they helped him off the table and handed him the revolver. He waited until he was sure that Montgomery regained consciousness. Then he stood over him and emptied a revolver into the man with a slow and calculated rage.

Six shots. Feet, hands, heart and head.

The loud reports drowned out the spook's last screams. When it was over, Taggart fell on the floor beside him. His rage had gone and the pain had come back.

Pain that lived with him still, but at least he was alive.

Taggart had been with Grail ever since. He owed him his life, and he repaid it several times over. He learned from the younger man how to assume and discard identities and personalities as needed.

Outwardly Burne Taggart appeared to be healed.

He could wear the mask of civility and tune out the cosmic-toned chatter that filled the air at Winston Grail's conference centers.

But inwardly he was still seeking revenge on the man he'd slain long ago and the government that spawned him, and just about everyone else who had done him wrong.

It was a long list, and it was headed by the ghost of Preston Montgomery.

As the raging thoughts and memories filled his head and brought him dangerously close to overloading his circuits, Taggart found himself humming one of the chants he'd heard during the meditation sessions. That was the beauty of it all. You didn't have to believe in the myths to get the benefits. It was simple physics. When the mind was distracted by breathing and chanting, it achieved its own temporary harmony. Just like those TV commercials that got stuck in his head.

WINSTON GRAIL SAT in near darkness, illuminated by a flickering bank of TV monitors and the shadowy pool of moonlight that poured through the skylight. The communications suite that served as his private office in THEM headquarters had practically become his living quarters.

It was located on the top floor of the Trans Human Evolution Movement broadcast center, the glass-and-steel monument to serenity, wealth and deception.

It was here in the command post that he felt most at home, walking around the premises at night when there were only one or two key members of the security staff on duty, looking out at star-filled skies while all around him was the cool electronic hum of high-tech communications machinery.

From the rooftop of THEM headquarters, an array of satellite gear sent out the cable programming that perpetuated the empire. The New Age mix of programs had quite a range: *Soul Healing through Harmony, The Solitary Shaman, Emerging the Shadow Self, Tapping into the Tao.*

The list was endless. Whatever trend came along, THEM would put out a videotape for it. Sometimes they would create the trend; sometimes they would follow it. But they were always current with the latest New Age practices. The catalog included courses in weight loss or sin loss through meditation, chanting and soothing videotapes of desert or ocean scenes accompanied by instrumental soundtracks.

Seminars featuring Winston Grail or other leading lights of the New Age were offered on videotape or in person through one of their traveling shows that brought his grace and his greed to most corners of the country.

THEM programming targeted an upscale clientele with plenty of spare dollars and unlimited interest in self-help, self-realization, rune stones, crystals, I Ching sticks and tarot cards. Any parcel of paradise that could be imagined could also be packaged and delivered to an audience that was restless for revelation.

Over the past decade, Grail's catalog had grown from a handful of print magazines and primitive audiotapes to slickly packaged videos, CD-ROMS, books and training courses. Along with original

THEM programming, the catalog now included a variety of material from other New Age practitioners.

No matter how esoteric the material, all of it was in keeping with the philosophy of THEM that Grail had created. It was an all-purpose philosophy that allowed you to take the best from every belief system and create your own. An instant sundae of satori, garnished well with the followers' favorite beliefs.

Like every other discipline he undertook, Grail sank himself into the New Age milieu twenty-four hours a day. He traveled across the country to sample the best that sanctuaries, sects and motivational gurus had to offer. Before unleashing his own mix on the world, he mastered the subtleties and psychology of religious movements, as well as the high-tech machinery that was used for everything from brain-wave synchronization to sound-scape therapy.

It wouldn't have worked if a part of him wasn't capable of believing it. On some level Winston Grail had to be able to revel in the mythical and mystical knowledge he'd gathered and packaged. But it was a level that could be submerged at a moment's notice, an aspect of his personality that he could easily deny.

Sometimes he liked to just sit and view the videotaped offerings of THEM on all of the monitors, absorbing the flood of New Age imagery and trancing out in an electronic Babylon of mysticism.

But he could just as easily watch the cold and brutal imagery that was now beaming from every screen on the editing console that took up one wall of the communications room.

He sat in the phosphorescent glow and watched the opening shots of the war against an enemy that believed it extinguished the Cohorts when they extinguished his parents so long ago.

Almost like a Hollywood celebrity who was hooked on press clippings, Grail had assembled every bit of news footage possible about the Cohort campaign of terror. From the first day of the assault in Manhattan to the latest nightly updates, the media had responded with their typical overkill. And thus they had created a minute-by-minute documentary about Winston Grail's covert movement. And so far they didn't have the slightest idea he was the force behind it.

The tapes of the broadcasts from the very first day were markedly different from the nightly follow-ups. These days the reporters were wondering what had happened to the violent Cohort offensive, almost as if they were thirsting for another offensive to begin. They had enjoyed it so much the first time.

Grail worked the levers and keyboard of the video-editing console with the skill of a network producer, conjuring up a rapidly changing sequence of electronic visions, beginning with the initial outbreak of war.

Nearly every screen showed news announcers who believed they were about to have some of their finest hours. They were apparently so outraged by the senseless slaughter in a Manhattan jewelry store that they had to cut to footage of the massacre every twenty seconds or so.

Their voice-overs recounted the litany of death and destruction as if they were play-by-play announcers at a playoff game.

"An atrocity was committed in one of Manhattan's

finest jewelry shops today. A shop where, instead of looking at bright and shining diamonds, some unlucky customers found themselves looking right into the barrel of a gun. The first to die was…''

''Massacre in Manhattan. That's what some police insiders are calling the horrendous attack.…''

''It looked like a war zone outside the Madison Avenue shop where several police officers and security guards met a grisly end…''

Grail found his attention drawn to a screen that showed a computer-generated schematic of the store's layout, complete with separate icons representing each of the participants. A series of animated dotted lines and arrows appeared on the screen to show the path of the gunmen. Big wide *X*s marked the spots where the victims met their deaths. Throughout the recreation, a digital clock was superimposed in the corner of the screen to show the timeline for each stage of the hit.

Film clips from another screen caught Grail's eye. Tracking shots panned across the dark red splotches on the floor where the bodies had fallen and their blood had congealed. The camera moved in for lingering close-ups of the trashed display counters that had been denuded of their gems.

The next screen over featured grainy photographs taken from the security cameras. The blurry enhanced photos showed Chandler in a series of shots: holding the gun, grabbing the salesgirl, firing at the guard. Even if the pictures were of a better quality, Chandler's face was hidden by his leather cap in every one of them.

Another screen featured a reporter for a network

affiliate, a rising star known for his crime-beat reportage. He stood outside the shop in a light gray trench coat and spoke urgently into his microphone like a war correspondent reporting from behind enemy lines. With the wreckage of the shop as a backdrop, he was interviewing alleged eyewitnesses whose knowledge of the street battle seemed as limited as his own.

Several screens showed similar scenes, as if all of the reporters had lined up one after the other to get their moment in the limelight. One of the most common money shots was the alcove outside the store where Chandler had taken out one of the SWAT team officers. Blood from the man's exit wound had spattered a mural of red across the wall, a Rorschach blot that inspired plenty of doom-and-gloom prophecies from the media savants.

Grail sat there quietly scanning the mosaic of television screens with its flickering gallery of local reporters and network news personalities. The veteran newscasters faked their sincerity pretty well, but many of the younger reporters showed their real emotions. Despite the apparent shock and sadness on their faces, it was impossible for them to totally mask the undercurrent of glee in their voices as they promised more in-depth reports.

In-depth reports, Grail thought. That meant a parade of news analysts, commentators and psychologists would give their spin on the story for days on end, providing endless speculations for the great unwashed. And they'd deliver instant-replay footage, performing autopsies on the videotaped violence while speculating about what it all meant.

The media circus was developing just as Grail had expected. Long ago he'd mastered the art of peddling his New Age wares to the media. Now it was just a matter of promoting his private war, giving it the right kind of allure and hook that the producers and reporters could hang on to.

Grail had given the media a new mystery to play with, and each station wanted to be the first to solve it. Even the footage from the first days of the campaign showed how close some of the reporters were closing in on the truth.

Ever since one reporter mentioned the possibility that the armed robbery in midtown Manhattan had more than one objective, most of the other reporters followed suit. They fixated on the idea that rather than merely getting away with the crime, the gang that hit the Etruscan Gem Company wanted to inflict damage on the security force.

That led to even more questions. Was it a personal vendetta? Or were they killers without a cause?

Some of the more connected reporters dug into the background of the slain men and discovered that the chief of security had once been an FBI special agent. Eventually they uncovered some of the operations the agent had been involved in, including the pursuit of the Cohorts.

The coverage shifted to speculation about how the two gunmen killed inside the shop were connected to the Cohorts in some way. Other reporters mentioned rumors about a shoot-out with police along a thruway rest area, but so far the authorities hadn't released any information.

The media did their best to turn the midtown massacre into a miniseries, covering each morsel released by the FBI or NYPD spin doctors with growing dread and delight. Yes, the reporters said. According to their sources a revolutionary group was plotting against the government once again. An underground phoenix was rising, and they would do their best to keep it in the spotlight.

Even with the losses they'd suffered on the first mission, Grail considered it a success.

Already several other armed robberies and atrocities committed by subjects unknown were being attributed to the mysterious group of Cohorts. Eventually there would be copycat killings just like the Etruscan hit. It was only a matter of time, considering the extensive news exposure the media had given him. Loose cannons attracted by the publicity and glamour were bound to concoct their own bloody spectacles, using the Etruscan footage as a primer.

And the government would have to squander its resources more than it already was, by chasing down every possible clue from every crime scene.

The media would play it up and label them all as Cohort killings. Bad for the country, good for the ratings.

Grail tapped a couple of keys and brought up some of the more recent news reports.

Other issues of the day had pushed the Cohorts to the back burner. They were mentioned in passing, almost treating it like an unsolved mystery. A reporter would mention the Cohorts as if he were testing the audience's memory, coaxing their notoriously short attention span to recall that Technicolor terrorist act. And there would be a quick flash of a photo or a clip of video footage bringing it all back. Then the reporter would go on to the death of the day or the interview with the movie star who found his current role more challenging than anything else he'd ever done in the past.

Soon it would be time for the real Cohorts to make the news again. By now some of the FBI security teams were at the end of their rope, worn out from the multitude of targets they had to cover. And their presence was so obvious to Grail's field teams that it would be a simple matter of planning the next hit.

It would have to be soon, he realized. The ratings were down, and the Cohort miniseries was becoming old news.

A sudden electronic chirping took his mind off the carnage on the screen. The double rings of his office phone announced that it was an inside call. He reached across the console and punched the button for the speakerphone. ''Yes?''

Taggart's soft voice sounded from the speaker. ''Chandler's here.''

''Who's he with?'' Grail asked.

''Just himself,'' Taggart said.

''How does he look?''

''Like he wants to kill me,'' Taggart finally said. ''Or at least give it a try. The man is none too pleased about our new security measures.''

Grail smiled. They were living in wartime now. That meant a healthy dose of paranoia was called for. From here on in, no one could come up to his top-floor suite without first checking in with Taggart or any other Cohort who was on watch. It was a double safeguard. Even if a visitor had an electronic pass card, he couldn't get through the door until Taggart activated the system.

"I meant how does he look physically?" Grail asked. "Is he wounded? Would he attract attention on his way here?"

"No more than usual," Taggart replied.

"Send him up," Grail said.

A couple of minutes passed before Chandler stopped outside Grail's office and ran his card through the security slot. There was a loud click, then the door swung inward.

Grail turned and watched Chandler walk into the room. His gaunt face was rigid, strained, and his eyes were cold.

Fortunately he wasn't wearing his leather cap, which reassured Grail. Ever since the Etruscan security photos had been delivered to the reporters, Chandler's leather-capped image had made him a media celebrity.

Chandler stopped near the end of the console, then leaned against the edge and folded his arms in front of him.

"How are the ratings?" Chandler asked, nodding toward the flickering screens. Though he tried to act casual, his voice couldn't hide the anger that had been building up inside of him ever since he entered the complex.

"There's been a noticeable decline," Grail said, flicking levers on the soundboard to mute the voices from the screens. "We went from leading every newscast to little more than a twenty-or thirty-second blip. Apparently the authorities have no new leads.

And as far as the newsmen can tell, there is no Cohort action on the horizon.''

"Yeah," Chandler said. "That's one of the things I came to talk about. But first—" he glanced behind him at the door that he had to use his electronic pass card for "—you're going off the deep end with all the security, aren't you? It's not like I'm going to turn on you. Christ, without me—"

"I wouldn't even be here," Grail answered, cutting off Chandler's protest. "Without you I would have been captured long ago, killed alongside my mother and father. But you got me out alive, you guided me through those first few years."

"Damn right," Chandler said. "And now I need a ticket to get an audience with the guru?"

Grail raised his hand, gesturing for silence. "You taught me well. So did the Army."

"Yeah, but—"

"But now we are at war," Grail said. "And I can't take any chances."

"Even with me?" Chandler said.

"Even with you," Grail replied. "What if you were under duress when you called me earlier? You could have been a prisoner. Or maybe just wounded and not thinking straight."

"That's a chance we all have to take," Chandler said.

"Take it a bit further, then," Grail suggested. "Say you *were* hurt and your erratic actions caused you to be followed. What if they came right in the front door after you?"

Chandler nodded. "That's an even slimmer possibility. But maybe, just maybe it could happen."

"Maybe it could," Grail agreed. "Remember how it used to be in the early days? The precautions you insisted upon us following…that was what kept *us* from being brought in. You took zero chances back then."

"Back then it was the only way," Chandler said.

"It's that way again."

Chandler shrugged. His anger started to fade. He knew the harsh security measures were required in the past, just as they were required in the present. "All right," he said. "I guess you get no more argument from me."

"Good." Grail gestured toward the bank of monitors. "Now you can sit down, and we can figure out our next move."

Chandler pulled up a chair next to the console and took a closer look at the screens. He shook his head at the familiar onslaught of images. His men. His mistake. "I should have chosen a better crew," he said. "A crew that could have maintained discipline. Rivers would still be alive if I did."

"Rivers was with us for a long time. His spirit will be with us still."

Chandler dismissed the suggestion with a wave of his hand. "Save that stuff for the marks," he said. "Rivers is dead and gone, and that's all there is to it. But he went before his time, and he went because of me. I should have vetted the crew a couple more times before I brought them in."

Grail shrugged. "You never know how people will act in a real war. Blood frenzy gets some. Greed gets others. If they do what they're told and they survive, you work with them again. If not, you get rid of them.

Fortunately, Crews and Lucierre took care of that problem themselves. Right?''

"As far as we know," Chandler said.

"Can you be a bit more definite?" Grail asked. "Any more luck in finding out what happened to them?"

Chandler gave him an expanded briefing on his intelligence gathering in the east. From their earlier phone conversations, Grail knew that the two were gone and presumed dead, but he didn't know many of the details.

While he'd been looking for suitable FBI targets and identifying the security teams covering them, Chandler also kept pursuing any leads he could about the two men who'd vanished with the suddenness of an alien abduction.

One minute they had half of the country after them, and the next minute they were gone.

While there'd been no physical sign of them when Chandler showed up at the original rendezvous site at the retreat, he believed he knew what happened. The place was empty, but a quick check of the cabin showed that the two men had stayed there. Not only did it look lived in, but the cache of weapons had also been removed.

While driving away from the retreat, Chandler heard enough activity on the police scanner to know that something was going down. Then there were all those choppers in the sky and the fleet of state police cars racing to the thruway stop.

Chandler thought it had all the markings of a containment operation, not a run-and-gun thing. The shooting match was over by the time he got there, and the army of lawmen was sanitizing the scene. If Crews and Lucierre *had* been in the area, they'd probably been put down. Maybe they didn't listen to orders too well, but neither man was the type to go out easy.

As he drove by the rest area, Chandler had been waved on by several stern-faced troopers. He'd put on his best citizen face and kept on driving at a reasonable speed. He continued north for two more exits before he left the thruway and took to the back roads.

Chandler spent the next few days talking with the locals in the taverns and cafés, but he hadn't picked up anything worth reporting. Just stories of a friend who knew a friend who said someone took a shot at him while he was driving into the rest area, and there were a couple of lunatics firing at each other. Everyone seemed to know the friend of the friend, but no one actually knew the person it happened to. After a while Chandler gave up the search, figuring that the Feds had covered this one up tight and turned it into another urban legend.

"So we still don't know for sure what happened to Lucierre and Crews," Grail said.

Chandler shook his head. "No one will know until twenty years from now when someone digs up a report from the goddamn FBI," Chandler said. "Until then we have to assume our guys got their hands on the M-61s—and that means the government's got them now, along with whatever gems they were carrying—because my other assumption is that the government transcended their asses out of their bodies. Those boys are gone."

"That's your final conclusion?"

"Yeah, it is," Chandler said. "Unless you can contact them on the astral plane and tell them to check in."

"You'll never make a good convert if you keep talking like that," Grail said.

"Only thing that'll ever convert me is a bullet. Convert me to a fine-looking specimen of dust."

Chandler filled him in on a few more details about his recons of known FBI agents involved in the original Cohort action. Then he drummed his fingers on the console and rocked slowly back and forth in the chair while he looked up at the monitors where the reporters were silently chattering away.

"So what do we do now?" Chandler asked.

Grail looked over at the man who'd shepherded the remnants of the Cohorts and brought them from extinction. He almost looked beaten, and his face was heavy with guilt. Not guilt over those he'd killed, but guilt at losing a man who'd fought at his side for years and helped him keep the Cohort dream alive.

Chandler needed penance.

Grail gestured at the talking heads on the bank of monitors. "Now we give them something they can really talk about."

CHAPTER EIGHT

Salem, Virginia

The driver of the eight-seat modified van rolled through the green stoplight in the center of downtown Salem, Virginia, then pulled over to the curb and parked in front of a glass-walled pub and waited for their last passenger to arrive.

The driver's name was Bo Davis, and he had been in and out of jails and other institutions for almost the entire first half of his life. Since then he had been in the regular Army and the Cohort army.

Davis kept the engine running and waited, knowing that the passenger they were about to pick up would be watching them long enough to determine whether it was safe.

Typical spook stuff. The van was supposed to wait for five minutes, no longer. If the man didn't show up by then, the operation was off and Davis was supposed to bring the crew back to the airport. But he doubted that would happen. So far they'd spent about ten grand in airplane tickets, wheels and meals and front money.

The man in the front passenger seat lit a cigarette

and looked out at the pub with studied nonchalance. Davis knew him slightly, from one previous operation. The guy had done what had to be done, made no bones about it and that was that. The other passengers were a different story. Davis didn't know a thing about them, other than they liked to complain a lot. They complained about food and planes and driving, and now they were complaining about the man they were supposed to meet.

Davis fiddled with the knob of the dashboard stereo unit, trying to pull in a jazz station. It was like trying to find a skating rink in the middle of a desert. Not a hint of jazz, not even a touch of blues could be found on the airwaves.

"Christ," he said. "Evangelical preachers, country-western crooners, all news all noise all the time. Nothing but every damn thing I don't want to hear. Where the hell is the real music?"

"It's about nine hundred miles away in New York City," the man in the passenger seat said.

"We're farther than that, man," Davis replied. "Figure it out. New York to Pittsburgh. Pittsburgh to Roanoke."

"I don't want to figure it out, man. I just want to get this thing done." He looked over his shoulder at the men in the back. "And drop them off for good."

The men in the back of the van were restless and starting to grumble. They'd taken buses and cabs from the airport to the mall and loaded up on fried steak and a couple of beers and coffee at a franchise pub with art deco lighting, waitresses in retro roller-girl outfits, and a constant rush of chatter from the overcrowded booths.

They'd gone into the mall pub in separate groups and pretended that they didn't know one another.

It wasn't too hard for Bo Davis. He didn't want to know the others, not really. Most of the other Cohort operations he'd been on were simple matters that required two or three men at the most. Military-style hits. They'd be given a time and target and they'd take it down, just the few of them. Not a whole crew like this. Not when they hadn't been told what the target was. Too many things could go wrong when you threw this many gunmen together, especially when they were none too clear about their objective.

Initially they'd all been given the summons from Chandler, who'd called them and suggested they get themselves to JFK Airport in New York. There were seven of them in all. The Cohorts had come from separate cells, and when they caught up with Chandler in NYC he'd given them just enough information to get them down here. Unlike other operations, he wasn't going with them this time. Instead they were sent down to Virginia to meet the man who would lead them into action.

"How will we know him?" Davis had asked.

"He'll be the guy who scares the shit out of you," Chandler replied. "And that's if he's in a good mood."

Chandler had then sent them all down to Virginia on a flight filled with businessmen who all seemed to have laptops propped on the trays from the back of the seat in front of them. They were fiddling around with pie charts and presentations and solitaire games on their four-grand keyboard gizmos. They killed some time at the Pittsburgh airport, walking through mile after mile of coffee shops, bars and boutiques while they waited for their connection to Roanoke. The connecting flight seemed no bigger than a tractor trailer with wings and felt just as comfortable. They'd hit a few bone-jarring pockets of turbulence just before they reached the Roanoke Valley.

And now they were here, waiting at the address Chandler had given to them, sitting back and waiting for the man to show up.

When the grumbling started up again, Davis flipped the radio dial back to the religious station and gave them a few strident chords of righteous indignation from a high-pitched Holy Roller. The preacher had the idea that the only way for them to save their souls was to send in a love donation directly to him.

It sounded obscene to Davis, but then again, nearly everything other than jazz—where the instruments did the talking—seemed like an obscenity to him.

But the voices in the back could be heard even over the evangelical tirade. "Where the hell is he?" the youngest one said. "Think the guy was God or something, keeping us waiting like this."

"Maybe you should get out here," said the guy sitting in the last seat, a guy named Duke Holland, whose bulk took up considerable space in the van, "if you're so nervous."

"Fuck nervous," the younger man said. "I just don't like waiting without good reason."

Holland looked out the small, quarter-moon-shaped tinted window and saw a dark shape coming out of the alley beside the pub. "Shut up, man. He's here."

The man in dark clothing drifted across the sidewalk, then pounded a black-gloved fist on the side of the van.

Holland leaned forward, pulled on the door handle, then rolled the door open. A cool breeze and a snatch of music from the town park's open-air folk festival drifted into the van.

So did their newest passenger.

WINSTON GRAIL'S HAIR was slicked back, tied in a knot and tucked under his collar. He wore a pair of tinted glasses that hid the piercing eyes so well known on his videotaped seminars.

Although his outward physical appearance had been sufficiently altered for the occasion, there was no mistaking the aura of command from the moment he stepped inside the van and rolled the door closed behind him. It slammed shut with a loud click that echoed inside the van, a cue for the Cohorts to fall silent.

Grail sat on the last remaining seat and draped his hand over the back, then, without saying a word, looked around at the group of men he and Chandler had picked for the operation. He scanned their eyes from behind the dark glasses, staring at them just long enough to take their measure. He saw strong faces that reflected a mix of confidence, contempt and just the right amount of impatience.

"You all ready for this?" Grail asked.

Most of them nodded their assent.

But a familiar voice from the back of the van said, "We've been ready for about twenty-four hours now. Ready and waiting to find out where we're going."

It was Duke Holland.

Grail looked back and grinned thinly at Holland. "You know the drill. You'll find out soon enough."

Holland and the driver were the only men in the group that Grail had worked directly with in the past. They hadn't known he'd be the one leading the mission. Along with the others, they'd been given sketchy details by Chandler. At best they knew that a cell leader who was much higher up in the organization than Chandler would take them into action.

Now these two men knew just how high up.

Holland had been involved on the periphery of Grail's operations for years now, stretching back to the Contra days. He'd been a mercenary then and he was a mercenary now. Like many of the Cohorts, he didn't have the same burning desire that Grail did.

To Holland, the government wasn't an evil presence that had to be toppled. It was a faceless entity that from time to time had reached its giant hand down to embrace paramilitaries like Holland or swat them off the earth. In fact, its very existence gave Holland a reason to ply his trade, back when he working for it and now when he was working against it.

Grail nodded at the driver. "Let's go," he said. He gave Davis directions that took them out of town and deep into the rich farm country that surrounded the Roanoke Valley.

Along the way he gave them the details of their targets. The main target was Gene Fleming, a veteran FBI agent who'd served with distinction during his long career.

Fleming had penetrated Mafia operations up and down the Eastern Seaboard and had also been one of the main forces behind the pursuit of the Cohorts.

He'd been there at the Vermont site where the old leadership died and the new leadership was born. After his years of service, Fleming and his wife returned to the area they were raised in and bought sixty acres of farmland and forest.

The other targets were members of the FBI plainclothes security team that had been protecting Fleming for just long enough for them to lose their edge.

An advance team of Cohorts led by Burne Taggart had arrived in the area several days before the other team. They had conducted enough surveillance to determine all the patterns in the security team's routines. And now the rest of the Cohorts were there to perform some fatal choreography.

THE FARMHOUSE SAT on the crest of a high green hill that rolled down to the heavily forested acreage that made up the bulk of Gene Fleming's lush property.

A long driveway rose straight up from the main road. It ran past the house and carport, and ended in front of a large gray barn that had become a garage for the old roadsters that Fleming was constantly rebuilding and taking to the car rallies. He'd invariably sell one of his restored vehicles and come home with another project from the forties or fifties. With so many classic cars in the garage, there was no room for the tractors or any other heavy farm equipment. It was no longer a working farm. It was a walking farm.

Fleming and his wife spent most of their time walking the land and traipsing over the well-worn trail that followed along the creek. Every night they would walk the creek to a ten-foot waterfall. They would linger there and talk, have a smoke, sit down and think in the comfortable quiet that came to man and woman who'd been together for so long. And every night one of their armed escorts would accompany them, although he stayed a considerable distance back to respect their privacy.

It had been a lot tougher in the beginning when the escort was almost always by their side. But as the days passed and the threat began to fade, the escort became more of a discreet presence. Whenever they stopped at the waterfall, he would walk past them and continue to patrol the area.

IT SOUNDED LIKE A HAIL storm. One moment there was just the sound of the early-evening breeze sweeping up the hill, then there was the strangely repetitive chocking sound. Like chunks of hail hitting glass.

The first wave of 7.62 mm hail rained into the driver's-side window of the primary watch car. The fusillade began immediately after the driver parked it between two shady elms on the right side of the house. It was facing the road so the driver could quickly intercept anyone who drove up to the farm. But the only thing the man behind the wheel intercepted was a bullet from Burne Taggart's Parker-Hale Model 85 sniper rifle.

The first 7.62 mm round had drilled a hole through the window and sent a crown of splintered glass over the man's head. The second round entered the man's temple and exited the back of his skull, taking a good amount of gray matter with it.

Taggart fired several more rounds from the silenced sniper rifle just to make sure his man was gone for good. The 7.62 mm rounds took out just about an inch of the wraparound glass.

While Taggart had been firing from a sniper's post two hundred yards to the right, two other Cohort snipers opened up from their hidden post in the woods directly across the road. They poured several rounds into a second unmarked car just as it slowed at the end of the driveway.

The second car carried two agents who'd just gone off duty, the time when they were most psychologically vulnerable. Anticipating no problem at the end of their shift, they'd already shifted into a more relaxed mode. As a result, they became permanently relaxed.

Though there was hardly any traffic on the road, the driver had tapped the brakes just before the driveway came to a T-intersection with the main road.

They slowed just long enough for the two snipers to take out their targets. The Parker-Hale sniper rifles they'd brought with them from the van had 10-round box magazines, more than enough to do the job.

The snipers laid down a steady stream of focused firepower that smashed the windshield and rear window into shards of glass that sprinkled the autumn air. The now unpiloted vehicle continued rolling across the road, only coming to a stop when the nose of the car butted against the low embankment.

Two other Cohorts who'd been hiding in the tall grass on the other side of the road got to their feet and sprinted toward the car. They unhooked the driver from his blood-spattered seat belt and pushed him toward the middle of the seat. Then one of the Cohorts slid behind the steering wheel, pulled the gear shift into Reverse and guided the vehicle back across the road and up into the driveway.

The sudden downpour of lead had accomplished its task in just a matter of seconds—and had attracted the attention of a fourth guard, who'd been walking around the back of the barn. The sound of the silenced rounds punching through the windshields restored the alertness that had been rapidly fading from him these past few days.

The agent's hand fell to his side arm, and he had cleared it from its holster by the time he neared the front edge of the barn. He peered around the corner and saw the car backing up the driveway. And then he saw the gutted windshields that could only mean one thing—the Cohorts had come for their target.

A sudden blur to his right yanked his attention away from the car. Three men rose up from nowhere and stood before him like phantoms.

He shouted out a warning—to Fleming, to any other agent who still might be able to hear him—then started to train his automatic on the Cohort assassination squad.

The sound-suppressed Skorpion barrels sought him out first. With staccato coughs, the 7.65 mm rounds raked his body with full-auto fire that shredded through his upper torso and punched holes through the barn behind him. The fusillade of bullets continued even after he began to fall, and he could dimly hear them striking the classic cars within.

Then he heard nothing at all.

"WHAT IS IT, GENE?"

Fleming turned to his wife. "I'm not sure." But he

could feel something was wrong. It was the same way he used to feel when he was on an operation and could sense an imminent confrontation in the air. A person could always tell when he was closing in on a target, just as he could tell when he was the target. "I thought I heard something from the barn."

Her face paled and her eyes widened with fear. She searched his face for whatever truth she could find there. She knew that during his long career with the FBI, he'd often kept her unaware of the dangers he'd faced. And even though he was no longer an active agent of the Bureau, she knew he would try his best to keep her from worrying.

"Where are they?" she asked.

He knew whom she meant. The guards who had recently been a constant presence were nowhere to be seen. Fleming turned in a half circle, taking in the trail by the creek and the trail that led through high grass toward the house.

"I'm not sure," Fleming said. "Maybe they're back at the house. Waiting for us."

"Gene..." she said, shaking her head. Her voice had a slight tremor in it. "It's not like them to get this far away from us. Ever."

Suddenly he felt like a fool for risking her life like this. It would have been so easy to take her away from here, to go on the vacation to the Bahamas that she was always talking about. Or maybe they could have just rented a van, got on the road and gone wherever their whims took them. They had the money, and they had the time.

He hadn't taken the Bureau's warnings seriously enough. Although from the very beginning he went

along with the security arrangements the Bureau rec-
ommended, Fleming never thought they were actually
necessary. He figured on letting the Bureau watch-
dogs do their jobs until the situation played out and
everything went back to normal.

But now he knew that wasn't going to happen.

The sounds that had drifted into his consciousness
were distant reminders from the days he thought he'd
left behind him.

A shout.

Fleming had definitely heard a shout. And silenced
weapons?

He couldn't tell if he was imagining things or he'd
heard the distinctive cough of automatic weapons. No
suppressor could completely silence a weapon. There
was always some kind of report, however muffled or
distorted, and it was just like the sounds he'd heard
carrying over from the barn.

"What should we do, Gene?"

He gripped her shoulders and kissed her lips. Whatever was out there, he didn't want it to find her. "Stay
here for now. I'll go take a look around."

"But what if—?"

He kissed her again. There was no answer for *what
if*? Or it was an answer he didn't want to give.

As he walked away from her, unarmed and
strangely unafraid, he thought back to the days when
they first moved here. He always used to walk around
the farm with an automatic at his side, thinking he
never knew what he might run up against in the
woods. Animal or man.

But she gradually got him to change his siege mentality. She worked on him in her subtle ways, and as

he got to know the land and felt comfortable with it, he stopped carrying a side arm with him.

It had been a good feeling that brought him a deep, rewarding trust in his fellow man. A trust betrayed.

No gun. No escape.

Fleming still carried a knife, however. It was only common sense to carry some kind of weapon. Little good it would do him against what he was facing, he thought.

WINSTON GRAIL WAITED in the shadows, listening to the sound of former Special Agent Gene Fleming surreptitiously hurrying through the underbrush. The older man was staying off the path and keeping close to the shadows.

Grail watched the man pass him, totally unaware of the Cohort leader's presence. Fleming still had a formidable look to him. He was in that stage where most of his bulk was still muscle, although he was carrying more weight than he used to.

But Fleming was out of practice. He'd been away far too long from the predatory world he once belonged to. From his vantage point, Grail could see that the former agent was unarmed except for the hunting knife sheathed on his belt. Probably hadn't wanted to carry a side arm to keep his wife from being alarmed.

Agent Fleming was a real family man, Grail thought. Two children. Both successful. One in Florida, in real estate, of course. The other was in politics. They'd grown up on the straight and narrow, bringing a lot of joy to Agent Fleming and his wife.

Yes, Grail thought. A real family man. But even Grail had been a family man at one time.

Until the time Agent Fleming took his family away.

He stepped out of the woods thirty yards behind the man.

And now Fleming sensed the Cohort's presence. He stopped and spun as if he'd triggered a mine, staring at Grail as though he were some kind of wraith who'd been stalking him for years. Perhaps Fleming had always known this day would come.

Other shapes stepped out of the woods beyond Fleming. They were carrying Skorpion machine pistols, and they were casually aiming them at the former FBI agent.

Holland was the closest Cohort. His massive physique towered over Fleming as he watched him with an impassive face, waiting for the agent to make any sudden moves.

Farther back in the shadows, Grail could make out Burne Taggart's silhouette. Taggart was staying deep in the background so he could keep everyone in his sight and make sure no one made a move toward Grail. He'd been watching over him for years, ever since the moment Grail had given him a chance to literally save face and rejoin the land of the living.

Fleming took in the group of cold-eyed men, then returned his gaze to the man who was obviously their leader. The man who brought these nightmarish killers to his home.

"Who are you?" Fleming asked.

Grail took a few steps closer toward the trapped man. "I'm the seed you planted years ago."

"What are you talking about?" Fleming snapped.

Grail came even closer, carefully noting exactly how much distance there was between him and the knife that was sheathed at Fleming's side. He took off his tinted glasses, snapped the frames shut and tucked them into his pocket.

Fleming studied Grail's face, trying hard to recognize him. "I don't know you," he said. "I don't know what you want."

"You probably wouldn't recognize my face," Grail said. "But there's a chance you'd recognize the back."

"You're not making any sense," Fleming retorted.

"Oh, but I am," Grail said. "The reason you should recognize my back is because that's what everyone was shooting at the night you and the rest of the storm troopers showed up at our house."

"Where?"

"Think hard and it'll come to you. Unless you're trying to block it from your memory. It was up in Vermont. A house near the lake. An army of special agents swarming the place in the dead of night."

Fleming nodded.

"Now you remember?"

"I was there," Fleming agreed.

"You admit it—"

"And I'm glad I was there," Fleming said. "But I don't recall shooting at anyone's back. Nor were we the first ones to fire."

"But you were at the house from beginning to end," Grail said.

"Yeah," Fleming acknowledged.

"That means that you were part of the hit team that came for my parents. A hit team that fired out of control at anything that moved, without even knowing who was there. Could have been parents, could have been a house full of kids. You didn't know what you were shooting at. And all we wanted to do was leave that place.''

''It was a bit late for walking away,'' Fleming said. ''Not after everything that was done. Bombings, killings, maimings. Kidnappings. You don't suddenly walk away from all that like it was just a mistake you made, a small misunderstanding that you want to put behind you.''

''You murdered them,'' Grail said. ''You tried to murder me.''

''Your father was a soldier, or claimed to be one. Same thing with your mother. They went looking for a war and we brought it to them. They deserved what they got. And if you were of age and you were traveling with them, then you deserved it, too.''

He studied Fleming's face. The former special agent didn't turn away from his death, didn't rush to meet it. He just spoke the truth as he saw it.

Perhaps the man was right, Grail thought. Maybe he deserved to die back then for not turning in his parents. Maybe it would have been a wonderful world without him. But it was impossible for him to say, not after he'd seen life through an entirely different viewpoint.

Before he was old enough to vote he'd been a fugitive, a soldier, a man without a family or a country. It gave him an alien perspective on things, an ability to do what others couldn't conceive of doing.

''I guess everyone who was at the house that night deserved to die,'' he said to Fleming. ''On both sides.'' He glanced toward Holland and nodded for him to come forward.

Grail reached out an open hand for what had become a ceremonial weapon in his mind. Holland handed the Skorpion to him.

Grail stared impassively at Fleming. The last time they'd been near each other, Grail had been running for his life. A frightened man-child whose parents had been killed in front of him. Fleming had been one of those who pulled the trigger.

"Those shots you fired so long ago…" Grail said, lifting the Skorpion and pointing it at Fleming's head. He stepped forward until the barrel was almost touching the man's left ear. "Listen closely and you can still hear the echo.''

Fleming craned his neck and pulled away. "My wife," he said.

"What about her?"

"Leave her out of this.''

"Why?" Grail asked.

"She had nothing to do with this. Nothing.''

"You can't expect me to change the rules of engagement now," Grail replied. "Not after the treatment you gave us. You killed my mother.''

"We don't know who killed her," Fleming said. "It could have been anybody.''

"But you were there," Grail said. "You know what happened. No one was going to let them get out of there alive.''

"She was a soldier," Fleming protested. "She knew the risk she was taking. Just leave my wife alone. She's—"

"She's what?" Grail asked. "Innocent? We'll decide that."

Fleming made a sudden grab for his sheathed knife. He'd unsnapped the safety flap earlier so he'd have a better chance of getting the weapon out, but it was of no consequence.

Both men knew it was an automatic reflex that had no chance of succeeding.

Grail reacted with a subconscious deflection. His left hand shot out and struck Fleming's wrist, then his hand curled around it, squeezed tight and twisted it sharply.

The knife dropped to the ground. Its sharp steel blade sunk into the earth right next to Fleming's foot so it stood straight up like a grave marker.

Grail held the barrel an inch from Fleming's ear and pulled the trigger, sending a 3-round burst into his head.

The agent dropped to the ground, leaving a fountainlike spray of blood that followed after him.

Grail signaled Taggart and the others to go, then handed the Skorpion back to Holland.

Holland turned and started to follow the others until Grail called him back.

"What?"

"The woman," Grail said, nodding at the trail that led toward the waterfall. "Take care of her."

Holland didn't move. "She's not a legitimate target."

"She is if I say she is."

"Then you can do it," Holland said.

"I'm telling you."

"And I'm not listening," Holland said. "The guy,

I can understand that. You had reason to hate him and now he's gone because of that. But like he said, his wife's got nothing to do with it.''

"We can't leave her here,'' Grail said. "She'll bring in outside help before we can clear the area.''

Holland shrugged. "You want me to put her under wraps until someone comes out here and finds her, that's one thing. But killing her, that's not in *my* rules of engagement.''

"You're willing to trade her life for yours?''

"No.''

"Because if something bad comes from this, if they get a lead to the group because we didn't erase her, then you'll pay the price.''

"Maybe,'' Holland said. "Maybe not. If you really wanted her dead, you wouldn't give me that option.''

"You're pretty sure of yourself, Holland.''

"I'm pretty sure of what you're about. The day I find out different, that's the day I'm gone.''

"That's all I can ask,'' Grail said. "Go ahead, then. Do it your way.''

East Mount, Connecticut

AT THE SAME TIME that Winston Grail was leading the raid in Roanoke, Virginia, Jacqueline Spears was running across the quad of East Mount College with the easy rhythm of a natural born runner.

Her arms pumped in an unforced cyclic motion, and her feet lightly touched the ground for a split second before lifting off again and softly propelling her across the freshly mowed lawn.

She was in sneakers and shorts, and a halter top

that was soaked with streaks of sweat. A gray East Mount College sweatshirt with its red block-letter logo was wrapped around her hips, with the long cotton arms flapping in tandem with the movement of her exquisitely muscled legs.

When she reached the end of the quad she kept on running, slowing a bit as she crested the small slope that led up to the road that made a meandering circuit of the gated campus.

She changed direction and ran parallel to the narrow ribbon of road. There were bright yellow speed bumps that limited traffic to five miles per hour on most stretches of the loop. Even the campus patrol car that was now making its early evening rounds had to keep to the safe speed.

Spears paced herself alongside the car for a while, making sure that the driver had plenty of time to look her over as she jounced along next to him.

Then she looked over as if she'd seen him for the first time. She smiled at him, receiving a broad smile in return as he gave the attractive woman an appreciative glance. It was moments like this that made his job worthwhile.

She picked up her speed and quickly passed the patrol car as soon as it entered the gallery, a section of road that was bordered by tall, elegant pines on both sides. It gave an old-world atmosphere to the Ivy League college. And it also gave her plenty of shadows to work with.

When she was about fifty yards ahead of the patrol car, Spears stopped at the side of the road. She bent in the traditional runner's pose and placed her hands on her knees while she took a few rapid breaths. A few moments later she straightened, looked his way, then suddenly clasped her hand to her side as if she was stricken by a muscle cramp.

As the campus patrol car neared her, Spears flagged down the driver.

He flicked on his directional signal, tapped the brakes and eased to a stop right next to her.

After shifting into Park, he rolled down the window and leaned toward her. "Are you okay?" he asked. He was young, maybe five years older than most of the students at the college.

"Yeah," she said, gasping for breath. She stepped closer to the car and rested her hand on the open window to support herself. "I just need something."

"What?"

"Your car."

He cocked his head at her, unsure if she was joking or if she really needed help. "I can take you to the infirmary if you want."

She glanced around her, keeping one hand behind her back and one hand on the door. "Sorry," she said. "I just need the car." Before he had a chance to say anything else, she whipped out the hand that had been hiding behind her back. It came up holding a .22 automatic with an integral sound suppressor built into the professional hitter's weapon of choice.

The gun coughed once and the stunned face of the campus cop turned away, propelled by the silenced round that was traveling through the middle of his skull.

The impact of the shot toppled his body toward the passenger seat. She fired one more time into the back of his head just to silence any last-moment death cries.

With a quick tug Spears yanked open the front door and slipped behind the wheel. It was a tight fit until she dug her clenched fingers into his belted waistband and pushed him out of the way.

She shifted into gear and drove straight toward the black gates of the main entrance. Tall Gothic fencing with sharp iron spires sealed off the college from the rest of the town, but the gates always stayed open until ten o'clock in the evening.

Since it was still early, she drove right through the main gates, then drove four blocks to the self-serve car wash where Nick Chandler and two other carloads of Cohorts were waiting for her.

Chandler was going through the motions of washing one of the cars. Two Cohorts in dark blue uniforms were sitting in the back seat, and one was sitting in the front. They stayed there until Spears drove the campus patrol car into the stall next to theirs. She then stepped out while the men did their stuff.

To give themselves more credibility with the students and anyone else on campus, the college's security force drove vehicles that were almost identical with the colors of the East Mount town police cars. When the Cohort ''cops'' slapped a couple of decals onto the side doors, it looked even more like the real thing.

After another Cohort dumped the slain campus cop into the trunk, Chandler rapped his hand on the hood of the car. ''All right,'' he said, ''we're good to go.'' He got back into his car, a nondescript station wagon, drove out the car wash exit and turned left toward his designated target.

The new "police car" turned right and drove off with one blue uniformed officer behind the wheel and two more sitting in the back with their prisoner, Jacqueline Spears.

They drove straight to the home of Professor Norman Leopold, a former FBI agent who was now a popular lecturer on criminology at East Mount College. There was something about the old war stories he told that always kept Leopold's classes filled.

The modified patrol car stopped in the middle of the road in front of Leopold's house, a grand old Victorian that fit in well with the other houses on the block.

Anyone who happened to be looking out their window at the police car saw two cops drag Spears from the back seat and march her up the steps of Professor Leopold's house. Her hands were apparently cuffed behind her back, and she looked as if she were giving them a bit of a struggle.

By the time they reached the top of the porch, the front door opened suddenly. A dark-suited FBI agent stepped onto the porch and blocked their way. Before the agent had a chance to demand what was going on, the Cohort holding Spears's right elbow launched into his rap about an apparent stalker they caught rifling through Professor Leopold's office. The Cohort rattled off more information about how the stalker claimed to be one of Leopold's students, and they wanted to check with him personally.

The agent stopped listening to him and started to go for his weapon, knowing there was something off about the story, just as there was something wrong about the manner of the "officers."

Spears's hand came out from behind her, and she cut loose with three quick rounds from the silenced .22. The first one caught the agent in the gut, the second one got him in the chest and the third one got him in the underside of the neck as he fell backward.

The two Cohorts raced toward the porch and fired silenced Skorpion machine pistols through the screen door, right into the startled face of Professor Leopold, who'd come to see what the commotion was about.

Two more cars came to a stop behind the doctored campus patrol car, and a handful of Cohorts jumped out onto the sidewalk. They laid down a covering fire that swept first across the porch and its tall white columns, then across the first- and second-floor windows, sending a blizzard of silenced 7.65 mm rounds into the home of the late professor.

Spears and the Cohort cops ran into the street and dived into the back seat of the nearest car.

Both cars drove off in a screech of burning rubber, leaving behind a host of stunned neighbors who were running out of their houses to see what had happened on their quiet collegiate avenue.

ONE MILE AWAY at the motel where the off-duty agents were staying, Nick Chandler slowly cruised the station wagon down the parking lot.

He stopped right below the adjoining second-floor rooms.

A few motel guests were walking along the upstairs balcony. He waited until they came down the stairs and vanished through the alcove that led toward the main office.

With a nonchalant manner that he'd perfected over the years, Chandler opened the driver's-side door and took another quick look around to make sure there were no would-be heroes in the area. Then he opened the rear door and lifted one of the two Czech-made RPG launchers that were lying side by side on the back seat.

They were utilitarian models, long metal tubes designed for lots of bang and quick disposal. Each launcher was loaded with an 85 mm high-explosive shell. A box in the back of the wagon held a couple more rocket-propelled grenades, but Chandler didn't figure on hanging around long enough to use them.

As calmly as if he were going to snap a picture, he rested the back of the launcher across his shoulder, then sighted in on the picture window of his first target. He pulled the trigger and thumped the first grenade home. It smashed through the window, then sent a spray of flame and smoke shooting up through the shattered roof.

He dropped the launcher on the floor of the wagon, grabbed the second one and fired the RPG into the remaining target.

Both rooms were reduced to smoldering caves of flame by the time he climbed back behind the wheel and drove away.

SHORTLY AFTER the first calls came in about a shooting at Professor Leopold's house and explosions at the East Mount Motel, the small-town police station had a crisis of its own to deal with.

The gas tanks of the three patrol cars in the police station's parking lot exploded with such force that the vehicles were temporarily airborne before they came down in sheets of twisted metal. The timed charges had been set by Cohort mechanics who'd been able to move freely across the open-air parking lot.

A few minutes later, at their rendezvous point on the edge of town, the Cohorts drove off in several fresh vehicles that quickly vanished into the Connecticut countryside.

CHAPTER NINE

Barrows Lake, New York

His head broke through the surface of the dark cold water with barely a ripple. He slowly looked left and right as he scanned the jagged horizon like a creature of the deep in search of prey.

The Executioner trod water in the middle of the spear-shaped bay at the north end of the lake. The glacially formed trough, which had been gouged out of the Adirondack Mountains aeons ago, was about three hundred feet deep. It was a wild and desolate body of water surrounded by countless treetop spires that scraped against the moonlit sky.

Scattered along the shore were a few small clearings with lakeside cottages boarded up for the season. But there was one "camp" that was still active, and its lights were burning bright in the distance. It glowed like a lantern, casting a large reflection on the lake.

Bolan's position was about two hundred yards from shore and about one hundred yards south of the target. As the screen of water fell from his goggles, he got a clearer look at the rustic lodge that sprawled along the water's edge.

There was a boathouse and a long trident-shaped dock, as well as a wraparound porch, shingled turret windows and a carport. Several vehicles were parked nearby.

Like many of the great camps that once thrived on the shores of hidden Adirondack lakes, the lodge was large enough to serve as a hotel. In recent years it had served as a preserve for wealthy refugees from New York City and Boston. It changed hands several times since then. For a while it had been a bed-and-breakfast, then a rural conference center and now it was in private hands again.

Extremely private, Bolan thought.

The guests were members of an exclusive club with a closely guarded membership list.

To anyone else who happened upon the scene, it would look like just an isolated getaway from city life, perhaps a staging area for a group of men on a camping or a hunting expedition. A family reunion where everyone had a chance to renew old ties and cut loose in the great outdoors. But to Mack Bolan it was definitely a house full of the Cohort faithful. Just as Brognola's intel had indicated, the troops were forming for another strike.

The Executioner trod water a few moments longer, got his bearings, then dropped several feet below the surface and continued swimming toward shore.

His scuba gear, a rebreather apparatus that was safe down to thirty feet and left no telltale trail of air bubbles, made it easier for him to carry the waterproof satchel that contained the tools of his trade. To keep from losing his grip on the precious cargo, he'd wrapped an extra utility strap around his wrist. The satchel hung low in the water like a heavy-duty shopping bag.

He swam toward the shore at a steady pace, breaking the surface a couple times to make sure he was following the right course. Then he emerged about twenty yards from land near a fallen tree that spiked into the lake like a thick arm.

Its long forked branches were full of bird nests, rings of moss and a murky carpet of weeds. Bolan kept low as he pulled himself along the half-submerged waterlogged tree, reducing the chance of anyone seeing his silhouette. Even at that distance he didn't want to take any unnecessary risks.

The Cohorts were known to employ a mixture of top-flight soldiers along with rank-and-file gunmen. You never knew who was manning the watch or who could have you in his sights.

When he reached the landward end of the ancient fallen tree, where its thick and splintered roots were embedded deep into the water, the Executioner stood fully for the first time. Like a primordial creature emerging from the deep and venturing into strange territory, he scanned the forest edge for any sign of a predator.

Standing perfectly still in the pocket of water that came up to his knees, with the satchel floating lightly at his side, Bolan listened long enough to accustom himself to the nocturnal sounds of the forest. There was no sound that didn't belong. The only predator in the immediate region was the Executioner himself.

Making no more noise than the sound of waves

sloshing against the shore, Bolan stepped onto the small stretch of beach. The moment he emerged from the water, he felt the full weight of the waterproof satchel and the full weight of the business ahead of him.

Bolan removed his fins, mask and wet suit, then unzipped and unstrapped the waterproof satchel. A cold autumn wind knifed across his skin as he began to remove the contents to prepare himself for war.

He slipped a dark assault vest over his night-black combat suit, then strapped the Beretta 93-R into an underarm sling. From the Velcro tearaway harness around his neck he hung the lightweight Heckler & Koch M-69 A-1 grenade launcher. The four-pound pistol-shaped launcher had an extendable shoulder stock that was about the size of the handle on a bicycle tire pump. When the stock was fully extended, it gave just enough leverage to deal with the kick of the grenade gun.

With the launcher hanging from his neck like a talisman, Bolan loaded several grenade rounds into his vest pockets. He was carrying an assortment of smoke rounds, tear gas and high-explosive shells and antipersonnel fléchettes.

The Executioner peeled the sides of the satchel completely open and lifted the last item, a canvas travel kit that was about the size of a gym bag. Inside was a Chartered Industries Ultimax 100 short-barreled machine gun. The weapon weighed less than twenty pounds, but delivered a ton of firepower.

Bolan evenly distributed the rest of his ordnance in the slanted vest pockets designed for quick access. Steel bolts for the minicrossbow were wedged into the canvas case, as well as spare mags for the Beretta. Everything he needed to walk into a hell zone.

When he was ready to move out, he lifted the calculator-sized satcom unit from a side vest pocket. He telescoped the antenna and made sure there was nothing between him and the geosynchronous satellite tasked to the operation. Then he typed "Landfall" on the small keypad and watched the corresponding characters appear on the tiny digital readout screen. With a push of his thumb, he bounced the encrypted message off the satellite to the task-force units gathering in the nearby mountains.

The first stage of the operation was under way. He'd reached the shore and was on his way to pay the Cohorts a visit.

Bolan stashed his scuba gear in the now empty satchel, secured it in the brush, then headed for the target.

As he made his way down the shoreline, he carried the canvas case in his left hand. His right hand was free in case he ran into a welcoming committee and had to draw the Beretta 93-R in a hurry. If he had a choice, he preferred not to use the weapon in the opening stages. Even with the sound suppressor, the Beretta made a noticeable cough that could alert other Cohorts in the area.

It was rough going and a lot slower than he liked. Barrows Lake was a wild lake, and that meant very little had been done to keep it from reverting to its natural state. Two hundred years ago the shore may have looked exactly the same.

The thin corridor of land that Bolan had to traverse was crowded by a jagged wall of forest that ran right up to the water's edge. It was an impenetrable mass of wilderness, sprouting spiked branches and thorns that clawed at him every step of the way.

Several times he almost lost his footing and had to steady himself by clinging to the branches and vine clusters that draped overhead. It was no easier at ground level. Only a few patches of wet sand interrupted the long stretches of slick rocks, jagged branches and snarelike roots that coiled around his feet.

Bolan let his subconscious mind take over for him, gliding across the terrain instead of making sudden, jerky movements that could end up with his foot trapped in a crevice. There wasn't much a one-legged man could do against the armed fortress of Cohorts.

When the woods finally thinned out, Bolan headed inland where he could move faster over the much more navigable ground.

He passed the remains of a cinder-block foundation dug out of the earth. Only one wall of the cabin that once sat on the foundation was still standing. Tall and spindly saplings grew through the empty window-frame. Except for the eroded shell, it looked like a roofless bunker.

The Executioner noted the position of the ruined cabin in case he had to make a stand later on. Some cover was better than none.

Twenty yards past the cabin, he came across a rotting wood shed that sat in the midst of a new growth of trees. It was full of logs that had merged together in a rotting and crumbling mass, obviously untouched for years.

Bolan stayed by the wood shed for another minute

to listen for the sounds of any other nocturnal predator, then moved on toward the veil of trees and brush
that marked the edge of the forest. Through the thick
forest growth, he saw the lights of the lodge.

He stopped and listened once again, then smelled
the air. Billowing streams of wood smoke drifted toward the sky from two fieldstone chimneys.

He pictured the group of Cohorts settling in for the
night, maybe sitting by the fire and killing time until
they were given their assignment and sent into battle.
Rest well, he thought. Then rest in peace.

Bolan eased forward through the brush and took
shelter behind an oak with a massive Y-shaped trunk.
He lifted the side-pocket flap of his combat vest and
took out a small monocular night-vision device, then
flicked on the hot button. His hand fit easily around
the contoured finger grip of the NVD, a compact
model that performed well even under minimal star-
light levels.

Tonight there were few stars in the sky and a massive bank of clouds that occasionally obscured the
moon. But the NVD gave him everything he needed.

His first sweep of the grounds turned up no bodies
on the green screen. However, the scope did reveal
an array of infrared beams that crisscrossed the dock
area. If anyone tried a direct assault from the lake,
climbing up the wooden stairs from the water, he
would have triggered a host of buzzers and bells. And
maybe even an antipersonnel mine or two would have
welcomed him the instant he stepped onto the dock.

Another IR "fence" was set up by the stone gates
at the end of the long gravel driveway. Anything that
came through the gate, man or machine, would be

tagged instantly by the IR beams, giving the occupants plenty of time to prepare a welcome.

Outside the gate, a late-model car was parked in the shadows of the trees. The engine was turned off and a man sat behind the steering wheel. Bolan zoomed in on the man. From that angle he couldn't make out the features. But the guy sat as still as a gargoyle, waiting for something to trigger him into life.

The man in the car was the known security Bolan had been informed about. The SIOC recon team that had first picked up on the Cohort gathering had noticed the man driving up and down the Barrows Lake back roads and logging trails at irregular intervals, checking for any unexpected traffic. Then he would drive back and park near the gate. Sometimes he'd make his rounds again after ten minutes. Other times a half hour passed before he went out.

It was an effective and low-maintenance security measure. Sound carried far in the Adirondack north country. A car door slamming or a set of radial tires whining on the tar roads could be heard from a long way off. When the Cohort guard was sitting in his car, he could hear anything approach, and when he was prowling the roads he could investigate anything that didn't belong there.

That was why the task force was coming in slow and sure, and why Bolan had come in from the water. He'd been dropped off on the opposite side of the lake from a government vehicle with a finely tuned engine, a matte-black finish with no chrome to reflect the moonlight and no headlights to give the driver away.

Bolan scanned the rest of the grounds and saw nothing moving. But he felt a presence just the same. He couldn't tell where it was coming from. He just had a sense that something else was out there in the darkness. Something lethal.

A lot of effort had gone into quietly infiltrating Bolan into the midst of the Cohorts. And now that he was there, he expected to find some serious security waiting for him. But aside from the mobile guard out near the road, who seemed totally dedicated to security patrols outside of the gates, there was no visible patrol within.

Perhaps they believed there was safety in numbers, Bolan thought. It was conceivable that the well-armed, well-trained Cohorts considered themselves an almost untouchable, unstoppable force. In their minds they were the predators. Who in the world could go against them?

But the Executioner took precautions just the same.

He moved up and down the perimeter of the woods, scoping out as much of the territory as possible while fixing the layout of the lodge in his mind.

It had a long wraparound porch with stone columns and wooden railings. Multiple windows lined the lower floors, while cathedral-shaped windows looked out from the upper floors. There had been so many additions made over the years that the rooms of the lodge were stacked like the layers of a birthday cake. Attics, corners and private balconies provided plenty of avenues of escape and entry.

The slant-roofed back porch opened out onto a patio with a marble walkway leading to the long driveway. Several cars were lined up along both sides, positioned with their front ends facing the driveway so they could make a fast getaway if necessary. Some of them were sport utility vehicles, while others were late-model sedans. However the Cohorts lived in their daily lives, Bolan thought, they certainly traveled in style. With a fleet of cars like that, they obviously weren't short of cash.

Along with offering a quick means of flight, the Cohort vehicles also provided plenty of cover for the Cohorts.

Another area that offered cover was a garden on the side of the house, which was cordoned off by a fieldstone wall.

And then there was the boathouse. It was a basic blockhouse shape trimmed with white, with an upper deck that looked out onto the water. Broad ladderlike staircases led down to the docks that flanked it on both sides, where two razor-hulled powerboats floated in the water. Any Cohort who made it to the boathouse deck could hold the high ground and have a clear field of fire.

After committing the landscape to memory, Bolan envisioned the near future with the cold eye of a technician.

The Executioner calculated the various points of attack and figured out where some of the Cohorts would head when they ran for their lives in the opening moments of the assault. No matter how well trained these irregular troops were, there were bound to be some who would panic. A few well-placed shots could boost that panic and spread chaos to the other troops. Throughout the battle, though, some Cohorts would be able to keep their wits about them and launch a counterattack. He meant to be ready to shut it down.

The Executioner lifted the 100-round drum magazines one at a time from the canvas case and planted them at strategic intervals at the edge of the woods. He positioned them alongside rocks and in the crevices of tree roots, making sure that he always placed them to the right of every landmark he chose. That way there would be no vital seconds lost in scrambling for the Ultimax ammo. To convince the Cohorts they were facing a small army, he needed to change the magazines with split-second precision. Any delay meant they wouldn't hesitate to pour in the woods.

The Ultimax had only one setting. It was a full-auto, finely machined piece of killing equipment. There was no pretense about what it was designed for. When you flicked off the safety and pulled the trigger, it spit out a steady stream of 5.56 mm rounds. If he did it right, the Executioner could turn the area between the lodge and the forest into a killing field. Whether they were panicked or not, the Cohorts wouldn't get much farther than that.

Bolan cupped his hand over his watch and glanced at the passively lit display. It was twenty minutes before midnight, which gave him exactly one half hour to play with. Any time until ten minutes past midnight, he could launch his attack according to plan.

But if the soldier didn't signal the rest of the team before the designated time ran out, they would assume that he was dead or unable to lead the assault. And then the rest of the team would come into the compound in full force.

Bolan forced himself to wait. That was always the

hardest part. Seconds seemed like minutes, and minutes could seem like hours. Every sense was heightened, and every inner thought was telling him to jump into action, to get it down before it was too late. But he waited just the same.

A few minutes later a car engine kicked into life. It was the guard outside the gate. He flicked on the lights and drove off down the road.

In all likelihood, Bolan thought, the man wouldn't be coming back. At least not on an earthly plane.

NICK CHANDLER LOOKED out at the pool of darkness beyond the dock, then at the jagged shadows on the other side of the bay. He blew a stream of cigarette smoke and watched it drift across the glass of the second-floor window like mist.

He was sitting at a long wooden desk, a regal old-world slab of carved and filigreed wood that occupied half the room. It had been an office once, when the place was a bed-and-breakfast.

Now it was a safehouse, he thought. And possibly a tomb.

He didn't like it out here in the middle of nowhere. It was too quiet and too dark. There were no city lights to paint the horizon, and there was no traffic for miles around. Except for the lights of the lodge, there was nothing but darkness. Nothing but the cold, quiet wilderness closing in on him.

Out here a man could hear himself think, and that was the real problem. On nights like this he tended to do too much thinking.

But it would be over in another day or two. The Cohorts who were selected for the mission had been arriving in groups of two and three. Many of them had worked together, including the group from the Roanoke raid and the team he led in Connecticut. They had performed well in battle; otherwise they wouldn't be here tonight.

Even with their battle experience, Chandler wasn't sure they could pull this thing off. Few of the Cohorts had ever gone on an operation of this size before. Most of them had no idea of just how many Cohorts there were and weren't used to acting as a large force.

Grail had intentionally kept his recruitment to a manageable level, just as he'd done in the old Contra days. Back then he kept a pool of trusted men he could call upon as needed. They would group before the operation, carry out their assault, then disband until the next time. He'd done the same with the Cohorts but on a much smaller scale.

Until tonight.

Tonight it was Chandler's turn to field the armies. He was the common denominator for all of the groups. While Grail had worked directly with some of them, Chandler was the one who gauged their readiness for direct action. The one they would follow.

Although Chandler excelled at hit-and-run guerrilla strikes, that was an entirely different arena than the one he was about to enter. Now he was like a field commander about to send his troops into war. The assembled group was going to sweep through the north country and hit the targets who were laughing in their faces.

Every night the television news shows ran film clips of veteran FBI officers working side by side with new agents, quoting them about how they'd taken down the Cohorts before and how they would take them down again.

It was probably a trap, Chandler thought.

He'd talked it over at great length with Grail, who finally agreed that the enemy was just making it too easy for them. The FBI wasn't known for broadcasting its intentions, especially after it had lost two of the agents they were supposed to be protecting. And they'd suffered several casualties from the group of protectors.

Their nightly news routines were either designed to calm the public or enrage the Cohorts.

In nearly every news clip, the agents told the world they were waiting out in the open for the Cohorts to show themselves, but the Cohorts were still skulking in the shadows. Many of the clips focused on how the Cohorts were little more than low-life thugs who were great at making attacks on retired agents. But they were obviously too cowardly to face serious threats.

The Justice Department's message was parroted by news anchors and reporters until it became common knowledge that the Cohorts would never dare to attack professional units face-to-face.

It was a macho tactic, a slap in the face, Chandler thought. Unfortunately that tactic was working. If it was a trap, they were going to walk right into it. But with the ordnance Chandler's crew was bringing, they were determined to make sure that the Cohorts were the only ones who walked away.

The war was escalating, Chandler thought. But the Cohorts had enough troops to do it right. As long as he did his part.

He took one last drag and stubbed out his cigarette, then went downstairs to the large common room on the left side of the lodge. Two tall and narrow stone fireplaces stood at opposite ends of the room, filling the air with crackling heat.

Cohort soldiers were sprawled out everywhere he looked. Some slept on couches. One man sat in a wicker chair by the front window, reading one of the old classic leather-bound volumes he'd taken from a rough-hewn bookcase. Back when it was a bed-and-breakfast, the shelves and library were stocked with hundreds of old books that were purchased by the pound at auctions.

There were several other irritating reminders that this had once been a great lodge catering to the elite: ornately carved furniture, old Tiffany-style lamps, cabinets with pieces of china and glass, Adirondack sketches from old-time artisans. It was full of everything that Chandler hated. He would be glad when this was over and they could leave the lakeside museum piece behind.

The others didn't seem to be in a hurry to get out, Chandler thought. In fact, they welcomed the reprieve, the chance to loaf around and do nothing at all. A few of them were sitting closer to the fire, smoking and drinking. Tobacco, not weed. Coffee, not alcohol. Chandler had seen to that. In the old days he'd seen too many Cohorts get wasted or captured because they were in a haze. In those days the Cohorts celebrated before, during and after their clandestine operations.

Chandler wiped the back of his neck as he walked down the hallway past the common room. The air inside of the lodge was parched from the fire. It felt suffocatingly hot and stale from the breathing of so many men who were on edge, men who couldn't help but wonder if they would still be alive the next day.

He went out the front door onto the porch and stretched his arms wide, inhaling deep breaths of cold autumn air. At first the crisp air felt like a tonic that revived him, but the feeling didn't last for long. Steady winds drifted in from the lake and tipped the rush-woven porch rockers back and forth as if they were occupied by ghosts.

He was on edge, but not from the thought of holding so many lives in his hand. More important to him was whether he won.

Still unable to get rid of the restless feeling that had been dogging him all night, Chandler walked down to the dock. His feet made a rumbling sound on the thick wooden boards as he strolled to the mooring at the end of the dock. He leaned against it, listening to the waves crash against the wet wood. He lit a fresh cigarette and looked across the lake. Then he looked north toward the distant battlegrounds.

The following day one of his Cohort recon teams would drive north to scout out the Saranac Lake operation where the FBI task force had made such a public show of their stalwart presence. The Feds were operating out of a government building just outside of town, a regional state trooper HQ that supposedly was the focal point of their ''antiterrorist'' operations.

Another Cohort recon team would drive to Plattsburg and check out the FBI task force that had set up shop near the closed air base.

Chandler knew that it was no accident the task

force was setting up in those towns. The Feds were sending a message, daring them to respond. Their old haunts were now occupied territory, Chandler thought, remembering how the original Cohorts made use of the area. The Adirondack area had plenty of wilderness to get lost in, but it was still close enough to the major cities that harbored their urban safe-houses. Once you crossed the border with Canada, Montreal was just a short drive north. Burlington and Boston were to the east, and New York City was directly south.

He'd known the region well in those days. It was strange territory to many of the new recruits, but that would change soon enough. The recon teams would come back with photos, maps, escape routes. Diversionary targets. Potential hostage sites. If it was a trap, they'd figure out the best way to spring it. And then the Cohorts would go in with everything they had.

Chandler didn't waste time worrying about the physical effects the battle might have upon him. Once he went in, he would be on automatic pilot. He would either be dead or he would be victorious. And the world would know that once again the Cohorts were a force to be reckoned with.

A soft click sounded behind him.

Chandler immediately stepped away from the mooring and dropped his hand to the SIG-Sauer pistol in his holster.

But then he saw the source of the sound. Holland was coming out the front door of the lodge. There was no mistaking the silhouette of the barrel-chested man who followed the same path that Chandler took just moments ago.

Holland walked to the edge of the dock near him and looked out at the lake. Quietly.

"Something on your mind?" Chandler asked.

Holland shrugged. "Should there be?"

Chandler thought back to the recent Cohort operation Holland had been sent on. Grail told him about the incident at the farmhouse when Holland refused to do a clean sweep. Instead of following orders without question and erasing everyone at the site, Holland made a fuss about how the wife of the old FBI agent was a noncombatant and should be spared. As it turned out, Holland had been right. The woman hadn't been able to offer any leads to the Cohorts involved in the attack.

But now Holland was at it again, wondering about their attack the next day.

"Don't worry," Chandler said. "Your conscience can rest easy. We'll only be hitting hard targets. No civilians." Chandler had no idea if that was true or not, but he said it with enough conviction that he almost believed it himself.

"Then I guess I'll stick around a little longer," Holland said.

"Glad you feel that way. Keeps *my* conscience clear."

"How do you mean?" Holland asked.

"Can't make it any plainer," Chandler replied. "You know the score. When you come into the Cohorts, you come in for life. Stick around and you'll have nothing to fear."

"I'll keep that in mind," Holland said. He turned and started to walk slowly back up the dock, with his hands in his pockets and his mind a world away.

Holland was a hard man to figure out, but he was a good man to have around. Thanks to his vetting in the mercenary world, he didn't get shaken up under fire, but somewhere along the way he'd obviously picked up some kind of conscience virus. Holland thought a bit too much about his enemies, and that kind of thinking could get a man killed.

Such concern for the other side was an outlandish concept to Chandler. Those kinds of thoughts had been totally absent from the world view of the Cohorts who once led the movement. He remembered the cutthroat competition between the members of the old guard when it was a badge of honor for a Cohort to show no quarter to anyone on the other side. That included men, women and children. The idea was to kill anyone who even remotely stood in the way of their goals.

That attitude stemmed from the belief that the only thing that truly mattered in the world was for the Cohorts to keep on living and opposing the government. As if they were the only ones who'd earned the right.

Everyone else was expendable. Even reliable old soldiers like Holland, he thought as the stocky Cohort stepped back into the lodge.

HAL BROGNOLA WAS twenty miles east of Barrows Lake and two feet above treetop level. Or so it seemed to the big Fed as he sat on the back bench of the Bell 206 helicopter. Though he was still running the logistics end, he wore the same kind of protective gear as the two men in the front of the chopper—antiballistic helmet and vest. Chances were good that before the night was over, Brognola himself could become a target.

Captain Kitchener and his copilot were flying the chopper just above the treetops. They were relying on instinct, experience and the night-vision screen to keep them a safe distance above the dark green carpet of forest.

Neither one of them seemed bothered by their proximity to the sharp and jagged peaks that could get tangled in the struts or spear into the fuselage. They were quiet and intent, locked on the task ahead of them. Brognola had been on similar missions before, flying at extremely low levels, but it was one of those things that you didn't get used to unless you were constantly exposed to it. The sky wasn't his territory anymore, the Justice man admitted to himself. He was more at home flying a desk, now and then manning a computer keyboard.

Brognola rested against the thrumming wall of the cabin and looked out at the windblown treetops that rolled below them like waves. Somewhere out there on the horizon were other airborne state troopers attached to the north-country operation. The aviation unit had several other recently outfitted helicopters converging on the same destination.

Battle platforms had been added to the scout helicopters to transfer them into airborne attack units. A pair of Sikorsky choppers was also on hand to move the heavy equipment and special-ops troops into the battle zone. The Cohorts had long fancied themselves a military group. Now they were going to find out once and for all what it meant to come up against a real army.

It was an army that Brognola had fielded with considerable speed, thanks to the preparations he'd made ahead of time. Now that they were down to the final hour, it was a matter of coordinating the communications and command for the joint task force. It was up to him to prepare all of the airborne and ground units for the moment when they would drop in as uninvited guests at the lodge.

State police units, sniper and tracker teams from the U.S. Marshals and FBI Hostage Rescue Teams had been positioned around the north country. Along with beefing up the protection for the FBI agents who had been hung out as bait, the special units had been preparing for a hit like this.

It had been a long time coming, Brognola thought, remembering all the endless hours he'd spent with the SIOC task force in Washington, night after night sifting through the raw intelligence that came pouring in. But now it was finally paying off.

The first break came when the desktop brigade added the fresh intel from the Czech Republic operation into the SIOC database. Along with several names of go-betweens used by Cohorts and their monk armorers, a wealth of financial records was delivered into SIOC hands.

By sifting through decades of old and new Cohort connections, the SIOC analysts uncovered a web of small but cash-heavy companies that were linked together. The small corporations were managed by a holding company that had been set up by a known Cohort associate years earlier. One of the businesses was a chartered tour outfit that arranged visits to sacred sites in Germany and England. Another was a realty company that managed a group of properties spread out across New York and New England, including the lodge on Barrows Lake.

While the SIOC number crunchers tried to unmask the real owners behind the businesses, a SIOC surveillance unit had kept a discreet watch on all of the Cohort-connected sites.

Meanwhile, by working from the profiles of past and present Cohorts, Doreen McKenna had created a series of public relations news clips that were designed to draw out the underground troops. She saturated the media with features about the north-country task force of veteran FBI agents that was operating in the very same territory that had once been considered a stronghold of the Cohorts.

Knowing the image the Cohorts had of themselves as noble warriors, McKenna laid out a psychological minefield for them. Even if they knew where the mines were planted, they would still place their men in the field. If not, they had to admit to themselves that they were no match for the government and were just a bunch of disgruntled losers who knew how to pull a trigger on innocent victims.

The media offensive worked like a charm, ultimately bringing a squad of Cohort soldiers to the lodge at Barrows Lake. The secluded site was the perfect gathering place for the Cohorts. The nearest towns, Saranac Lake and Lake Placid, were far to the north and they had no reason to suspect anyone was on to them.

When the first Cohorts arrived, the SIOC surveillance unit immediately flagged Hal Brognola. In turn he put together the various units of the quick-reaction force that was now moving toward the lakeside hideout where Bolan was already in place.

It was Bolan's job to make sure there was no time for the Cohorts to prepare for the invisible army that was about to descend upon them.

Brognola glanced at his watch, then looked out into the darkness ahead, knowing that at any moment the night could explode into flame. When it came time for Bolan to knock on the door, he was going in hard.

THE EXECUTIONER HEARD the sound shortly after the Cohort who looked like Nick Chandler walked back into the lodge.

He'd been concentrating so hard on trying to make a positive ID on Chandler and the man who joined him on the dock that he almost hadn't noticed the guard's approach. That, or the guard was a well-trained woodsman who knew how to move almost soundlessly through the brush.

But now that the man was closer, Bolan could hear the soft footpads cutting a path behind him.

The Executioner didn't move, aware that the slightest motion might put the man on alert. Instead he listened until he could pinpoint the man's location. He took a quiet breath and slipped his hand around the handle of the Beretta 93-R, mentally rehearsing the split-second act of tearing it free from its harness and taking aim at the sentry.

The man's death was foretold as Bolan's combat instincts kicked in.

Then he heard the man move on.

The Executioner turned his neck slowly and watched the dark shape filter through the trees. It was a roving patrol. So far just one man. The soldier waited a few moments longer to see if there was a backup before he crept sideways through the brush.

He matched the rhythm of the guard's movements through the curtain of forest and used the sound of the man's footsteps to cover his own.

Bolan followed his progress right up to the edge of the woods, then came to a complete stop and watched the man walk out into the open. He could hear the Cohort singing to himself, totally relaxed now that he'd reconnoitered the woods and found no sign of danger.

The danger had found him.

The Cohort was silhouetted in the moonlight and showed absolutely no concern as he walked back toward the lodge. He wore solid khaki pants, a dark sweatshirt and a ranger's patrol cap. He had a holstered side arm but no other visible weapon.

He stopped once, scanned the area in a full circle, then continued on his way. He still hummed to himself as he continued going through the motions of sentry duty.

If the guard had really been alert, Bolan thought, he could have totally derailed the raid. But the Cohort hadn't been expecting any kind of action, so he simply didn't look hard enough.

Bolan watched the man walk across the grass, apparently heading back to the house. But then, when he was almost halfway to the lodge, he made a sudden detour toward the brick-walled garden. As soon as he walked through the opening, he started talking to someone. An unseen guard.

The second Cohort sentry had been sitting quietly

inside the walls of the U-shaped garden, which offered him a perfect view of the lakefront approach. If Bolan had made his move earlier, he would have walked right past his sights.

The Executioner drifted back into the woods and angled to his left, moving toward the water until he got a glimpse of the second man through the night-vision scope. The gunner sat with his back against the wall and a machine pistol cradled across his legs.

The two men briefly talked in hushed tones before the man in the ranger cap headed back toward the woods to make a countersweep.

Bolan calculated where the guard would reenter the woods, then hurried to intercept him. He crouched in a pocket of woods where the moon couldn't cut through the branches and the night painted him with shadows.

A few seconds later the guard parted the branches at the edge of the forest. He ducked his head and blinked his eyes like a man entering a dark room, then stepped cautiously into the shadowy woods.

Bolan sprang up at him before the man's eyesight could adjust to the change in light and decipher the shape coming at him from the darkness. His left forearm swept behind the Cohort's neck while his right hand pistoned upward.

The palm-heel strike clapped the man's jaw shut and pushed him back against Bolan's forearm at the same time. The impact nearly raised him off the ground and left the tips of his feet scrambling for traction.

The move stunned the guard for the crucial few seconds it took to finish him off. Bolan continued pushing upward and levered the man's neck against his rigid forearm until there was an audible crack. And then the man was dead.

Bolan caught the full weight of the sentry's limp body and gently lowered him to the ground.

He took off the man's cap and placed it on his head, tugging on the bill until it was a snug fit. It wouldn't deceive anyone very long, but in the darkness it would serve his purpose long enough.

The soldier walked toward a small clearing in the forest where there was enough unblocked sky above him. He pulled out the satcom unit and tapped out another word on the keypad: ''Siege.'' Then he sent the encrypted message skyward to alert the group that the next stage was beginning.

It was time to take the stronghold.

The Executioner drifted back through the woods to the spot where he'd positioned the canvas drum case and the lightweight Lexan-molded machine gun. He took the last remaining weapon from the case, the Barnett minicrossbow, and cocked a bolt into the groove.

He grabbed the chopped machine gun and propped the butt under his left underarm, then closed his fingers around the forward hand grip. Even with the drum magazine it wasn't hard to carry. The Ultimax's abbreviated stock and the thin barrel that was less than a foot long made it an extremely portable weapon.

Bolan stepped quietly out of the woods and headed for the walled garden. He moved at an angle that covered his approach almost until he reached the U-shaped opening.

The guard looked up and saw the familiar silhouette of a man wearing a ranger's cap.

"That was quick," the guard said. "Find something?"

Bolan moved closer without saying a word. He stepped into the garden with his hand clutched tightly around the pistol grip and leveled the gun at the man's forehead.

By then the guard was looking up at him in total surprise. The shock of recognition scrambled his senses and made him squander the little time remaining to him by trying to do three things at once—grab the Skorpion machine pistol, scramble to his feet and try to shout a warning to the others.

Bolan raised the crossbow enough to track the man's split-second scramble and pulled the trigger. The crossbow sang and the steel bolt cored through the middle of the gunner's forehead.

It was at such close range that the razor-sharp point of the bolt continued through the back of the guard's skull. The impact send a few bone fragments skipping across the grass, carrying the Cohort's last few thoughts with him.

The slain guard bounced against the brick wall, then crumpled sideways to the ground. He flopped onto his back and lay there on the damp earth with the end of the bolt protruding from his forehead like a bloody red seedling.

Bolan dropped low and sat back against the brick wall, scanning the grounds to see if anyone had noticed the encounter. The house was quiet and there was no sign of movement through the windows.

Two down, he thought. And an army to go.

CHAPTER TEN

The Executioner raised his head above the garden wall, scanned the field between the lodge, then looked back up toward the gate. Nothing was moving.

Propping the minicrossbow against the wall, Bolan left a few bolts alongside it, just in case things didn't work out as he'd planned. He tugged the Heckler & Koch grenade gun from its harness and extended the small shoulder stock. He fished out a few 40 mm cartridges from his back vest pocket, loaded a high-explosive round into the weapon, then dropped the remaining cartridges in the front pocket where they'd be easy to reach.

The Executioner pushed himself up from the ground, gripping the Ultimax in his left hand and the grenade gun in his right. Crouched low, he drifted close to the house, close enough to hear any sounds coming from within.

It was still relatively quiet inside the lodge, but he could hear muffled snatches of voices, and from one of the upper windows came the sound of a radio tuned to an all-news station. Every few seconds he could hear the sound of shutters creaking in the wind and banging lightly against the windows.

The house seemed to be shut down for the night, Bolan thought. The Cohorts were secure in the knowledge that armed guards were patrolling the grounds and watching the roads. Besides, in their minds they were the invaders, and it was hard to imagine anyone mounting a hit against them in the middle of the wilderness.

Bolan quickly scanned the windows of the main floor. No one appeared to be moving inside.

He carefully set the Ultimax machine gun on the grass with the barrel pointing toward the lodge, then headed toward the back of the house, glancing up one more time to make sure the mobile guard hadn't returned.

Standing just to the left of the walkway that led from the patio, the Executioner propped the stock of the grenade gun against his shoulder. He took aim at the double windows at the upper part of the back door and pulled the trigger.

The high-explosive round shattered the glass window on the back door and rocketed inside the lodge. The blast shredded the panel walls, caved in some of the ceiling beams and sprayed the room with molten fire.

The sudden blast echoed like cannon fire across the lake, alerting anyone in the vicinity that the firestorm had begun.

While the first blast was dragging some of the Cohorts from a deep sleep into an even deeper and more permanent one, the Executioner took several steps back to the side of the house. Before anyone inside had a chance to recover from the thundering blast that breached their stronghold, Bolan fired another HE grenade through one of the middle windows on the bottom floor. Moments later the glass, the window and the side of the lodge turned red as a volcanic flash of fire and brimstone ripped through the long room.

The concussion from the blast knocked out the rest of the windows and ripped jagged holes in the walls, tall ribbons of flame leaping from the splintered openings.

He half expected to see men spilling from the lodge, but so far none of them had gathered their wits or their weapons. Almost none, he thought as he heard the sound of breaking glass coming from somewhere at the front of the house. The torrent of falling glass wasn't due to the aftershock of the explosion. Someone had bashed his way out of the two-story trap.

Bolan dropped another 40 mm grenade into the Heckler & Koch grenade gun and aimed toward the front of the house. Seeing nothing moving on ground level, he fired a round into the second floor. The grenade thudded through a second-floor window and burrowed deep inside. The blast ripped apart the turret on the front of the house and sent it crashing to the ground. Flaming splinters and shards of wood pinwheeled in the air as the rocket-shaped structure drowned the ground with fire.

Sudden instinct propelled the Executioner to move closer to the house. Without questioning the impulse, he took several steps forward just before a trio of bullets thudded into the ground behind him. Divots of grass flew into the air from the first volley, followed by a second burst of slugs that chewed into the ground closer to him. As Bolan took cover in the flickering shadows of the besieged lodge, yet another burst of slugs singed the air nearby.

He couldn't get back to the forest. Not yet.

The gunfire was coming from the front of the house, but for now the angle was too sharp for the shooter to get him.

Bolan couldn't ignore the threat.

He snapped the shoulder stock back into place and harnessed the weapon. Then he picked up the Ultimax machine gun and sprinted alongside the house to reduce the angle of the unknown shooter's kill zone.

To Bolan's right, flames and smoke belched from the shattered windows, but no return fire was coming from that direction. His main threat was the shooter at the front.

The gunner had fallen silent and was probably even now tracking Bolan from his last known position, waiting for him to come out into the open.

As he neared the front of the house, the Executioner triggered a burst that swept from right to left. He squeezed off several more rounds in the same direction, conducting a recon by fire that covered the ground between the lodge and the woods.

Staccato flashes erupted from the barrel of the Ultimax, puncturing the darkness in flickering streaks that made him an easy target for anyone who was still at the front of the house. But the fusillade had done its work, suppressing any of the gunners who'd reached the front of the lodge.

The Executioner eased up on the trigger and jogged several yards to the left, scanning the shadows as he moved.

There was no sign of movement. No dark shapes

on the ground. But there were too many places the enemy could have sought shelter. The shooter had either been hit and was lying low, made it down to the docks or back into the lodge or had managed to reach the woods.

Bolan didn't waste time wondering. He cleared the wide kill zone in front of him with a long trigger pull, holding the Ultimax like a Tommy gun as it spit out a heavy metal blizzard of rounds.

He pivoted to strafe the woods behind him in case the shooter had reached the shadows. The 5.56 mm rounds thwacked into the thick tree trunks and severed dry branches that were just about the height of a man's chest. He hosed the barrel in an up-and-down motion that sent another lethal spray into the woods. That was one of the reasons Bolan had been the only one to come in from that direction. For now it was his territory, a free-fire zone that none of the backup units would stray into.

The assault had been planned so Bolan could come in and inflict maximum damage, then step back while the rest of the teams came in to do their stuff. As soon as the fighting started, they would hit the lodge in full force.

Which meant that even now they were on their way.

Bolan raked the side of the lodge with the last rounds of the Ultimax, then backtracked to the woods when the drum clicked empty. He hurried to the first cache he'd planted and locked a fresh drum magazine in place. With a couple of quick steps he was back at the edge of the woods and ready to welcome the Cohorts with a hundred more rounds.

By now screams and shouted orders came from every area of the lodge. Some Cohorts staggered into the open, their clothes blackened by smoke or stripped by flame. Some were holding their faces, unable to see, while others were falling onto the grass, only giving in to their wounds now that they had made it out of the death trap.

A handful of Cohorts made a run for it down toward the dock, and Bolan let them go for now. He'd been lucky so far, and he wasn't about to push it by chasing after them into the open.

Several shapes filtered into the night from the other side of the lodge, heading for their cars, which were parked along the driveway.

Even though they couldn't see any of their attackers, many of the Cohorts were firing their machine pistols wildly into the air, stitching the phantom army with full-auto bursts.

The Cohort soldiers knew they were under attack, but they didn't know the source. Even without any clear targets they felt safer by burning off as many clips as they could, hoping their wild fire would get the attackers to reveal themselves.

The source of their troubles quickly became apparent a few moments later when a squad of U.S. Marshals opened up with Remington 870 shotguns from their position just across the road from the gate. The bright flashes and the concussive blasts stopped most of the Cohorts in their tracks.

The short-barreled 12-gauge weapons cut down a Cohort who was beating it on foot through the gate, determined to get out of the compound before any reinforcements arrived. Instead he ran right into the enemy and the wall of lead they threw at him. The shotgun barrage practically cut him in two.

Several other Cohorts dropped to the ground to avoid the steady onslaught from the chopped-down special-purpose shotguns.

A few of them sought shelter behind their vehicles, but they quickly found out that the shotgun loads could easily punch holes through thin metal fenders and still tear a hole through them.

While one line of marshals riddled the cars with shotgun fire, a second reloaded their Remingtons with fresh loads, then stepped up and took their place.

After the first waves of one-sided fire ripped into the Cohorts, the marshals dug into the ground and kept low as the Skorpions sought them out in the darkness.

Volleys of 7.65 mm rounds buzzed through the air in the desperate full-auto rhythm so common to the Cohort gunners. Most of them were conditioned to slap a magazine into the weapon, pull back all the way on the trigger to burn off the entire clip, then start all over again and hope for the best.

Several loud blasts of Remington shotgun fire drowned out the chattering of the Czech machine pistols, but both sides were forced to duck from all of the lead scything through the air.

Through all of the chaos three of the Cohort vehicles managed to get moving, two cars and one compact SUV. The first vehicle headed straight for the gate until a shotgun blast took away the windshield and a good portion of the driver's head.

The steering wheel spun out of control and whipped the vehicle sideways against the gate. The passenger who'd been unlucky enough to catch a ride out with the doomed driver found himself barricading the gate. His panicked face was pressed against the window, and he was trying to aim his Skorpion when another shotgun blast took out the window in front of his eyes.

The remaining two Cohort vehicles split up at high speed. Both of them drove around the gates, digging ruts in the rough terrain and bouncing across the short ditch that ran parallel to the road.

The bumper of the lead car clipped one of the marshals in the leg and sent him flying in the air. He came down hard on his head and lay there in the middle of the road, stunned and too weak to get out of the way.

Two Cohort gunners stuck their Skorpion machine pistols out of the car windows and sprayed the roadside with full-auto volleys.

As the downed marshal tried to scramble to his feet, he took several shots in the chest. Another burst dug into his shoulder, and a third burst riddled his arm.

A second marshal jumped up from the ditch, lost his balance, then started to aim the shotgun at the driver. He was a split second away from taking the Cohort out. But before he could trigger a blast from the Remington, several rounds punched into his armor-plated vest and knocked him backward.

The falling marshal clutched onto his shotgun, but only managed to fire it straight into the air. As his 12-gauge round rocketed toward the stars, he teetered off balance and for a moment was suspended there, rocking back and forth until a burst of Skorpion slugs drilled a bloody line across his neck. The full-auto burst threw him down to the ground with his head nearly severed.

As the lead car unknowingly drove toward a convoy of marshals coming from the lakeshore road, the compact sport utility vehicle rocketed down the road in the opposite direction. It was moving at close to one hundred miles per hour when it hit a solitary marshal's car that was trying to block the road. The car spun like a top, then flipped into the ditch.

Farther down the road, as the SUV gunned past them, two marshals pulled out from the side of the road where their car had been hidden under the trees. They roared off after the fleeing vehicle, but it was already out of sight. They kept up the chase, knowing there was little chance of the SUV getting away, not with all of the chase cars swarming the ground and the helicopters that were swooping in from above.

But the driver of the SUV believed in making his own chances. Bo Davis had spent his life behind the wheel and if need be, he was going to end it there. About a mile away from the lodge, he slammed on the brakes, skidded sideways, then spun off the tarred road onto a narrow rutted lane that promised to be their only possible escape.

By now they all knew that they weren't going to ride out of there without being checked at every crossroads.

Davis kept his foot pounded to the floor, gunning the vehicle along an old logging road that carried them high up onto the mountain. His passengers didn't dare say a word, even if they'd been able to. Though Davis was taking them as close to death as they'd ever been, at least it wasn't the certain death that had been waiting for them back at the lodge.

As the hill grew steeper, the SUV's tires spun wildly in the soft soil, jerking left and right and losing speed, but it made it to the top of the hill. It went airborne as soon as it crested the uppermost ridge, shooting across a small pond and flying just low enough for the tires to ski over the surface. Then it came down hard, bouncing on soft ground, sliding back and forth before it buried its blunt nose into the dirt wall of a ten-foot cliff.

Davis slammed the gearshift back and forth from Forward to Reverse to Forward again while he smashed the gas pedal to the floor. But the SUV just kept on sinking. Its tires tore ruts in the muddy ground that were at least two feet deep before the SUV sank and they had to abandon it, stranded in the middle of a mountainside.

Bo Davis and Duke Holland piled out of the front doors and ran toward the woods. A moment later the back door opened and the tall, gangly Cohort who'd risked his life twice in the space of a single evening found himself risking it once again as he followed the Cohorts into the darkness.

At the first sound of battle, Nick Chandler had grabbed the holstered SIG-Sauer pistol that was hanging over the back of the chair. He slung it around his shoulder, then opened the file cabinet by the desk and took out one of the Skorpions that had been stashed away.

The entire lodge was full of the weapons, having

become a temporary armory during the past twenty-four hours.

But now it sounded as if the entire armory were exploding right beneath his feet. The floor below him shook and shuddered as if it were about to lift off the ground.

The blasts continued, echoing one after the other, apparently moving from the back of the lodge toward the front. The lodge could cave in at any second, or worse, the next sequence of explosions could go off right in Chandler's office.

Chandler turned out the lights, jumped on top of the desk and slid across the smooth polished surface with both feet straight out in front of him and pointing at the glass. He kicked out the windows on the front side of the lodge, then found himself momentarily weightless as the momentum carried him straight through the jagged aperture and dropped him onto the slanted roof.

He stayed in a half crouch as he slowly moved down the roof and tried to pinpoint the direction of the attack. It was coming from the side closest to the forest.

Chandler slid down the roof until his feet extended over the edge, then gripped the overhang and stretched to his full height before dropping to the ground below.

He landed with a heavy thud and a loud crack in both knees as he bent forward to absorb the impact. When he regained his balance, he found himself in the startled midst of several Cohorts who'd poured out the front door and were standing there trying to orient themselves.

Among them was the stocky figure of Duke Holland. He and the others fanned out alongside Chandler, nosing the air with their weapons as they peered into the darkness in search of their attackers.

They saw nothing but shadows and flame.

No army. No horde of government agents. Nothing to shoot back at. The clandestine corps had come for them, Chandler realized, and with the Cohorts all gathered in one place like this, the government wasn't about to take chances. By now they'd have almost every avenue of escape cut off.

"What do you want us to do?" Holland shouted.

"I want you to get the hell out of here," Chandler said. "They know we're here and there's no use staying. Get out with as many of our people as you can."

"How?" Holland asked, glancing down at the water and weighing his chances of getting away in the powerboats. "The water or—" He saw Bo Davis, the wheelman from the Roanoke raid, walking around the side of the house.

"Whatever way you choose," Chandler said. "Just get away. I'll stay here and cover you."

Holland looked surprised, but then he saw the stern look in Chandler's face. He also saw the SIG-Sauer pistol in his left hand and the Skorpion machine pistol in his right, looking every bit like a suicide commando who was ready to stay behind.

Holland nodded and took off after Davis. It wasn't a cause that he was in a hurry to die for.

Chandler watched them go, knowing that whoever had attacked the lodge would certainly be prepared to deal with any of the vehicles that were gathered along the driveway.

How could they miss attractive targets like that?

Chandler gave similar orders to another group of Cohorts who looked to him for instruction, sending them out to the cars or down to the docks, knowing that both sides would soon be host to a demolition derby.

They weren't getting out of there easily.

Neither was he.

A short dark missile streaked through the night and plowed into the forward turret on the lodge. The explosion ripped apart the supporting struts and sent the turret flying into the air like a thousand-pound rock heading straight for Chandler's head.

He swore and scrambled out of the way. And then, without thinking, he found himself running across the grass and firing at the assailant. Chandler couldn't see anyone, but he could sense where the person had struck from.

Even though he'd figured out where the point of attack was, Chandler couldn't counter it. After he fired several more bursts from the Skorpion and the SIG-Sauer, Chandler thought he could still see the shadow of a man moving around out there.

The shadow never stayed in one place long enough for him to take aim. And with the smoke and flames casting a fiery and inconstant illumination on the ground, it was impossible to tell if he was firing at a real man or a figment of his imagination.

Then the figment fired back.

The lodge started to disintegrate in front of Chandler's eyes as bits and pieces of wood and plaster flew into the air. He dropped to the ground as the machine-gun rounds burned through the darkness overhead.

Chandler inched back into darkness and kept low to the ground. Looking toward the forest, he saw that it was just a short run to the relative safety of the trees. But however short it was, there was no way he could outrun the machine-gun blizzard.

With a quick look to the opposite side of the lodge and the more distant forest beyond, Chandler figured that he had a better chance of making it there.

He nosed the air in front of him with the SIG-Sauer pistol, then sprinted across the clearing. Behind him the lodge was in flames, and a pitched battle was raging at the gates. Above him he could hear the sounds of rotors. Choppers were en route, and who knew what else they were carrying. More men, more firepower.

Chandler kept on running. It wasn't cowardice, now was it courage. It was simply a fact of life. The old rule that had kept him alive for so long was once again coming into play. While the Cohorts were all equal, some were more equal than others.

He couldn't afford to be caught. If he was, part of the movement would die with him.

He made it to the woods on the far side of the house. As soon as he got under the forest cover, he dropped to the ground and hugged the dirt. He stayed there and listened, then started to crawl. He stopped and started over, snaking his way into the darkness.

After moving for about five minutes, Nick Chandler realized he was in the middle of a picket line.

He heard voices calling to one another and footsteps slashing through the brush. When the first man came into view, Chandler saw that he was dealing with a sniper-observer team. The guy was in woodland fatigues and had brush wrapped around him from head to toe so that he looked like a human scarecrow. Chandler kept his head down and saw similarly camouflaged shapes knifing through the woods.

They'd been waiting in the wings in case the Cohorts made a mass exodus toward that side of the forest.

Once the first wave of snipers passed him, Chandler could barely discern their movements. He tried following them with his eyes, but they glided so slowly and blended in so well with the splintered shadows of the forest that they might as well be invisible.

Since they were making hardly any sound, Chandler had a hard time tracking them by ear. There was damn little he could hear above the rapid thumping of his heart. His subconscious mind knew that this was the first time that he had come this close to death, and his subconscious mind knew that death hadn't passed him by yet. His temples were pounding, his blood was pumping, and a strident little voice in his head was telling him to rise up and run.

But conditioning took over.

Chandler stayed low and slow until it seemed that the wave of snipers had continued by him, ready to wreak havoc on the remnants of the Cohort strike force he'd abandoned.

He was just about to get to his feet when he heard one more nocturnal hunter prowling through the woods. This one wasn't part of the sniper team, though. Not a special forces type. A trooper maybe, or a Bureau man who had some experience in covert ops but not a lot. That's why he was a backup, and that's why he was making a bit too much noise.

He was also coming right at Chandler.

The Cohort lay still, forced himself to breathe softly and quietly and got his heart to slow down.

But the man kept on coming, unknowingly leading himself closer and closer into combat. He was holding a Heckler & Koch submachine gun before him. One hand was on the forward grip and the other was wrapped around the pistol grip. But his finger wasn't on the trigger.

The man didn't expect to have to use it. Not after the team of snipers had cleared the way for him.

Chandler was going to let the man pass, figuring it was better not to make any sound that might be picked up by other troops in the area. But the man gave him no choice when he continued to walk directly toward Chandler's prone form, almost as if he were being drawn to him by a magnet.

The Cohort hesitated just a shade too long. Instead of taking him out with a silenced burst from the Skorpion, he'd played possum until the guy was right on top of him, literally standing over him and about to step on him.

Chandler rolled to his side, formed both hands into a double fist, then hammered the sentry behind the kneecap.

He went down as if his legs had been cut out from under him. He landed in a heap, flailing at the wild animal in the brush who was clawing at his feet, the wild animal who was a Cohort chieftain fighting for his own survival.

As soon as the man landed on his back, Chandler rose up and shot a heel-palm strike toward his temple, aiming to crush him into oblivion with one blow. But his target moved fast and avoided the full brunt of the strike. With his instincts ignited by the sudden proposition of death, he made a grab for his weapon.

By then Chandler was looming over him. He stamped one foot on the submachine gun and pressed it flat into the ground, then swept the Skorpion toward the man's face.

"No," the man pleaded.

"Yes," Chandler replied. He pulled the trigger of the machine pistol and drilled a silenced 3-round burst through his forehead. "Yes, three times."

CHAPTER ELEVEN

Three helicopters crested the horizon of the dark forest. They were flying in a low-level pattern that kept them just above the treetops until they came out into the open and soared across the deep cold water of Barrows Lake.

The trio of choppers headed straight for the burning lodge at the end of the lake, where tall and bright crimson tongues of flame lapped against the sky like a beacon.

Down on the ground there was a cluster of bright barrel flashes, indicating the firefights taking place near the woods and around the boathouse. Other flashes punched through the darkness on both sides of the gate where the battle was winding down.

Several overturned cars had piled into the stone gates and lay there like smoldering wrecks from a fatal traffic jam. Hoods were blown off, tires were scattered on the ground and several would-be drivers were merged with the metal. Beyond the gates a fleet of federal vehicles was prowling the main road, throwing spotlights into the woods.

Ground units were moving inside the gates, taking

control of the area around the lodge, tightening the noose and sealing off avenues of escape.

Now that the land battle was over, it was up to the airborne unit to take control of the water.

The three-unit helicopter squad was composed of two heavy-duty Sikorskys and a combat-ready Bell 206. In case they needed assistance, they could call upon another backup squadron that was flying over the nearby hills, ready to conduct search-and-rescue or search-and-destroy operations.

The pair of Sikorsky choppers carried two kinds of deadly cargo. Inside the belly of the forward Sikorsky was an eleven-man BCI strike team. They were decked out in full armor and carried a wide range of automatic weapons and breaching devices in case there was anything left of the lodge to breach.

The pilot of the lead Sikorsky chopper intentionally overshot the lodge, then turned hard to the right to reduce its forward speed. He brought it around in a half circle, hovered above the larger field between the forest and the lodge, then quickly touched down on the grass. The strike team spilled out into the night.

Inside the second Sikorsky was an elite Riverine unit that was ready to man the high-speed chase boat hanging down from the chopper, a Zodiac Hurricane with a .50-caliber machine gun mounted on the front. The pilot made a quick recon over the water, then headed back toward the mouth of the bay where the unit could cut off any of the Cohorts who were unlucky enough to make it that far.

The Zodiac hung from the Sikorsky hoist wires like a sleek gray torpedo sailing twenty feet above the water.

The third helicopter, the armored Bell scout that carried Hal Brognola, took a couple of hits of sporadic gunfire when it roared past the dock, the thrumming sounds of the rotors adding to the panic of the trapped hardmen.

The small group of Cohorts had gathered on the dock, pushed there by the battle lines that were constantly closing in on them. Their choices were extremely limited and possibly fatal. They were either going to stay on the docks and make a last stand or surrender to the dark shapes moving about the lodge. Or they could try to make a run for it in one of the powerboats that were floating alongside the docks.

Two of the powerboats were visible, and a third craft floated inside the boathouse. Each one of them was almost fast enough to take them to freedom, a temptation that was too hard to resist for men who'd spent a good portion of their lives on the wrong side of the law. If they stayed put, they were facing a short and quick battle or some long and hard jail time.

The Bell 206 continued to fly low along the shoreline, then looped around the end of the bay. By the time Kitchener made his approach to the dock complex, one of the powerboats was already jetting out toward the middle of the lake, its hull raised high as it pounded across the waves.

Only a few Cohorts were inside the second powerboat as it started to push off from the dock. Two more gunmen made up their minds at the last possible second and dived headfirst into the boat. Before they had a chance to get to their feet and regain their balance, the Cohort in the cockpit spun the wheel and gave the engine full throttle. The powerboat's nose lifted out of the water as it gunned away from the dock. It shot across the lake like a bullet and left a wide churning wake behind it.

The Bell recon chopper followed the same course.

Captain Kitchener decided to zero in on the second boat, knowing that the other craft was going to run into a .50-caliber surprise from the Zodiac. The pursuit boat had been dropped into the middle of the bay with a veteran crew waiting for the Cohorts. Nothing was going to get by them or the Hurricane.

Kitchener glanced briefly over his right shoulder to catch the eye of Hal Brognola. The big Fed was leaning forward and peering at the Cohorts cutting across the water.

"Sir?" Kitchener said into his mike. "In light of your capacity as the commander of this operation, we should probably set you down somewhere. If we want to go by the book—"

"The hell with that noise, Captain," Brognola said. "I wrote the book on this operation. You set me down when this thing is over."

"Yes, sir," Kitchener said. "That I can do."

The powerboat kept dangerously close to the shore, narrowly missing several rocks that jutted from the lake bed. The Cohorts were obviously trying to stay within swimming distance to land so they could make a run into the forest if the chopper got too close.

If they overcame the hypothermic shock from jumping into the icy lake water and made it to the shore, they just might get free.

To change their minds about making that swim, Kitchener dropped low and flew a short distance behind the boat. Staying between the powerboat and the shore, he lit it up with the Nightsun searchlight.

As the bright cone of light illuminated the boat, several Cohorts jerked their heads back and looked up at the aircraft, feeling painfully exposed by the bright light.

The two Cohorts in the back of the boat covered their eyes, but the man in the middle aimed a Skorpion toward the light. He staggered back and forth, losing his balance from the bucking motion of the hull slamming up and down against the waves. He held his fire, perhaps realizing that the small rounds from the machine pistol might provoke a much deadlier response from the Bell. When another Cohort began to yell at him, the man lowered the machine pistol completely.

"Smart man," Kitchener observed.

So far the Cohorts in the powerboat were holding their fire. It was impossible to tell whether any of the men who'd fired at the chopper earlier were on board. Until he had reason to believe otherwise, Kitchener was going to give them the benefit of the doubt.

As he flew in a zigzag pattern so he wouldn't overtake the fleeing boat, he turned toward Brognola again. "How bad do you want these guys alive?" he asked.

"If you can do it without too much risk, go ahead," Brognola said.

"Nothing's without risk," Kitchener replied. "We might take a few more hits."

"And they might get away if we waste any more time."

"All right," Kitchener said. "There are two ways

we can go. We can get on the bullhorn and hit them with words of wisdom from the loudspeaker, or we can fire a few warning shots across the bow. That usually does the trick.''

''It's your call,'' Brognola said.

Suddenly a group of bright flashes cut through the darkness. Two Cohort gunners were firing at them. ''Guess not,'' Kitchener said, as several more flashes of autofire erupted from one of the Cohorts in the cockpit. The hardmen had made the call and now they had to live with it, if they could.

''Light them up,'' Kitchener ordered.

His copilot was already in motion, thumbing the button on the M-134 minigun and sending a stream of 7.62 mm rounds into the powerboat's bow. The boat slowed as the front of it started to disintegrate from the ceaseless burst of firepower. As it lost its momentum, the line of fire from the minigun dropped back just enough to take out half of the crew.

Two of the Cohorts were knocked off their feet by the heavy rounds and found themselves flopping overboard. A third gunner hugged the wheel, collapsing around it as the slugs from the strafing run took their toll.

Kitchener turned hard to the right and brought the chopper around in a half circle. He bore down once again on the remains of the boat, prepared to make a final strafing run if necessary.

First he released two flares on their approach, casting a large furrow of light above the stranded boat and letting the survivors see just what brilliant targets they made.

The boat was taking on water and keeling to the

right. More than half of the crew was dead, and the remaining men were just a few precious seconds away from joining them.

One wounded Cohort was tangled up in the extender ladder and was stuck half in and half out of the frigid water, unable to make a swim for it or to climb back aboard.

The last Cohort had a machine pistol in his hand, but it stayed there for only a moment. As the Bell 206 droned closer, he flung the weapon over the side and raised his hands over his head.

"Looks like we've got two of them," Kitchener said. He was about to make a pass toward the mouth of the bay when the sudden chatter of the .50-caliber machine gun echoed across the water.

It was followed by a bright fireball that flashed across the water where moments ago the other Cohort craft had been. They'd taken their chances with the Zodiac crew and lost.

"Looks like that's all we got," the copilot said, looking toward the fading ball of flame that extinguished the Cohort crew.

THERE WERE TOO MANY for Bolan to count.

The furtive shapes that filtered through the woods were moving away from the blare and blast that enveloped the lodge. Anywhere in the immediate vicinity of the lodge had become a minefield for them, a kill zone where automatic fire zipped through the air and explosives rocked the house, turning much of the grand old structure into deadly sheets of shrapnel.

It was no safer down at the docks or up by the

main road. The gate to freedom had been shut down by an army of well-equipped marshals.

Helicopters were droning overhead, troops were dropping into the field and reinforcements were pouring in from almost every direction.

The only possible escape route was the forest on the side of the house where the attack had been launched. Only one man was covering that area and even though he could cover much of the ground with the machine gun, the Executioner couldn't cover all of it at once.

After the initial strafing rounds, Bolan had found himself outflanked by Cohorts who streamed from the house with only one thing in mind, and that was to get away from the hell zone and kill anything in their way.

He'd been able to empty two more of the 100-round drums from the Ultimax before the Cohorts came out en masse. They caught him in a cross fire with their Skorpions, forcing him to pull back into the woods.

And now that they knew the Executioner was in there, they were conducting a recon by fire. The moving and shifting ranks of the Cohorts chopped the air in front of them with full-auto bursts, then darted ahead and repeated the process.

Some of the hardmen wielding the machine pistols moved with the quiet and confident gait of military men. Other Cohorts were less effective in their movements. They stopped and started with awkward motions that gave away their positions as they rushed from one bit of cover to the next. Then they burned off their clips in a single direction instead of sweeping the field before them.

Many of the gunners were unfamiliar with the chaos of a full-scale battle. In the past their idea of a military action had been a quick descent on an unknowing target. They'd make their hit, then run. Now they were the ones who'd been hit, and they were reeling from it.

But no matter how disorganized the Cohort force was, unless he took control of the field, sooner or later one of those Skorpion sweeps was going to take the Executioner off the field for good.

One thing in Bolan's favor was the absolute knowledge that no one else from the task force was in the zone with him. He knew that everyone in the vicinity was fair game, and he didn't have to worry about taking out any friendlies.

But there was also one major disadvantage with that battlefield situation. For the immediate future there was no one else he could count on to deal with the Cohorts.

The plan had been for Bolan to go in hard from one side of the lodge, seed chaos with the grenades, then take out anyone who came toward his side of the battleground. No one else from the assault group was coming into the kill zone until the Executioner came out.

"Over there." The hushed voice came from off to his right. "See him? He's moving just up ahead."

"I got him," said another voice. This voice was also hushed, but there was a strained urgency in it. It belonged to someone who was at the end of his rope. Or would be there very soon, Bolan thought.

"Come on," the first man said. "Let's take him on *three*."

The Executioner pressed against the tree he'd been leaning against as the two Cohorts coordinated their attack, thinking that they had spotted him. There was no way he could tell for sure, but from his position pressed into the curved hollow of an aging oak, it didn't seem that there was any way they could see him.

And it seemed as if they were going after a moving target. That, or they were playing a hell of a mind game.

But he'd find out soon enough. The Executioner got ready to push himself into the open and chop away with the Ultimax. He planned on using a 360-degree arc for his killing field. If they *did* have his location pinpointed and were centering in on him, then he'd make sure they went down with him.

"One."

The voice sounded closer.

"Two."

He could hear heavy footsteps snaking through a cluster of vines.

"Three."

The Cohort jumped forward and triggered a full-auto burst from his Skorpion, holding the machine pistol straight out in front of him.

But he wasn't shooting at Bolan. He'd run several steps past the tree that sheltered the soldier and was firing at some unseen target ahead of him. His hand moved from left to right and scythed the air at a level that was waist high.

The other Cohort opened up from about ten yards to the left.

Bolan didn't move. He waited for a half minute while the two hardmen searched the ground for his body. Then he heard them call out to several other Cohorts. The band of gunmen was regrouping, getting ready for another sweep of the forest.

The Executioner didn't wait around to get swept. He started to move back through the forest again, concentrating on keeping his own motion undetectable while he listened for the sounds of pursuit.

He drifted over the terrain until he came to the temporary stronghold he'd noticed before.

The cabin ruins.

From behind him came the sounds of a handful of Cohorts who had clustered together and were now making a more systematic sweep through the forest. And then he saw a smaller group of shapes moving through the woods about thirty yards away.

They, too, were heading for the ruins of the cabin.

Bolan suddenly jogged forward, aware that he was attracting attention from the enemy.

Unlike them, the Executioner knew the lay of the land, and that there was a gap in the terrain that would swallow him up if he got there in time.

Bolan ran to the edge of the foundation and took a running leap into the air while he held the Ultimax over his head with both hands.

A half-dozen barrel flashes lit up the dark forest as several full-auto bursts zeroed in on him. But Bolan was six feet underground by then, getting ready for the inevitable rush.

The enraged Cohorts finally had a focus for the

vengeance that was due to them. They'd been cut to pieces everywhere they turned and now that they'd trapped the transgressor, they were eager to pay him back in kind.

Bolan stood perfectly still and took the brunt of the charge, listening to the slugs buzz through the air overhead. They were shooting at his last known position as they advanced toward him. Keeping up the chaotic chatter of full-auto fire, they rapidly burned through their magazines, then slapped in fresh clips.

Before they could get off their second volleys, Bolan stood to his full height. He raised the barrel of the Ultimax at a thirty-degree angle and pulled the trigger. He hosed the area above the front wall with a long burst of automatic fire that decimated the enemy.

Some of the bodies tumbled into the foundation; others fell back to the ground screaming.

Before the Cohorts had a chance to realize where he struck from, Bolan unleashed another burst from the Ultimax. He strafed just above the edge of the foundation and took down anyone who was still standing.

From his earlier recon the soldier remembered how the bunker could easily become a tomb. If he lingered too long, he just might stay underground permanently.

He backed toward the far wall of the foundation and levered his left arm on the edge of the crumbling wall. While pushing down with his left hand, Bolan quietly leaped into the air and vaulted over. He landed on the soft grass and stealthily backed away.

The Executioner waited until the remaining Cohorts went on the move again. They stood at the edge of the bunker and fired straight down into the shadows. After burning off several clips, they climbed into the underbrush and followed the same path he'd previously taken.

When they were caught up in the search through the ruins and the thick undergrowth at the foundation, the Executioner stepped forward.

Bolan planted one foot on the edge of the foundation, then leaned forward and pointed the Ultimax barrel downward. He pulled hard on the trigger and drilled the hardmen below him, making sure that one more group of the revolutionary underground would never surface again.

CHAPTER TWELVE

The Adirondack Northway ran about 150 miles from Albany, New York, up to the north country. It went by the tourist town of Saratoga Springs, continued past Glens Falls, then ran alongside Lake George for thirty miles. It followed the shoreline of Lake Champlain for another ninety miles before cutting through Plattsburg and coming to an end at the Canadian border.

It was flanked by woods and water, resorts and retreats, summer camps, college towns, loghouse taverns, amusement parks and historic old forts dating back to the Revolutionary and the French and Indian wars.

The Northway was the main artery for commerce, travel and tourism for the eastern Adirondacks. And it bordered only a small portion of the wilderness area known as Adirondack Park.

The Adirondack Park region was dotted with small communities and countless lakes. Though connecting roads and trails had been carved through the north country, much of it was still claimed by mountains and forests that looked as untouched as they had thousands of years ago.

Nearly six million acres of wilderness territory spread across upper New York State. Enough wild country to fit several national parks and a couple of small European countries. That was the area Hal Brognola's task force was scanning for the Cohorts who fled Barrows Lake.

Teams of U.S. Marshals and Forest Service rangers conducted grid searches of the hills and mountains. State police helicopters and search planes patrolled the region from the skies.

Fleets of unmarked cars prowled the Northway and the narrow back roads that wound through the wilderness. It was the largest manhunt in the history of New York State, and the men who were running for their lives were aware of the resources devoted to taking them in dead or alive.

DUKE HOLLAND HEARD the helicopter before he saw it. At first it was just a murky thrumming sound on the edge of his perception, then it grew into the harsh mechanical droning of rotor blades whipping the high mountain air as it came over the ridge from the north.

Through the green veil of forest, the thick-set Cohort saw the scout chopper's dark silhouette heading his way. He dropped down, burrowed through a leafy overhang and sat with his back against the nearest tree.

With one hand shielding himself from the bright afternoon sky, Holland watched the helicopter approach. It looked like a black metal wasp painted on the sun.

For the first time in years he wished that he hadn't bulked up so much. But it was a pattern he'd followed ever since his high-school days. First he'd added some pounds so he could make the football team, then he moved on to the wrestling squad, where his agility and bulk proved to be a winning combination.

Holland had thrived on the constant regimen it took to be a champion wrestler. Their coach put them through three hours of conditioning every day. Then, after those monstrous workouts, they would match up against one another and go all out, just as if it were a regulation match. That kind of conditioning shaped him for the rest of his life, teaching him that no matter how tired he was and how close defeat was, if he could endure just a little more than the other guy, he could put him down.

Wrestling was a one-on-one sport, and though it was nice if his teammates won, it didn't really matter how well they did as a group, as long as he had a chance to go against his man.

He'd been going against the other man for more than twenty years now and always came out on top.

Until now.

The power and presence that Holland had prided himself on for so long could very well turn out to be a fatal condition for him. He wasn't the type who could get lost in a crowd, or in a forest.

He and the two Cohorts traveling with him had managed to make it through the night, cold and wet and miserable, but alive. Just about when they thought they'd got away, the helicopters had appeared.

From mountain to mountain they'd moved under cover of the thick forest, splitting up from one another and seeking shelter whenever the helicopters hovered nearby.

This particular helicopter seemed to be spending more time in the area than any of the others. For a while it had been flying in wide circles around the mountaintop. Then it suddenly changed its pattern and flew in straight lines that cut across the treetops, almost as if it were trying to scare the prey on the ground into motion.

That meant they had a reasonable idea where the trio had gone, Holland thought. They'd either narrowed the search area by the process of elimination or maybe they got lucky and picked up a flash of movement on the ground.

Keep going, keep going, Holland chanted, willing the helicopter to pass him by.

But it didn't. Instead the sleek Bell observation craft banked to the left and began a low circular prowl over this section of the forest.

The downwash shook the boughs overhead as the aircraft carried out its slow and careful search. Like a hawk that had sensed his presence, Holland thought, it was biding its time until he was vulnerable. The steady thrumming of the blades was its war cry.

The sound brought back memories, both good and bad. Sometimes Holland had run toward choppers or evac from a hot zone. Other times he'd run away from them. It all depended on what side of the law he was at the time.

Very rarely did he stay perfectly still when a helicopter moved into the area. But now his instinct was making him hold his ground. Death was in the air, and any moment it would come for him. He assumed an almost statuelike pose and tried to breathe nice and easy while keeping his eyes on the path of the chopper.

The scout bird now patrolled the mountaintop in a figure-eight pattern, rising and lowering over the jagged treetops like a droning insect. Whenever the sound of the rotors began to recede, Holland caught some additional echoes that shouldn't be there.

The sound of the first chopper was either bouncing off the hilltops or there were other helicopters in the air. But he couldn't afford to think about them now. Not while the observation craft was meandering back his way.

The helicopter-shaped shadow painted the woods off to his right, then made an approach right toward him. Forward-looking infrared radar, he thought as the shadow momentarily washed over him. The Bell pilot had him on FLIR. Any moment Holland's thermal-imaged mug shot could light up the green screen.

Though he thought it unlikely the Bell had a surveillance system capable of filtering his heat signature from everything else that was scurrying in the woods, he knew there was a chance he'd been tagged. It was a remote chance, but maybe it was time for fate to catch up to Duke Holland.

Without moving his head any more than was necessary, Holland followed the arc of the helicopter as it drifted away. When it looped off to his left, he could see that the cabin door on the copilot's side was open. All he could see was some movement inside the dark oval shadow of the cabin door.

That was more than enough for him to conjure up the image of a man taking aim at him. Even worse than the thought of the door gunner was the brief glimpse of armament Holland caught as the chopper had passed overhead. There was a 7.62 mm minigun mounted on the fuselage. With that kind of war machinery the pilots didn't have to get too exact a fix on their quarry.

Holland had ridden in military versions of the Bell 206 before and knew there were a couple thousand rounds of ammunition all boxed up and ready to feed the minigun. A weapon like that could do some serious recon by fire.

The Bell helicopter also had a Nightsun searchlight, which Holland could make out from the glinting of the sun on the lens, but he couldn't distinguish the rest of the heavy metal add-ons.

When the Bell made a lazy turn and started to head back toward his section of the woods, Holland had a feeling he was about to see some more weapons up close.

He slid his hand down the harness that held the Skorpion, mentally rehearsing the next few moments, which easily might become the occasion of his death.

He would aim for the windows, the open cabin, the fuselage, hoping to drill for oil and maybe send it crashing to earth in flames. It was an improbable thought, the dream of a dying man. Or a man about to die. Holland had no doubt he had been seen.

His hand tightened around the Skorpion.

And then the helicopter moved away. Somehow his unvoiced prayers had been answered.

Thank you, Lord, he thought. Times like this made him feel close to a higher power. Too close, maybe. He wasn't sure of the reception that waited for him on the other side.

He collapsed against the tree and exhaled, realizing that he'd been holding his breath. The tightness in his chest broke, and he felt himself laughing as the silhouette moved away.

The danger hadn't completely passed. The helicopter was patrolling in an ever widening circle in its search for fugitives. There were two more of them out there, two more potential magnets to draw fire from the minigun.

When the sound of the rotors began to recede, Holland thought he could hear distant echoes of heavier rotors drumming against the sky. Other helicopters *were* in the air.

Not a good sign, Holland thought. If somehow they made it off this mountaintop, there was another hill to cross and another helicopter to evade. Never mind the ground teams that were no doubt swarming through the forest in their grid patterns. If they had to, they would cover every inch of the mountains before marking it off and moving on to the next one.

Sooner or later Holland and the other Cohorts would end up in the grid. The two Cohorts who'd fled with him were now spread out on both sides. Neither man could be seen just yet. Good, Holland thought. If he couldn't see them, then the pursuers in the chopper couldn't, either.

Holland waited another five minutes before he got to his feet. It was time to round up the crew again.

They'd been splitting up whenever they heard the sound of helicopters echoing across the mountains. Hell of a way to run a revolution, he thought, rushing blindly through the woods like field mice scurrying away from a winged predator.

It was better than taking a chance at being spotted together. If the three of them were gathered in one location, it would be a lot easier for a thermal imager to pick them up. He had no idea just how intricate the gadgetry in the searchers' arsenal would be, but considering what happened at the house by the lake, he figured it would be top-drawer stuff.

Holland shook his head as he walked off into the forest and wondered just how the hell he ended up here. It certainly wasn't the companionship that kept him in the Cohorts. Aside from his immediate crew— what was left of it—he felt there were few people he could trust.

Before going on the Virginia run to take out one of the Cohorts' ancient enemies, Holland had worked mostly on small-group fund-raisers. He and a cell of veterans would take down an armored car or rip off an unconnected drug gang, a source of quick and ready cash that was always on the periphery of Holland's world. Though the other cells were competent, there was no real bond between them.

The Cohort leadership didn't inspire much trust, either. Holland had seen the headman just a few times before the man himself led them on the Virginia vendetta. It was long enough to sense the charisma that drew so many men into his orbit. But most of the time Holland dealt with Chandler.

Chandler was a cold one. The only time he really seemed alive was when he was ready to put someone down. Men like Chandler pursued a scorched-earth policy that left no possible witnesses behind, never thinking twice about whacking anyone who might be considered a problem.

Right now, unless Holland and his crew could find their way back to the fold, they were grade-A problems.

He kept close to the trees, moving in the shadows and avoiding the more open trail that zigzagged through the forest. A few minutes later he heard a sound behind him.

A footstep.

His hand reached for the Skorpion, and he turned, ready to drop whoever was there when he heard the voice.

"It's me," Bo Davis said, a split second before Holland was about to waste him. He stood there in his thin leather jacket, machine pistol slung over his shoulder. There was a half smile on his angular, high-cheekboned face. His probing eyes were darting around, looking past Holland for signs of the enemy or a trace of the third Cohort.

"You asshole," Holland said.

"What's wrong?" Davis asked, raising his hands. "We're alive and well, man."

"Just barely," Holland said. "Another second and you would have been a dead man."

"If I didn't know you better, maybe I would," Davis said. "But you always look first and shoot later, man. That's something I know for a fact. You always make sure of your target."

"In some situations, yeah," Holland replied. "But not out here. Not when we've got so much company." He nodded at the sky in the direction where the Bell chopper had gone. "They'll be coming back in a while, and they'll keep coming back until they find us."

Davis shrugged. Men with guns were looking for him. That was the story of his life, and somehow he always got by, no matter where the battlefield took him. Although Davis was mainly a wheelman and spent as little time as possible in the great outdoors, he was holding up well in the wilderness, considering how ill-prepared they'd been to make the uneasy flight across the mountains.

The two men headed for the third Cohort, who was relatively new to the organization and definitely new to being hunted like this. He was more at home when he was on the prowl. Point him in the right direction and tell him what to do, and he'd do it. Natural born fodder.

Weren't they all? Holland thought.

It took a few minutes before they came to the third man's nest. He was staying perfectly still, just as Holland had told him whenever there was a scout craft nearby.

Holland kept walking until he was close enough to raise the third Cohort with a whisper. "Ned?" he called out. "Come on out, man. We're clear for now."

Ned Waterman raised his head from the ditch he'd been hiding behind. He came through the brush slowly, almost as if he were coming out of hibernation with his legs and arms stiff from hiding for so long. His gun was in hand and he was studying both of them warily.

"You sure about that?" he asked, looking first at the sky, then back at Holland.

"Rest easy," the cell leader stated.

Waterman stepped toward them, brushing the muck

off his jeans and shirt, and running his hand through his wild and matted hair. He'd been lying in the mud, and it gave him a feral and frightened look.

The three of them stood there, stranded in the middle of nowhere with at least one high-tech helicopter roaming the skies nearby.

And there was probably a special-operations unit or two coming for them on foot. The Cohorts had attracted a lot of heat, and some of it was bound to be military. After all, the Cohorts had declared war. Whoever had come after them at the lodge had been prepared to wipe them out.

"What do we do now?" Waterman asked.

Holland took a deep breath. "We dig in for real."

"Where?" the younger man pressed. "The high ground?"

"This is the high ground," Holland said. "Best thing to do is set up a little picket line, dig ourselves a foxhole and wait out these bastards for a while."

"Wait them out?" Waterman repeated. "Wait for what exactly?"

Davis had stayed silent, watching the younger man get an education. Now he leaned forward with a cheerful countenance. "Wait for them to come and get us," he said. "Or pass us by."

Waterman froze. He looked at Holland, registered the grin, then looked back at Holland. "I don't see much of a game plan here."

"That's 'cause there isn't one," Holland said. "In case you haven't heard, there's more than one chopper prowling the woods." He'd heard the heavier thrumming of transport helicopters from the next mountain over.

"You think they spotted us?" Waterman asked, unable to hide the worry in his voice.

"Maybe," Holland replied. "But if they did, they couldn't land. Tree line's too high and uneven. Or maybe they didn't want to set down where we could see them. But they'll find a place to set down. And sooner or later the troopers and whoever else is in the posse will sweep through here."

Davis matter-of-factly outlined their situation. "They'll cover it in a basic grid pattern, cut up everything into neat little squares, and then they'll cover every single square in the grid. That'll gradually narrow it down until they know where X marks the spot."

"X," the man repeated numbly.

Davis nodded. "Right. That's us, man. We're the Xs."

Holland read the look on Waterman's face. Betrayal and fear were etched in the worry lines across his forehead. But there was just enough anger to possibly keep him alive, anger that things weren't working out as they were told. The Cohorts were the ones who were supposed to bring Armageddon to the FBI.

Now Armageddon was coming to them instead.

"What would Chandler want us to do?" Waterman asked.

Holland looked at him, disbelief on his face. "That's simple," he said. "He'd probably want us to die."

"What are you talking about?"

"Chandler's not the patron saint of lost causes," Holland explained. "He should have pulled the plug on this operation long ago. He must have known the intelligence wasn't solid enough, that it was a lure to bring us all in location. But he sent us in anyway.''

"Why?"

"Obvious, isn't it?" Holland said. "He was fighting a war of attrition. If we went ahead with his plan and stormed the FBI teams in their strongholds, we would have done a lot of damage.''

Waterman nodded, remembering the plan that couldn't fail and how Chandler had outlined every step of the way for them. The plan that had failed so horribly.

"But we also would have suffered a lot of casualties," Holland said. "Chandler was willing to have us die for the cause just so we could boost the body count."

"The cause?" Waterman repeated. "What the hell kind of cause is worth that?"

"The cause to keep Chandler alive and well and out of jail," Holland said. "If it costs our lives, well, that's a price he's willing to pay."

"You willing to pay it?"

"Not if I can help it," Holland said. "Let's dig in and hope they pass us by."

Holland held his counsel. There was no sense in letting the younger Cohort know everything that he was thinking. Like the real reason that Chandler probably sent them scrambling for the cars back at the lodge. It wasn't so Holland and the others could get away. It was so they could create a diversion that would make it easier for Chandler to escape.

The younger Cohort already knew that Chandler was a heartless bastard. But if he knew just how much of a bastard he was, it might distract him from the everyday concerns of staying alive.

In the meantime they had to get ready to deal with the chase teams that were scouring the mountains for them.

Two MILES AWAY the Bell 206 helicopter hovered above a wide brook that carved a crooked trail through the trees. Rounded rocks dotted the water like stepping-stones.

Captain Kitchener followed the brook until he located the bank he'd spotted from the air. He lowered the aircraft as much as he dared, until the blades churned up a froth of cold mountain water and he was hovering above a shelf where there just was enough room to make the drop.

The Executioner clambered from the cabin onto the skid, picked out as level a spot as he was going to find, then jumped into the high grass, bracing himself for the impact.

His feet hit hard on the ground and his knees bent as he toppled forward, intentionally spreading the force through his hands and then his shoulder as he rolled across the grass. The pack that was strapped on his back added several pounds to his drop, but also could add a few years to his life. It was packed tight with survival and comm gear, rations and magazines for the Beretta 93-R.

Bolan was in for the long haul. He wasn't coming out of the woods until he had the target in hand.

Until now the last known location of the trio of Cohort fugitives was the logging road that ran halfway up the mountainside across from the lodge. Their

SUV had come to a sudden halt when it buried itself into the soft clay face of a cliff.

Shortly after the firefight, a recon chopper that was flying over the area was able to spot the abandoned vehicle from the air. But by the time a search party landed, the fugitives were long gone.

And they stayed gone for the rest of that night and most of the next day, a lucky streak that was about to end.

The Executioner waved off Kitchener and the co-pilot. As the helicopter rose over the treetops, Bolan headed uphill, moving toward the spot where the captain thought he'd caught a glimpse of one of the Cohorts.

He covered the first mile at a good speed and glided over the terrain in an easy jog. As he drew nearer to the peak where Kitchener believed he'd spotted the fugitives, Bolan slowed considerably. He stopped several times to scan the terrain with a monocular thermal imager before continuing on his foray.

The first target flickered in his scope when he was about a quarter mile to the right of the heavily wooded mountaintop. It was half of a man. At least that was the signature that briefly showed up on the screen.

Several times previously Bolan had picked up the heat signatures of small creatures that were on the move in the forest, but nothing like the momentary target.

He stayed still and focused the imager on the same spot, a low ridge where some fallen trees had formed a natural barrier. And then he saw the face of one of the Cohorts rising above the barrier and looking for his pursuer.

Rather than move against the Cohort immediately and take him out of the picture, Bolan waited until the man dropped out of sight. Then he moved off to his left and tried to scope out the other two hardmen.

According to the short briefing that took place down on the main dock—one of the few remaining sectors that hadn't been scorched by the battle—it was believed that at least three of the Cohorts had escaped in the SUV. One marshal had seen a trio of men pile into the vehicle, and another marshal who got off a couple of shots before he had to jump out of the way thought that he'd counted the same number.

The footprints around the cliff where the SUV ended its journey were lost in a muddy pool that filled the basin after the rains had come. And though the tracks in the forest floor were just as washed away, with no telling how many men had fled, Bolan decided to go on the assumption that he was dealing with three.

Even though they were caught up in the heat of battle, the marshals were trained observers who were used to keeping track of the opposition. That meant there was one down and two more to go.

The Executioner found the second one higher up on the peak. He was at the apex of an inverted *V* and for some reason he believed that he was too far up on the incline to be spotted. He wasn't quite as security conscious as the first man Bolan had seen, the bulky Cohort who stayed low behind the barrier and only poked his head up now and then to scan the area.

The position of the second man clued the Executioner into the defensive pattern they'd chosen for him or any other stalkers who came for them on foot. There'd be one more gunner at the other end of the V. Anyone who walked straight up the mountain would have a Cohort on each flank and a third Cohort directly in front of him.

It was a reasonably good plan, Bolan thought. If you were new to the game.

He dropped back to a lower height and crept across the hilly terrain until he was able to pick out the third Cohort's heat signature. Like the other Cohorts, this man was also carrying a Skorpion machine pistol.

It was almost a religious thing with these guys, he thought, as if this sacred icon they carried into battle could cast a supernatural aura around them to keep them unscathed.

Bolan wasn't a firm believer in auras.

He flicked the selector of the Beretta 93-R to 3-round-burst mode, then extended the stock to its full length and tucked it into his shoulder. It was time to do some hunting.

Now that he knew where each Cohort was making his stand, Bolan pulled back until he came to a low ridge that was at the outer limits of the Skorpions' accuracy range. The earthen wall gave him enough protection for what he had in mind.

From his position deep in the shadowed woods, Bolan stood to his full height and tracked the Beretta across the jagged horizon. He stopped when the 93-R's barrel was aimed dead center.

He squeezed off a burst toward the Cohort at the apex of the V, then turned to his right and triggered two more bursts toward the Cohort on that flank. While the first two were seeking cover, Bolan pivoted to his left and sent a triburst of 9 mm rounds at the last Cohort.

With a couple more trigger pulls, he emptied the Beretta at the Cohort line.

His feint had the intended result.

The woods exploded with gunfire. There'd been a few seconds of delayed reaction, just long enough for them to recover from the shock of the Executioner's barrage, then they poured their return fire toward his position.

But the Executioner was no longer there.

He was on the move, circling the left flank as he watched the telltale flashes of their machine pistols. The barrels spit flame in sudden flickering bursts, stopping only long enough for them to slap a fresh clip into their weapons.

It was a deadly onslaught and from the way they were raking the area, he knew they probably would have brought him down if he'd stayed there long enough to fight a pitched battle.

Finally the Skorpions fell silent.

During the momentary lull, the Cohorts were waiting to see if there was any return fire.

Bolan held his fire and let them wonder if they'd gotten their man or if their unseen enemy was coming after them. He let the seconds tick away, knowing that the amplified sense of time would get on their nerves until fear joined his side of the equation. Each of them had plenty of time to paint the portrait of the reaper he knew was out there.

Out there and coming for them.

As the Executioner drifted slowly toward the left arm of the inverted *V*, he relied on an almost subconscious state of mind that shut out everything else but the immediate laws of survival.

Get them before they got him.

This was his territory and they were his prey. If he managed to bring in one of them alive, that was fine. If not, that was fine, too.

Bolan angled uphill and flanked the first gunner from the left. He dug softly and soundlessly into the earth, merging with the dark forest until he was a part of it. He moved hand over hand as he crept through the windblown brush.

His face was low enough to the ground to make out the thin spines on the fallen leafs, the branches on the forest floor that wove in and out until they became a soft mat, a carpet that he could crawl upon unheard and unseen like a creature of the hunt.

And then he saw the gunman holding down his end of the primitive Cohort defensive line.

The guy was young and scared. Scared dangerous. He looked as if he'd spent a week in the wilderness, hair wild and muddy, face heavy with fear and anger. The barrel of his Skorpion was waving in jerky motions from left to right, ready to hose down the kill zone as soon as he found a target.

Bolan flicked the selector from burst mode to single shot, then wedged the extended stock of the Beretta against his shoulder.

He pulled the trigger.

A red mist clouded the man's face an instant after the Beretta spit fire. He lurched back from his sentinel post with one 9 mm round through the center of his forehead and collapsed into the brush.

The Executioner stood and ran uphill. He crouched over the dead man, whose last act had been to coil his arm around a thin tree trunk for support, holding on to life as long as he could. Except for the trail of blood that ran down the man's forehead, he looked peaceful, like someone who'd fallen asleep at his post.

Bolan picked up the fallen Cohort's Skorpion along with a spare magazine. He fired a couple of chattering bursts from the machine pistol. The unmistakable sound of the Skorpion would convince the other Cohorts that their comrade was still alive.

Long enough until it didn't matter anymore.

Bolan plucked the man's wallet from his back pocket and scanned the contents—several fifty- and twenty-dollar bills and nothing else. No credit cards or social security card. Not even a driver's license. This one took himself seriously, Bolan thought. He'd gone into the field as a nameless soldier who could give up nothing if he was captured or killed.

Though there was no immediately useful ID in the wallet, there was a picture that might help them in the future.

It was a girlfriend. Or a sister. Maybe even a wife. She looked to be in her midthirties, and wore a pleasing smile and a bewitching gaze, almost as if she were sharing a secret with the person who had taken the photo. Whoever the woman was, she was obviously someone who'd known the more human side of the Cohort.

The Executioner moved to his right, firing the

Skorpion every now and then to make it seem as if the Cohort were pursuing the intruder through the woods. He rammed home the fresh magazine as he neared the brush-covered ridge where the next Cohort was dug in at the top of the *V*.

"Where is he?" the other man shouted as Bolan approached him through thick dense cover.

"Right here," Bolan said.

He emerged from the forest and triggered the Skorpion as the Cohort turned, fully expecting to see his friend but realizing at the last possible second that there was something wrong with the voice.

Three rounds caught the man in the chest, and he crumpled to the ground.

Now only one Cohort remained.

Bolan waited a couple of minutes before he headed for the last outpost.

The last Cohort's voice pierced the quiet as he called out to the recently departed gunmen for a situation check.

Situation dead, Bolan thought.

The Cohort called out a few more times before he fell silent, perhaps realizing that there would be no more answers to his call and all he was doing was giving away his position.

When Bolan estimated he was within forty yards of the Cohort, he crouched, held the Skorpion overhead and fired a sustained burst at the surviving hardman. Then he threw the machine pistol so it pinwheeled through the air and came down heavily on the ground. It thumped end over end, like rapid footfalls.

The sound provoked the Cohort to burn off a full

clip in the direction of the thrown machine pistol. He rapidly changed magazines and fired again, shooting at shadows.

The man was on the move and firing a lot of shots, Bolan thought, but he wasn't taking much aim.

The next burst changed the soldier's mind. A blizzard of metal slugs peeled off jagged patches of bark from the strip of evergreens off to his left.

Maybe the guy figured out Bolan's position after all. But then the gunner fired several bursts into the woods nowhere near the Executioner.

The machine pistol clicked empty.

By then the soldier was much closer. Close enough to hear thrashing and fumbling, then the sound of a fresh clip being rammed home. Then the process started over again—bursts of 7.65 mm rounds cut a choppy path through the woods as the Cohort hosed the dense undergrowth with lead rain.

This man had the same philosophy as the others. Throw as much lead in the air as possible and hope to take out the other guy with the sheer quantity of bullets. There was also a psychological effect at play here. The gunner was hoping to unhinge his opponent with a steady barrage of fire, each chattering burst an echo of death in the air.

But that only worked on civilians, not on pros who were used to the sound of war and knew its orchestrations more than most Cohorts ever could.

Another full-auto burst chattered through the forest, thrashing into distant trees and kicking up clods of dirt. Unfortunately for the Cohort, he was still firing into an area that Bolan had left behind. The Executioner had used the sound of gunfire to cover his approach as he moved even closer on the right flank.

Yellow spears of flame from another burst gave the gunman away. He was partially hidden behind the clawlike roots of a tree trunk that had been ripped out of the ground. The towering black walnut tree had fallen across a narrow trail in the woods where it lay like a giant rotting bar about four feet off the ground.

Though the roots covered him like a protective hand, the Cohort's face moved in and out of sight. Every ten seconds or so he peered through the thorny cover that enveloped the roots as he tried to gauge the damage he'd done. He was unable to stay still during those moments between burning off full clips, hoping that somehow he'd sent his adversary to join his late comrades.

Bolan was close enough now to get a good look at the Cohort's face. The man was in his late thirties or early forties and had short black hair and a weathered face. It was the face of a man who'd been in combat before.

The guy was extremely sturdy. Thick neck, muscular shoulders. Out on the street he would look like just another aging athlete carrying a lot of weight. But here and now he had the unmistakable look of a man who would do anything he could to survive.

Bolan watched him.

How many more magazines could he be carrying? The man had probably been given enough ordnance to last for a sustained engagement, but was squandering it in a short ten minutes.

The Cohort popped up again, like a woodchuck scanning the area for predators.

A single shot from the Beretta would do the job, Bolan thought. Or at most a 3-round burst would take care of him. But the soldier figured he had a good chance to take this guy alive.

As a prisoner, perhaps even a prisoner of war in his own distorted view, the Cohort could provide valuable information. As a casualty, he was just one less gunman in an army that was almost impossible to find.

Another burst erupted from the fissured shield of roots. A wind-driven branch, a breeze rustling through leaves, had led him to believe that something was out there in front, something coming for him. The man rummaged in his pack and grabbed at the pockets of his combat vest, then swore. He was out of ammo. Unless he had a backup weapon.

Bolan raced forward.

The sudden rush through the leaves drew the Cohort's attention. He snapped his head toward Bolan, saw the hard look in his eyes, the Beretta 93-R in his hands.

He let the Skorpion drop from his fingers. Even before it thudded into the ground his right hand moved in a blur in front of his face, ready to fend off his attacker.

By then Bolan was already airborne.

The Executioner's feet pistoned through the air in a circular motion, his left foot touching briefly on the tree stump, his right foot lashing out at an almost imperceptible speed. His heel powered through the Cohort's blocking hand and caught him squarely in the jaw. The impact clacked his teeth together and nearly lifted him off the ground.

As he soared past the falling Cohort, Bolan caught a split-second glimpse of the forest floor, just enough to position his feet for a balanced landing. As soon as he touched down, he pivoted to his left and swung his arm behind him in a circular blocking motion.

There was nothing to hit but air.

The Cohort hadn't risen.

Instead he dug his heels into the ground and somehow spun in a furious crabwalk that ended up with his hands right at Bolan's feet. One hand grabbed the soldier's ankle and twisted it hard. At the same time the other hand clamped down on the front of his knee so that his leg was as straight as a wooden post. With a sudden force that lifted him off the ground like a springboard, Bolan found himself flying backward in the air.

In the split second before he landed on his back, Bolan saw the thick-set Cohort charging him, ready to pin him for good. There wasn't enough time for Bolan to bring the Beretta 93-R into play to deal with him.

The Executioner let the Beretta fall from his fingertips as he slammed down hard on his back and raised his knee just as the stocky hardman dived onto him.

The knee strike caught him square in the chest, jolting him long enough for Bolan to clap his hands against the Cohort's ears. The double palm strike further dazed the heavyset man, and while his ears were still ringing, Bolan twisted savagely. It would either break the man's neck or flip him onto the ground.

The man flipped over and landed on his stomach. He groaned loudly and seemed a second away from unconsciousness. But then the man shook his head and pushed up off the ground into a kneeling position.

He was ready to spring up for another attack until he saw the Beretta aiming at his broad forehead.

"Stay right there," Bolan ordered.

"I guess I will," the man said. He didn't seem to be out of breath. And now that he'd had a taste of hand-to-hand combat, he seemed stronger than before. A regular Hercules syndrome, Bolan thought, as if the guy could touch the earth and draw strength from it. Whatever the source of his amazing recovery ability, he was glad he didn't have to go another round against him.

The Cohort had other ideas, though. Bolan could see from his eyes that the man's adrenaline was pumping, and he was calculating his odds. It was a feral look that Bolan had seen in several other prisoners who'd come to the end of their run. He was looking for another chance to move against his captor.

Bolan walked behind him. "Hands behind your back, face on the ground."

The Cohort tensed his body, signaling that he was going to make his move.

The Executioner's right heel shot out and thumped him in the middle of the back. The kick toppled the Cohort onto his face. He put his hands behind his back, formed into fists that were side by side.

"Cross your wrists," Bolan said.

The man did so immediately.

"Now that you're listening," the soldier said, "pay close attention to me. If you make the slightest, I mean the absolute slightest, move against me, it will be your last. Are we clear on that?"

"Clear," the man growled, his face muffled by the earth.

The Executioner crouched beside him and planted a knee in the man's back. Then he pressed the barrel of the Beretta 93-R into the guy's neck and dug it into the base of his skull as if he were about to core an apple. While the Cohort was temporarily frozen, Bolan looped nylon cuffs around his hands, then backed away and let the man sit up.

"Any other Cohorts out there?" Bolan asked.

"That depends."

"On what?" Bolan asked.

"On whether you killed the men who were with me."

"They're both down for good. They gave me no choice."

"That's it, then," the Cohort said. "There were just the three of us."

"You three got names?"

The man looked at Bolan, wondering how much room he had to maneuver. "That's hard to say. Until I know what it'll buy me."

"It might buy enough time to convince me you're worth keeping alive," the Executioner replied. "Otherwise I'll just have to see what we got from the other Cohorts who've been rounded up."

"You wouldn't just kill me out here—"

"Yeah, I would. Considering what the Cohorts have done, I'd do it in a second."

"Do what you got to do, then," the Cohort said. He was obviously still unsure of what kind of soldier he was dealing with. The kind who played by the rules or the kind who won the war.

Bolan nodded.

He slipped a small transceiver from his pocket and radioed Kitchener. The helicopter was halfway up the mountain, and its steady drone was getting louder.

"This is Striker. On Summit Six." He flicked a button so the Cohort could hear Captain Kitchener's voice from the small speaker.

"Go ahead, Striker."

"I have two down and I'm closing in on a third."

"Say again."

"Two down," Bolan repeated. "I'm closing in on the third. He's still on the loose."

The Cohort went rigid.

"Do you need assistance?"

"Not yet. Stay clear of the area. No more flyovers until I give you the word. And tell the marshals to hang back. I don't want them to risk getting hit by friendly fire. As long as I'm here by myself—" he paused and looked down at the Cohort "—I figure I'll be able to drop him."

"Roger that, Striker.'

"Figure on ten minutes to take this tango out," Bolan said. "Then you can come in and pick up the pieces."

The soldier signed off, then pushed down the antenna and dropped the transceiver in his vest pocket.

"It's up to you," Bolan said. "I got all the time in the world. You got ten minutes to decide whether you fly out of here in a body bag or sitting in the back seat."

"Hey man," the Cohort said. "Book me on that flight. I just had to see what was on the table."

"Give me some names," Bolan demanded.

"Sure," the Cohort said. "The young guy's name as Waterman. Older guy was Davis."

"And you?"

"Duke Holland."

"Is that a real name?" Bolan asked.

"As real as I'm sitting here. As far as the other names go, I got no way of telling. People in this crowd go by a lot of different names."

"Keep talking," the Executioner said. "I want as many names as you can give me. Start with the guy who runs the operation."

"I can give you the name I knew him by," Holland said. "But it won't be the real thing. He uses lots of cover names. Always has."

"Since when?"

"Since he ran a crew of mercs in Costa Rica. I did a few things for his outfit back then. Usually it was through a couple of cutouts. Later on he got in touch with me for some of the early Cohort operations. Ever since then, he shows up now and then and off we go."

"What name does he use?"

"Marshal," Holland replied.

Bolan thought back to the names of the Cohort leadership, the ones who were killed in the Vermont raid that started all of this. Provost, he thought. The guy's name was Provost. And the son who carried it on was Marshal. "Provost Marshal," he said.

"I don't know about the Provost angle. Just the Marshal. And that was just one of several the guy used."

"How do you know?"

"Different guys in different cells knew him under

a different name. No one knows what his real name is or where he operates from. Guy's a real nut about security."

"Let me get this straight," Bolan said. "You know what he looks like, but you don't know his real name. Or where he operates from."

"Right," Holland said.

"The way I see it, there's not much use in bringing you in."

"Hey, man," the Cohort protested. "Maybe I can't give *him* to you. Not directly anyway. But I can give you Chandler."

"Go ahead," Bolan said.

Holland saw the look of interest that flashed on Bolan's face and knew he had a card to play.

"No offense," Holland said, looking up at the Executioner, "but all I know about you is that you killed two men. One of them was a friend of mine. The other could have been. In time. If he'd had the chance to grow a bit older and get a bit smarter."

"He threw away his chance," Bolan said. "Don't you do the same."

"After that little stunt with the chopper—holding them off until you give them the go-ahead—what guarantee do I have that I'll get out of this alive even if I give you the names you need?"

"How do you want to play it?" Bolan asked.

"Take me somewhere where there are others around. Someone who can see that I was still alive when I came in."

"Deal," Bolan said. It wouldn't make much difference in the long run. The guy was ready to give up intel. Might as well have him do it where others could sit in. "Just so we're clear about this. If we bring you in and you suddenly decide to clam up, we're both going to take a flight back here so you can join your buddies."

"Look," Holland said, "I want to give Chandler up. He's got it coming. If I can do anything else to make this deal work for everybody, I will. Once we're out of here."

Bolan nodded.

He radioed Kitchener again. "I'm ready to come out," Bolan said. "Get in touch with the head Fed and let him know we're bringing an extra passenger with us. Guy's got a lot of things on his mind that he's just dying to share."

CHAPTER THIRTEEN

Washington, D.C.

Duke Holland wasn't the most welcome visitor to
ever set foot inside SIOC headquarters, considering
that he was a member of an organization devoted to
the destruction of the United States government. Its
primary target was the FBI, and now here he sat in
the midst of their most advanced intelligence-
gathering center.

Holland sat at one end of a long conference table,
aware that he was being studied by the other members
at the table as if he were some kind of creature who'd
been captured from the wilds and put on exhibition.

"I'm telling you the truth," Holland said. "Yes, I
was a Cohort. But no, I wasn't a follower."

"Yet you traveled with them and carried out their
orders," Bolan pointed out.

"Yes. But as I told you before, it wasn't as cut-
and-dried as all that."

Bolan sat directly to Holland's left, the closest man
to the defector. Initially it had been part of the security precautions. If Holland made a move against anyone, Bolan was there to stop him. But there was little

likelihood of that happening anymore. Not only were Holland's legs shackled to the base of the chair, restricting the powerful man's movements, but also the ex-revolutionary was no longer considered a serious threat to anyone in the room.

Holland had clearly thrown in his lot with the people dedicated to crushing the reborn Cohort movement and was now bargaining for the best deal he could get. That meant he was trading every bit of information he had at his disposal. On the slim chance Holland had any last-second impulse to became a martyr for the group, there was always a special FBI security detachment nearby. It was the same detachment that brought him to and from the clandestine apartment house on E Street where he was kept under wraps.

"Tell us again," Bolan said.

Holland looked from face to face. At the far end of the table sat Hal Brognola, who had spent the most time with him since his capture, first in the regional state police barracks in Saranac Lake and then here in the SIOC complex. Brognola listened repeatedly to his story and picked it apart until he knew it almost as well as Holland did. To his right sat Doreen McKenna, who made more connections between the myriad details of Cohort operations than he could possibly conceive.

These three were his most constant audience. From time to time Holland would meet with a forensic artist who would make one more pass at re-creating the image of the Cohort chieftain that Holland knew by the name of Marshal. And there would also be marshals looking for details of specific operations or com-

puter detectives who would suddenly burst into the
conference room and blister him with questions about
addresses, phone numbers, cars he drove on operations, airlines he flew on and any companies that provided services to the Cohorts.

Duke Holland was a six-foot piece of data, and he
was being analyzed by the best minds in the business.

"Okay, from the top," Holland said. "The Cohorts
were just a group I occasionally worked for. That was
in the beginning when they were still small. As time
went on, the group made more and more demands of
me. I wasn't happy about it, but in deference to my
health, I always went along with them."

Holland went over a summary of all of the Cohort
operations he went on, and then moved on to the subject that initially interested them the most. Nick Chandler, the man who gave him his marching orders.

"This is where we have a problem," Brognola
said. "Chandler was your main contact. Chandler led
most of the operations. You said you could deliver
him, but so far nothing's panned out."

"I know," Holland said. "I know. But I swear the
information I gave you was one hundred percent
true."

He went over it again, how he never really trusted
Chandler from the beginning, how he sensed that the
man would abandon them or liquidate them without
giving it a second thought. That was why he'd followed Chandler after going with him on a Cohort
operation. He'd managed to trace him to a residence
in Flagstaff, Arizona.

"Why'd you track him down?" Brognola asked.

"Like I said," Holland replied. "I always figured

that one day he was going to come after me. And if that ever happened, I wanted to know where he lived...so I could go after him first.''

"But he's not living there anymore," Brognola said. "If he ever did."

The SIOC teams had immediately gone into action upon learning that Chandler had rented a house in Flagstaff.

Several plainclothes units descended on the northern Arizona city, but Chandler was nowhere to be found. A quick canvas of the neighborhood turned up the fact that Chandler had been seen on and off during the past few months, but no one was sure of exactly when he'd last stayed at the house.

SIOC still maintained a strong presence in the area just in case Chandler returned. In the meantime they were gathering every bit of intelligence they could about the man who'd stayed at the Flagstaff safehouse. So far there wasn't much to know. Chandler paid for everything in cash, and he used a pseudonym for all of his activities. Like many of his ilk, he chose a patriotic cover name. Revere. But unlike his namesake, he wasn't warning anyone about the enemy. He was the enemy.

As far as anyone knew, Chandler seldom had visitors. The landlord believed that he was in sales or worked as some kind of travel consultant because he traveled around the country a lot. Other than a brief meeting with Chandler when he first made arrangements to move in, the landlord had rarely spoken with him. He considered him a model tenant who always paid his bills well in advance.

"Let's get back to our main problem," Bolan said

to the Cohort defector, "which is you. You promised us Chandler, but you didn't deliver him. You've got nothing else that really helps us. That puts you on a par with all the other low-level Cohorts who were caught in Barrows Lake. And that means you won't get a much better deal than they will."

"What do you want from me?" Holland asked.

"Something we can use," Bolan said. "Something that will make it worth bringing you in alive."

Holland glanced at the man who'd captured him in the woods. Though he now looked as official as the rest of the suits in the SIOC complex, there was still something about him that made Holland wary.

In the battle zone Holland had heard the man referred to as Striker. Here in the high-tech boardroom, the same man was referred to as Belasko. But no matter what name the man went by, Holland thought, he didn't suffer fools gladly. Or informants. From his near death experience at Striker's hand, Holland had the distinct impression that the guy might actually follow through on his promise to bring him back to the Adirondack hillside to join his slain Cohorts.

To avoid that visit to cemetery hill, Holland once again became a human encyclopedia, searching his mind for any nugget of information he could offer them. The more he went over the terrain, the more memories he could dredge up.

"Okay," Holland said. "Here's something that might help. I know you guys are interested in the early days of the Cohorts, right? I mean, we've only talked about them for about twenty-four hours straight. But this...this is something that's just coming back to me. Something strange about some of the conversations I had with members of the old guard. It might give you a lead you're looking for.''

"Put it on the table and we'll see," Bolan said.

"It only happened on some of the Cohort operations I went on," Holland said. "Now and then there would be some original members around. Riding herd on everybody, keep them from running scared."

"Veterans from the military wing," Bolan said.

"They were known as the Cohort shock troops," Holland stated. "I don't know how much real military training they had, but they were stone-cold killers who would do anything for the cause. They thought nothing of risking their lives or ours. Kind of like Chandler."

"Right," Bolan said. "So they had some tough crews, and you had some strange conversations with them. What about?"

"It's not so much what they were about, as what they sounded like," Holland said. "I know they were from the States, but a couple of them spoke with British accents—you know, like they'd spent a lot of time living over there trying to pass themselves off as locals.''

"Living underground in England." Bolan glanced at Brognola.

Holland nodded. "Right. They'd say things the way the Brits do, 'boot' instead of 'trunk,' small stuff like that. I got the impression they'd been hiding out there so long that it was natural for them."

"These shock troops were laying low in England and coming over to assist on operations?" Bolan asked.

"England mostly, maybe some in Italy or Germany," Holland said. "At least that was the impression I got. On the one hand these guys liked to be secretive, but on the other hand they wanted you to know they got some serious schooling abroad. Like they'd made the grade."

"And you saw these guys a lot?" Bolan asked.

"It was more frequent in the early days, back when the group always seemed to need money to look after its people. Like things were desperate back then."

"And now?"

"Now it's a going concern," Holland said. "Cohorts can fund two kinds of operations these days. The kind to get more money, or the kind to get revenge. And sometimes they try and combine the two, like that Manhattan thing that went down. But we don't see too many of the guys from the foreign wing any more."

"Why's that?" Bolan asked.

"Hard to say, exactly," Holland replied. "From a few things Chandler said—either he let it slip accidentally or he was giving me some inner-circle stuff to swell my head—I gathered the shock troops went back home long ago, wherever home is. But they'll be coming back soon enough. Our group was just testing the waters. After all the dust settled, the shock troops were supposed to come back in to handle the real attacks."

"A regular foreign legion," Bolan said.

"Yeah," Holland agreed. "But they'll be hooking up with their opposite numbers here. I got the feeling there's a whole other unit that we don't know about, one that hasn't taken the field yet."

"You may have something there," Bolan said. "Keep talking."

Duke Holland filled them in on the foreign connection until Brognola signaled a halt.

"Let's break it off here," he said. "We've got enough to go on for a while. In the meantime I want you to take another shot with forensics. See if you can come up with a better image of the Cohort Provost Marshal."

"I've already done that," Holland said.

"You can do it again. And you can keep on doing it until we can find a match." Brognola tapped a key on the speakerphone, then leaned toward the built-in mike. "Come on in," he said. "He's all yours."

Even before Brognola and Bolan left the room, it was in the process of transformation. A SIOC forensic artist came in and hooked a portable zip drive to the computer. Seconds later several images of a strong and aggressive face were displayed on the wall-length screen.

Each one of the images was a variation of the clandestine Cohort leader, based on input from Holland. The central image was the basic sketch of the Cohort. The images to the left and right were digitized versions that showed shadows, lines of age, mustaches, beards, long hair, short hair, no hair, sunglasses and prescription glasses. The images were morphed to show younger versions, current versions, and even versions of the face that were made to look a lot older. All the variations known to man and computer.

The artist jacked a light board into the computer, then grabbed the light pen that was attached by a thin cord.

The artist nodded at Holland. "All right," he said. "Let's get inspired."

The Cohort defector sighed, then went to work, trying to summon an even better image of the man he knew as Marshal.

Doreen McKenna came around to sit on the opposite side of the table, studying the images onscreen.

And standing just a couple of feet behind Holland was the SIOC security officer who'd come into the room a few steps behind the artist. Instead of glancing at the screen, he kept his eyes on the Cohort.

"WHAT DO YOU THINK?" Brognola asked as he sat behind his desk in the office adjacent to the conference room.

Bolan sat back against the couch with his arms folded in front of him and his long legs stretched out. "I think we're getting our money's worth from Holland," he said. "That bit about the British angle connects with the intel we're getting from Zizka. If Holland and the artist come up with a better mug shot for Marshal, we'll consider that a bonus."

Brognola nodded. He and Bolan had been playing the usual game with Holland. To make him work harder and not hold anything back, they convinced him that his information wasn't all that valuable or any different from the other intelligence that was rolling in. But Holland's intel was helping them round out the picture of the Cohort organization. A picture almost clear enough for them to plan their attack.

Bolan gestured toward the conference room they just left. "You giving him a deal?"

"Yeah," Brognola said. "Not exactly the one he wants. But under the circumstances it's enough to keep him happy and keep him talking."

The Executioner nodded. He never liked the deals they had to cut with men like Holland, but it was a simple equation. To get inside information, you had to deal with someone on the inside. In exchange for hard intelligence and full cooperation, the informer got shorter jail time or in some cases no time at all. Otherwise there was no incentive for them to offer up their brethren.

Holland wasn't the worst they'd dealt with. He was a hired gun, a mercenary who worked for whatever side paid him the most, but at least he had a code that he followed. Like the incident in Virginia. The widow of Agent Fleming corroborated Holland's account of events. While others in the Cohort crew wanted to silence her for good, Holland refused to let that happen. The man was willing to stand up for his principles, Bolan thought. A regular saint among sinners.

"Okay," Brognola said, shuffling through some of the papers and manila jackets that had recently accumulated on his desk. "Let's take another look at the foreign-legion angle."

Included in the mass of intelligence reports that had been provided from Jaromir Zizka were photo recon shots of a group of Cohort associates who'd taken up temporary residence in the southwest of England, near Glastonbury.

"Here's the latest intel that came in," Brognola said. "Take a look at some of these faces. I got a feeling you'll be seeing some of them up close real soon."

Bolan grabbed a handful of glossy sheets. Some of them were long-range shots of hard-faced men who were staying at an old English inn a short drive from Glastonbury. The men were mostly in their thirties and forties, and the photographs were obviously taken with a zoom lens. At the bottom of some of the photographs was a list of names. The top name was the subject's real name and the others were the known aliases the person adopted once he became a fugitive.

The first set of shots was totally candid and so were the faces of the men, who obviously hadn't gone to the Somerset countryside for rest and relaxation. It was a gathering of mercenaries, fugitives and hardmen who made up the foreign ranks of the Cohorts. Zizka had followed the chain from the Karlovy Vary monastery, both past and present, and uncovered the gathering of recent recruits along with some old-guard Cohorts that Zizka's monks had trained in the clandestine arts so long ago.

Apparently the Cohorts had maintained links with their comrades from other revolutionary groups who'd been driven underground when the police and intelligence agencies finally fought back with everything they had. Though the groups were forced to go underground, they never quite went away. Instead they became a subterranean species that thrived in a clandestine environment.

By providing logistics support such as weapons, documentation, safehouses and occasional outlays of cash, the Cohorts were able to buy considerable loyalty over the years. The surviving members of the Cohort organization set up a terrorist rat line, similar to the ODESSA group that helped SS fugitives adopt new identities after World War II so they could escape punishment for their war crimes.

In return for providing a safe haven and a network of support for terrorist fugitives, the Cohort organization demanded occasional services. The fugitives always complied. For one thing they were psychologically inclined to help achieve the Cohort aims. For another they realized that the Cohorts knew their real identities and could expose them at any time.

With Cohort help, the foreign connection had branched out from subversive guerrilla operations to armed criminal enterprises that now included kidnappings, armored-car robberies and the drug and weapons trafficking that plagued Europe. They could field a considerable number of hard-core soldiers for Cohort operations.

And now their next operation would be in America.

Bolan leafed through another set of photographs that showed the same group of Cohorts taken at a close range. There were several individual photos taken as they strolled along small village streets or stepped out of some of the local pubs. All of the village shots showed a different and less austere side to the men. They affected the easygoing "tourist" look of people who were on a holiday or tour. A good many of the faces showed the aftereffects of a few too many brews.

"It's good to see that Zizka hasn't lost his touch," Bolan said. "He's still got a capable network if he could come up with this kind of intel."

"Zizka pulled out all the stops on this one," Brognola agreed. "He's figuring he'll have favors owed to him for the next ten years. Along with covert help from our agencies, he'll be expecting a lot of overt financial assistance from Uncle Sam."

"Whatever it costs, it'll be worth it if we can finally put them away," Bolan said. He dropped the stack of photos back on Brognola's desk. "What's their cover story, now that they're all in one place?"

"Part of one of those magical mystery tours," Brognola said. "Guided tours to sacred sites all across Europe. Mostly castles, cathedrals, stone circles, grottos, monasteries. The last stop on the European tour is a circuit of southwestern England sites like Stonehenge and Glastonbury. A lot of standing stones, ruins and cairns. These are Druid, pagan and Arthurian sites that attract a lot of historians, real tourists and everyday pilgrims. And a lot of mysties."

"Mysties?" Bolan said.

"It's one of the terms that's used to describe them," Brognola explained. "It means mystically inclined. New Age types. True seekers. It's hard to keep track of the latest term or trends these days. But in general they're at the extreme spiritual end of the spectrum."

"And the Cohorts are masquerading as mysties?"

"That's part of their pattern," Brognola said. "Retreats. Monasteries. Sacred sites. All seem to be their safehouse of choice. It's like they're hiding in plain sight, selecting the last possible place where you'd expect to find them. It's also the perfect way to move a large group of people around without attracting too much attention. That's one of the angles Doreen's looking into right now."

"How many are in Glastonbury?" Bolan asked.

"The full count's not in yet," Brognola said.

"Some are still arriving in the village itself. Others are gathering at the inn."

"What do we know about the inn?"

"Enough to know it's a legitimate target," Brognola said. "The place they're staying at just happens to be a property owned by an outfit called TransCom Enterprises, which has some financial links to the same holding company that owned the Barrows Lake place. The holding company's turning out to be just as covert as the Cohorts. It was set up through the same offshore banks the cartels use to hide the real people behind them. But we're putting a lot of pressure on, and sooner or later we'll find someone willing to cooperate. Until then, we've got to stop the group before they make the next leg of the tour."

"Where's that?" Bolan asked.

"The sacred sites of the U.S.A."

"You mean like Las Vegas?"

"Close," Brognola said. "California. New Mexico. Arizona. The itinerary for the tour group isn't exactly fixed once they get here. It fits in well with the New Age philosophy. They'll be going wherever they're psychically drawn."

"Convenient for them," Bolan said.

"The plan is for them to wander around the country in search of enlightenment at retreats, spas, missions, caves, Native American monuments," Brognola stated. "Whatever strikes their fancy. But we're looking into the Arizona angle, just in case there's some connection to Chandler's Flagstaff digs."

"You've got enough people covering the Chandler end?"

"Enough to bring down a small army," Brognola said.

"What about the tour group? Do we let them come in?"

Brognola shrugged. "That involves a considerable amount of risk," he said. "And you'll be the one who decides if it's worth taking, Striker. If it's possible to let just a few come over so we can follow them to their destination, yeah, we'll try that. But if it means taking the chance of having them all come into the country and scatter for parts unknown, I think we're better off if you stop them before they start."

DOREEN MCKENNA STUDIED the two images of the man on-screen. The man who would be king—or at least chief Cohort. The computer artist had made some refinements to the original sketch that he created, based on Holland's latest pass at the Cohort he'd seen up close.

The images on the screen were light-years ahead of the old-fashioned police sketches. These sketches used a holographic stacking process that presented a three-dimensional image with accurate shading and skin tone.

The two versions of the man's face were nearly identical. One showed him with dark sunglasses that added an aura of menace to an already imposing face. The other image showed a man with piercing blue eyes that seemed to be looking right at her. The artist had practically captured a living man this time around.

"Who are you?" she said to the screen. "Who the hell are you?"

Her voice echoed in the cavernous SIOC conference room. She was alone at last, doing her best to psych out the face of the Cohort leader.

It was a strong, angular face. His hair was slicked back into a tight ponytail that made the skin on his forehead look taut. He almost looked like mob muscle. But there was something in the eyes, an amused quality like someone who knew something you didn't, someone who knew a secret and your life depended on finding out what it was.

Someone with a cause. An unholy cause, she thought.

The religious angle had a lot of promise. His connection to monastic and religious retreats indicated that he was someone with a mystical bent or at least someone who could mimic that personality type. On one hand he used it as a cover for his clandestine operations. On the other hand he saw himself as someone who was involved in a crusade. A warrior monk.

She went over the other things she knew about him.

Assuming that the current leader of the Cohorts was the same man who'd been staying at the house where the old leaders met their end, he was anywhere from thirty years old to forty. He'd been kept out of the system from an early age and though he'd been educated on the run, his parents schooled him with the same kind of commitment that they gave to their movement. By all accounts he was extremely intelligent, a quick study who could be charismatic or intimidating, depending on what the situation called for.

He was also someone with military experience. A mercenary or a Special Forces type. If he'd gone through the actual service, that meant he had at least one identity that satisfied government requirements. Good enough to pass more than a cursory check into his background.

There was also a psychological component at work here. Whoever he was, the Cohort leader had methodically plotted his rise from a very early age. He had the ability to discipline himself for the long haul and learn all the skills he needed to revive the underground movement. He either had delusions that let him think he actually could overthrow the government, or else he simply wanted to exact revenge on the entity that had destroyed his family. He'd been hit with overwhelming power when he was young and now he wanted to strike back with that same kind of power.

There was something else that McKenna knew about him that had to be added to the mix.

His right-hand man, Chandler, had some kind of connection to Flagstaff, Arizona. If it was a long-term address, and not just a crash house, it was reasonable to assume that Chandler was staying fairly close by so he could be available whenever the Cohort leader needed him.

She called up a map of the area on the screen. From Flagstaff it was a relatively short drive, probably two hours at the most, to the Nevada and California borders on the west, Utah to the north, or New Mexico to the east. Using Flagstaff as the epicenter, a computer search of all the retreats and spiritual centers within that circumference might turn up the location of the Cohort leader himself.

The only problem was that there were hundreds of those sites within that circle.

McKenna compiled an updated psychological and physical profile for the Cohort leader, added in the geographical fix, then with a push of a button, sent the data to the SIOC database team for another round of searches across the Justice Department's dedicated intelligence Intranet.

They would do the electronic search.

She and Belasko would search for him in the real world.

Sedona, Arizona

WINSTON GRAIL LOOKED at the faces of the latest batch of initiates who'd completed their first one-week stay and were now gathered in the small lecture hall for the meditation and the question-and-answer session.

A camera was set up just off to the side to tape the entire session. Bits and pieces of the session would end up on one of the promotional videotapes for the THEM experience. Grail looked from face to face, making eye contact with each one of them. Then he turned toward the camera and treated it exactly the same way, as if it were alive and listening to him, so it would appear as if he were looking right at the viewer.

"Remember why we are all here," he said to his small, intimate audience. "Every discipline you pursue can lead you closer to the truth, or it can lead you astray. The key to self-realization is knowing when to drop one path, and when to start another. That is the key we wish to hand to you.''

He lost himself in the rhythm of his words and savored the rapt expressions on the faces in the first few rows. The men and women had come here to find something missing in their lives and they had found it. So had he.

These days Grail needed the peace and tranquility of the sessions more than any of the guests. It was a question of balance. The raid at Barrows Lake not only depleted the ranks but indicated that the government was closing in on him much faster than he had predicted. He needed the overseas arm of the Cohorts. Though they were even now gathering in Glastonbury, he wouldn't feel at peace until they were here with him, ready to pick up the reins dropped by the regular troops. He needed the old-guard Cohorts to see him through.

There was another reason that Grail welcomed the brief moments of peace that came from these sessions. Chandler.

The man who had kept the Cohort dream alive was now dangerously close to becoming a liability. Two of the operations that Chandler led had ended in failure. And one of them resulted in the capture of several Cohorts who were no doubt providing the enemy with whatever limited intelligence they could.

On top of that, Chandler's face was all over the networks. Though he'd altered his appearance somewhat, it didn't help matters that he'd come back to the retreat. Instead of lying low, he was moving too freely around the complex. Sooner or later someone might recognize him.

As if he'd been summoned by Grail's thoughts, Chandler appeared in the back of the room.

He had the look of a haunted man, not the stalwart man who had shepherded them from the brink of extinction.

Grail stopped the question-and-answer session, guided the small group into meditation, then drifted toward the back of the hall. He nodded to Chandler, who silently followed him out of the room.

"What is it?"

"Nothing much," Chandler said. "I was just thinking of some things we should be doing."

"Maybe," Grail agreed. "And maybe you weren't thinking at all. It's not good for you to be seen like this."

"I took precautions," Chandler told him.

His precautions consisted largely of a change in hair color and clothes. But there was still the same atmosphere about him. It was the atmosphere of a man who brought danger wherever he went. And right now he was bringing danger into the heart of THEM.

"You're a wanted man," Grail pointed out.

"Yeah," Chandler said. "I have been for quite a while now. So?"

"So that means you're not wanted here. Not now, anyway. If anyone sees the news and then sees you, it'll be bad for business."

"You're getting too paranoid again," Chandler said.

"No, you're becoming too well known. Everywhere I look, I see your face on the screen. If I see it, *they* can see it, too." He gestured toward the hall he'd left. Everyone in the hall and everyone at the complex had plenty of time to see the news. When they weren't getting mystical input, they could still get their daily dose of media back in their rooms.

"That fits in with what I was thinking," Chandler said. "Instead of waiting around for the tour group to get here, I thought it would be a good idea if I took some of the troops and did some more recon—"

"No," Grail said.

"No? Just like that, no?"

Grail nodded. "Just like that. I can't have you roaming the country now. You're the link between the old and the new."

"Yeah," Chandler said.

"But I also need you to stay out of sight until the others get here," Grail stated. "You've been making yourself too visible. Instead of staying in your quarters, you're practically mingling with the guests."

"It's the waiting," Chandler said. "It's starting to get to me. I'm not cut out for all of this stillness and meditation. I've got to be out and about moving, setting up our next move—"

Grail shook his head. "What you've got to do is leave. Right now you're the only visible connection between us and the Cohorts. If anyone here recognizes you, it'll be all over."

"Then maybe *they* should leave."

"They will," Grail said. "They'll be gone by the time the tour group arrives. You can come back then."

"What'll I do in the meantime?"

"Do what you do best," Grail said. "Go underground."

CHAPTER FOURTEEN

Glastonbury, England

Doreen McKenna walked up the circular path that wound around Glastonbury Tor, the high green hill that provided a view of most of the fields and valleys of the west country in Somerset. She moved at a leisurely but steady pace that kept her ahead of the small groups of "pilgrims" who were stretched out on the path below her.

Bolan was several yards ahead of her, showing none of the effects of the steep climb that had many of the other "pilgrims" gasping for breath and stopping along the way now and then to gain the strength to keep going on.

Looming above them on top of the tor was the remnant of an old stone tower that jutted against the sky like a huge and ancient chessboard rook. There was a long gateway carved through the base of the tower that acted almost like a wind tunnel for the strong blasts of air that shrieked through it at the high altitude.

It was a fairly strenuous climb, but anyone in reasonable condition could make it without too much trouble. First there was the trek across the flat land that stretched from the narrow access road to the first slight hill. Once a person made it past the hill, the path veered toward the right and continued to rise until finally it came to the tor itself. Then it looped toward the peak at a gradual but constantly increasing angle.

The hill was just outside of the town of Glastonbury, and it had become as much of a draw as the town itself, one of the top landmarks maintained by the National Trust.

From a distance it seemed like a massive prehistoric hill fort that loomed five hundred feet above the surrounding area. It was so symmetrical in appearance that it was hard to imagine that it was a natural formation. Anyone making an ascent straight up the hill would be at a great disadvantage to any defender waiting on the crest.

Bolan reached the top of the terraced hill and stood there in the wind that snapped against his black windbreaker, waiting for her. He reached down a hand as she rounded the last sharp curve of the path and almost lifted her up to the level ground.

McKenna's red hair streamed wildly in the breeze that tugged at the hem of her light jacket. The wind had been blustery all along the trail, and she'd heard the keening sound it made as it rushed through the tower, but she didn't feel its full force until she reached the plateau of the tor.

The wind pushed them across the flat expanse, herding them closer to the tower. It felt as if it were alive, a giant hand sweeping them toward the site.

The effect of the wind suddenly died down when

they reached the side of the massive tor, a stone wind-
screen that momentarily protected them. As they
walked toward the opening, they saw a young couple
standing at the mouth of the tower. The couple were
holding on to the side of the gateway as the wind
buffeted against them and snapped their long hair
straight back.

An elderly couple in hiking clothes and boots sat
inside the gateway on a cold wooden bench, soaking
up the atmosphere and regaining their strength for the
walk back down to level ground. The man had a
gnarled walking stick that was weathered on the bottom and had obviously seen him across much of the
country.

On the edge of the hillside sat a youth in a leather
jacket and boots who was trying to light a cigarette,
ineffectively cupping his hand around his lighter
flame.

When the others cleared out, McKenna and Bolan
stood in the gateway long enough to feel the awesome
might of the high wind. It swooped down to the edge
of the plateau, then picked up speed and roared into
the tower gateway like the breath of some ancient
entity.

Then they walked toward the edge of the tor farthest from the tower.

From there they could look down on the surrounding fields and farm country that had once been an
inland sea, giving the site its legendary association
with Avalon. Supposedly the tor had once been the
island fortress where the king of Somerset held Guinevere captive for more than a year before Arthur came
to rescue her. And down in the town of Glastonbury

itself, in the sprawling ruins of Glastonbury Abbey, was the burial place of King Arthur and Guinevere. It was only one of several alleged burial sites. There were as many Arthurian graves spread across England as there were pieces of the One True Cross.

It was a place of myth and mystery and for a while, Doreen McKenna could almost forget the reason why they had come there. They'd been playing the tourist role to the hilt. First they'd visited Stonehenge on Salisbury Plain and made the circuit of the stones, listening to the canned narrative on the handsets provided to all of the visitors. After Stonehenge they took the short drive to Avebury and walked among the standing stones that spread out across the field and roads. It was more primitive and unfinished than Stonehenge, but a bit more immediate. The tall stones weren't cordoned off from the public and struck more of an ancient echo with anyone who walked in their shadows.

Finally they drove to Glastonbury itself, following in the footsteps of the Cohort tour group. That was the main reason they'd come to the tor.

"Here," Bolan said, handing her the binoculars. "Take a look." He pointed toward the west.

McKenna looked across the fields and the former inland sea known as the Levels, then out toward the farthest edges of the west country, where the wooded hills and the rolling moorlands stretched as far as the eye could see. Scattered among the hills were churches, farms and upscale inns that catered to the pilgrims.

On top of one of the hills was a long and broad structure that was more of a manor than an inn. It was made of local stone and had a honey color to the facade. There was one main building and a couple of smaller buildings. At one time it had been home to the landed gentry. Now it was the haven of the Co-horts.

That was the penultimate destination for the Cohort tour group, the last scheduled stop before they made the crossing to the United States so they could move on to their next sacred site. For some of them, Mc-Kenna thought, it would soon become the ultimate destination.

They lingered on top of the tor for a good half hour, scanning the surrounding country and withstanding the steady winds that roared across the steep hill. Part of the reason for staying was to soak up the ambience of the site. Part of it was to make sure that they hadn't been followed by anyone.

They studied the line of cars and campers, motor-cycles and old vans parked on both sides of the access road. The vehicles stretched all the way down the steep and winding road that cut through the forest before rolling down to the outskirts of the town.

There was no one there who seemed to be out of place. But then again, McKenna thought, neither she nor Belasko looked out of place. They appeared to be just a couple more tourists out of nearly a hundred others who were making the trek up the tor. If they were being followed by someone who was really good at his or her job, there was no way they could know.

Of course, they weren't the only ones looking for surveillance, she thought. Alexander Lux had been with them nearly every step of the way. Now that Lux was no longer the Summer Visitor in the Czech Republic, he was free to temporarily set up shop in the United Kingdom. He was Hal Brognola's main off-the-book logistics man. He'd handled liaison with Zizka's people, verified their intelligence, then set the itinerary for McKenna and Belasko. From the moment they landed at Heathrow Airport, the deep-cover operative had been shadowing them.

She'd first seen him standing at one of the currency-exchange kiosks inside the international airport, which was packed with passengers even though it was early in the morning. He stayed in the background of the mobbed airport, grabbed a coffee from a franchise shop, then nonchalantly left the terminal shortly after they did. He lingered at the taxi and shuttle-bus island while they picked up their car at the rental agency adjacent to the airport.

And then he followed them discreetly in his compact car as they drove into the English countryside, moving west from London.

And now Lux's car was down on the road, parked several spots behind theirs. At the moment he was performing one of the riskiest maneuvers of the day. He was buying his lunch from a mobile food vendor who had pulled up on the roadside to cater to the pilgrims.

McKenna and Bolan made the return trek to level ground and passed Lux, who was sitting by the side of the road, eating his lunch and drinking a soda. He barely looked up as they walked by.

They got into their car and drove toward town, aware that a short time later Lux would follow them.

They parked their car on the side street that ran

parallel to the fenced-in grounds of Glastonbury Abbey, which had a steady stream of visitors walking across the nearly forty acres of ruins. Many of them were long rectangular shells of ornate Gothic structures with floors of grass and crumbling stone window frames. Crypts, chapels and altars were exposed to the open air, giving them an unreal and hallowed aura.

It was late afternoon, and their appointment with the Cohorts was several hours away. To kill some time, they walked along the streets of Glastonbury, carrying out the tourist charade.

The streets were full of colorfully dressed latter-day pagans and Druids, staid academics and clergy, long-term New Agers with graying hair and bright eyes. In this section of town there seemed to be more locals than there were tourists, although from what they'd gathered, many of the tourists who'd come to the place felt as if they'd finally come home and so they quickly decided to become locals themselves.

They went past rows of alternative book shops and spiritual centers that offered everything from pagan rituals and tarot readings to secret mystery-school teachings.

The streets were a New Age arcade where the extraordinary had become the ordinary. Neo-hippy clothes stores flanked vegetarian restaurants. Hermetic healers had their metaphysicians offices right next to candle, crystal and aromatherapy shops.

After a light meal of exotically flavored eggplant, artichoke hearts and a glass of zero-sulfite wine at a main street restaurant, they retrieved their luggage from the rental car and headed around the corner to the rooms that Lux had rented for them under their married name.

To avoid spreading around the Belasko nom de guerre, especially since it had been recently used on the related operation in the Czech Republic, they were using another assumed name.

They'd checked into the room as Mr. and Mrs. Michael Braun. Each of them had a completely backstopped identity that was fully documented, stretching from their illusory days in grade school up to their recently obtained marriage license.

By now Bolan and McKenna had been together long enough that they were relaxed and comfortable with each other when they found themselves sharing a room. When they entered the suite of rooms that looked out on a row of Glastonbury shops, McKenna slipped off her jacket and draped it over the chair by the desk. It was a very natural and also a very calculated maneuver.

She stood in front of the mirrored dresser and looked back at him as he stretched his long frame on the bed, pushing aside the "loaded" suitcases that Lux had placed in their rental car back at the tor. He leaned back against the backboard and caught her reflected eyes in the mirror.

She continued disrobing, watching him watching her as his eyes were drawn to her smooth and taut skin.

"You know," she said, folding her blouse on the dresser, "we've got the license, so we might as well use it."

"I've been thinking along the same lines," he said. "I picked up on that."

"That's your job, isn't it?" he said. "Always supposed to know what the other guy's thinking."

"That's right," McKenna agreed. "In your case, it wasn't all that difficult."

Bolan grinned.

"So what are you thinking?"

"I'm thinking about one of the places we visited earlier," he said.

"Stonehenge?"

"No," he said. "Avebury. The standing stones we walked along. It took us nearly a half hour to make the circuit."

McKenna crossed her arms in front of her, once again drawing an appreciative gaze from him. "What about them?"

"Remember the legend that was associated with them?" he said. "The site was connected to fertility rites."

"Hard to forget a thing like that," she said.

"In light of that, we should probably take some serious precautions."

"I've got a talisman in my travel kit that will take care of that," she said.

"I've got a talisman or two of my own."

"Good," she said as she drifted toward the bed. "Let's see how well we know our rites."

Flagstaff, Arizona

CHANDLER DROVE slowly down the street. His mind was on the Sedona situation and the way that Grail had acted toward him.

Exile, he thought. He was being sent into exile like

someone who'd outgrown his usefulness. Or worse, someone who had become dangerous to those around him.

Was it possible? he wondered. He thought back to the operations he'd carried out for Grail, and he immediately thought how he could have done them better.

First there was the Etruscan hit. For that one he should have spent more time in picking out the team. More time drilling his colleagues in what their role was and limiting the actions they could take. That would have cut down on the last-minute chaos that descended upon everyone.

He could still remember seeing Rivers vanish in a hail of fire, and he could see the crazed look in the eyes of the two Cohorts who'd lost their discipline when they discovered so much loot at their fingertips.

They'd paid the price, but so had the Cohort organization. It had lost one of its long-term members, one of the men who'd been the soul of the organization along with Chandler.

And then there was the Barrows Lake incident. That was a much more costly fiasco. Instead of delivering a telling blow to the armed forces that were arrayed against the Cohorts, he had delivered his small army into their hands.

He remembered the flight out of there. The place had been surrounded. The grass was seeded with fresh bodies. They had been waiting for him, while all along he thought he was going to be the one to deliver the fatal surprise.

Men screaming, cars going up in flames, helicopters tracking them down like hawks swooping out of the sky. It, too, was an incident that could have been avoided. If only he'd held his ground and convinced Grail that it was too risky, that they were walking headlong into a trap. But he hadn't. He'd gone along and he'd taken too many good men with him.

Maybe he had outlived his time, he thought.

Chandler thought back to how it was in the early days of the Cohorts, and how he had felt toward the aging radicals who were constantly jockeying for leadership of the group. Aging radicals. At the time they were thirty years old, and to him that seemed like one step away from the retirement home. He remembered questioning their willingness to lay their lives on the line, to take the necessary risks to keep the Cohort cause alive.

Now, he wondered, what if he was one of those risks?

He was.

He felt it the moment he turned into his driveway and rode up the slight incline. He hadn't been paying enough attention to what was going on in the street. But now he noticed the neighbors that were out. Too many neighbors. Too many new neighbors.

As if some kind of inner clock had gone off, here they were lingering in their driveways, washing their cars or walking down the streets. The neighbor to his immediate right was standing just beyond the other side of the fence with a paintbrush in his hand.

Waving to him.

Though Chandler had never really made any effort at getting to know the neighbors, he'd seen them enough to say hello to. This man was someone he'd never seen before.

And in his rearview mirror he could see the man in front of his house across the street, the man who just happened to be walking up to his front door but made no sign of turning the key and going inside. Almost as if he were waiting for something to happen.

That something was Chandler. These weren't neighbors; they were infiltrators.

They knew.

Somehow they knew.

And if they didn't already have the entire block sealed off, he knew it would only be a matter of time. Maybe a few seconds more.

Chandler stomped on the brakes and hit the clutch as the car screeched to a halt. He yanked the gearshift into Reverse, rode the clutch, then roared back down the driveway.

The back end of the compact ran straight into a moving wall. A white reinforced wall of metal. The internal-security vehicle had rolled soundlessly to a stop behind him just as he'd started to pick up speed.

One moment the street had been clear, and the next there was a huge armored riot-control vehicle blocking his way. It was one of those special-purpose vehicles designed to look as innocent as a large modified van or a small bus. Instead of scaring the hell out of civilians it seemed like nothing more than a high-tech travel home, complete with a satellite dish and an array of antennae.

There was an armored crash bumper in the front, and the vehicle obviously had solid armor on the sides.

Chandler's car had barely dented it, although the crash squeezed the back end of the compact like an accordion. If he hadn't disabled the air bag, the impact would have triggered it and he would have been all wrapped up for them.

From his peripheral vision he saw that the street was filling with other vehicles. Christ, he thought, there was an army out there. There was no room for his car to get away, no way he could outrun them if he could make it to the road.

Footsteps sounded as the riot squad inside the security vehicle hit the street and pounded on the pavement.

Chandler shifted into first gear and jacked the car forward, hurtling once more up the driveway. As soon as he crested the driveway, he spun the steering wheel hard to the right, aiming straight for the neighbor who'd been painting his side of the fence.

The car smashed halfway through the wooden fence before it was impaled on the splintered slats.

And Chandler smashed into the windshield with his head. The glass cracked and formed a spiderweb halo around him. Blood spilled from his forehead down across his eyes. There was something cutting into his neck, a shard of glass that was still clinging deep into his throat. But he couldn't remove it now. Not when he had other things on his mind.

Chandler spilled out of the car and staggered across the yard.

He managed to draw his SIG-Sauer, but he knew he would never get to use it. Even if he could see.

The blood was cascading down his face, filling his eye sockets and painting the world a dark red. He swiped the back of his hand across his face and for a moment he could see what he was up against.

Along with the "painter" who had a Heckler & Koch submachine gun leveled at him, there were two other men drawing down at him with similar weapons.

"Drop it!" the painter shouted.

Chandler teetered back and forth, just a few moments away from unconsciousness.

"Drop it!"

"Get down, get down!"

The shouts came from every direction. He was surrounded, but the last victory was his. Even though he could no longer see them, he knew they would have no choice. He raised his gun to his side and was just about ready to fire when the first bullet slammed into the front of his skull.

Even as he was falling, he felt the other bullets thud into his body, opening up corridors through his flesh. But there was no pain. The first one had brought with it all of the pain in the world and poured it into his seething brain.

Chandler dropped to the ground, knowing that at least he had achieved victory.

He had prevented them from bringing him in alive and betraying the Cohorts any more than he already had.

He heard a few more words but couldn't really make them out. It was the language of the living, a language he no longer spoke.

England

THE ROAD BACK from Glastonbury was a bit of a blur to Norman Palmer. The pints had been flowing smoothly, the village girls had been pleasing to the eye and the rousing music from the slightly over-the-hill rock and folk minstrels had been a welcome change of pace from the peace and quiet of the old English inn he and the others were staying at.

The Olde Folks' Inn, as he thought of it. Currently it was home for several grizzled veterans of the underworld.

The crew that was assembling there had plenty of years on Palmer, and some of them were afflicted with some very strange beliefs. The old-line fanatics believed that the world was just ready and waiting for them to come marching in and lead them into chaos: revolution, subversion, the people's war.

All of those hoary old clichés he'd previously heard about on the news or in the history book had come back to life. The Cohorts at the inn were living, breathing proof that some of those ideas never died and went to their just rewards.

The Cohort dinosaurs were still fighting a war that was over long ago. Whether they knew it or not, victory had been declared and the Cohorts lost.

He was in no hurry to get back to the inn, growing tired of seeing the international who's who of terrorists like them and mercenaries like him. The tour group was growing larger every day.

Palmer had come along for only one reason. Money. He'd been part of a unit that had fallen under the control of the Cohorts, originally setting up the routes and protection for drug and weapon traffickers, occasionally carrying out some freelance hits.

It had been steady and profitable work, but now

that it was moving into the realm of open warfare, Palmer wasn't pleased.

Although he had plenty of experience in soldiering, both before and after his stint with the Special Air Service, Palmer was having second thoughts about throwing in his lot with the heavy mob gathering in Somerset. Moving against as yet unknown targets in the United States promised too much risk and too little payoff.

He was playing it smart, though. He'd kept his own counsel. He would make no fuss, no complaints and stick along for the ride. But once they got across the Atlantic, he'd vanish. For a man of his talents it should be a simple matter to get lost in a country that size.

As Palmer rounded another bend in the road that had been full of curves and close forests, he saw a pair of headlights in the darkness behind him.

The lights were coming up fast.

Lunatics, he thought. Some people were just born dangerous.

He sped up a bit, knowing that he was only a few miles from the inn and might not have to play demolition derby with some drunken road warrior or testosterone-fueled teenager.

The car continued to close.

Could it be a hit? he wondered.

Palmer doubted there could be any real danger. No one knew what the group was about yet. No one even knew they were there.

He decided not to speed up any more. He'd driven the road several times before and knew there were too many hairpin turns that couldn't be navigated at any greater speeds than his current rate. At least not in the sedate little sedan he was driving and not with his senses dulled by alcohol. If it was a hit, he wasn't going to do their work for them and kill himself.

Nor was he going to go out alone.

The boozy aura of contentment quickly faded as years of training took over. Palmer reached under the seat and removed the pistol that was lodged in the springs under the seat. The springs served as a perfect holster, almost as if the car had been designed for clandestine use.

Palmer looked in his mirror as the car behind him accelerated, riding in the slipstream and getting ready to pass.

He swore. Like many of the roads in this part of the country there was barely enough room for one car, let alone two.

Palmer drifted as far to the left of the road as he possibly could without losing control.

As the car pulled out into the passing lane on his right, Palmer slowed and lifted the automatic. He held it just at seat level, barrel pointing at the passenger door, ready to raise it a few inches and take out the man who was following him.

The woman in the passenger seat was smiling. She looked a bit tipsy and very attractive. Her eyes were inviting, making him think how the night might have turned out if only he'd met someone like her.

Past the woman he could see the driver, an older man. Some geezers have all the luck, he thought.

He grinned back at her and waved.

The car shot past him.

At the last possible instant it cut back in to the left

lane, but the driver cut in at too sharp an angle. There was a loud thump at the front end of Palmer's car, then the steering wheel no longer belonged to him.

It turned to the left, and a few moments later Norman Palmer was airborne. The car sailed off the road at the worst possible bend and plowed through the trees.

He held on to the wheel for dear life and managed to hold on to consciousness until the car came to a sudden and violent stop.

As the car crashed into a thick tree trunk, Palmer rocketed up from his seat and smashed his head against the roof. Then he was out cold.

It lasted only for a minute or two because he could hear the woman calling out to him, following the path his car had made into the woods.

Palmer grabbed the handle, pushed the car door open and started to step out onto the forest floor. It was moving under him much too fast, and the night sky was spinning. As the wave of dizziness overcame him, Palmer dropped back down on the seat.

He clasped the steering wheel to steady himself, then looked up at the woman who was standing just a few feet away from the car. Beside her was a man who had a concerned expression on his face.

"Are you okay?" the man said as he leaned into the car.

Palmer exhaled and shook off the dizziness. "Yes. I think so."

"That's a pity," the man said. The look of concern vanished, and a huge fist crashed into Palmer's head.

As Palmer fell back into the car, another fist caught him under the chin and propelled him toward the passenger window, where the back of his head smashed against the glass.

This time he went out for good.

PALMER WOKE UP in the middle of the forest. He was unable to move.

At first he thought it was a result of the accident, then he remembered the big man who'd leaned into the car and put his lights out. Gradually he realized his hands were bound behind him and he was roped to a tree in the middle of a forest. He looked around and tried to get his bearings, thinking that he was somewhere near the inn.

"He's coming around," the woman said.

He turned toward the sound of her voice and saw the big man who'd decked him. "Wakey, wakey," the man said.

Palmer groaned. Seeing the big man was bad enough. Seeing the guy next to him was worse.

The second guy was dressed in combat blacksuit from head to toe. A Beretta 93-R was holstered at his left armpit.

And the man was looking at Palmer as if he were something that didn't belong on earth.

"Name," the man in black demanded as he stepped forward and studied Palmer's bruised face.

"Palmer," he said.

The other man came in from the side, the man who'd already done considerable damage to Palmer's face and looked as though he might do some more. He leaned against the tree, flattening his large palm against the bark near his captive's neck. "Palmer?" the middle-aged man repeated. "Is that some kind of celebrity name? You're so famous in your line of work that you just need one name?''

Palmer knew the type. The larger and older one was the kind who would play games with him before he died. The other one would simply kill him. He turned toward the man in black, who seemed to be in charge.

"Norman Palmer," he said. "You can check it if you want.''

"We already have," the man in black said. "Good thing you gave us the right answer. Keep on doing that, and we might be able to work something out.''

Palmer thought back to the beginning of the night. If only he hadn't gone into town. If only he'd stayed home for a change. If he'd sped up instead of letting the car pass him and drive him off the road... But that was in the past now, and there was nothing he could do about it. The future, though, he thought, that was something that still hadn't been decided yet. Maybe he could extend it.

"What do you want to know?" he asked.

As soon as it was obvious that he was going to cooperate, the middle-aged hardman took his hand away and stepped back from the tree. The woman moved next to him, both of them deferring to the man in black.

"I want to know who's worth keeping alive," the man said. "That includes you and anyone else up at the inn.''

"I'll cooperate," Palmer said.

"I know. But that might not be enough. What I need is some hard information about your final destination. Where's the tour group headed for?''

"America," Palmer said.

"Whereabouts in America?"

"I'm not exactly sure."

The man nodded. "Then tell me someone who is sure."

"Leighton's the guy you want," Palmer said. "Hugh Leighton. He's running the operation, but he's keeping closemouthed about it. Everyone was supposed to go to the States, somewhere in the Southwest. It was going to happen in the next few days, as soon as the rest of the crew arrived here. Once they all get there, he'd give them their targets."

"You keep on saying 'they.' Does that mean you're no longer with them?"

Palmer shrugged. "For what it's worth, I planned on parting company once we got there. I don't expect you to believe that now."

The man in black shrugged. "Try me."

"It seems like it's going to be a one-way trip for a lot of people," Palmer said. "I'm not quite ready for that. I've got a lot to live for."

"We'll see."

The interrogation continued for a few more minutes with the man in black firing several questions at him, trying to catch him off guard to see if his story held up.

"All right," the man in black finally said. "We're going to take Leighton down and see if he's got the answers like you say."

Palmer nodded.

"Before we go, is there anything we should know about? Any special precautions they took?"

Palmer shook his head. "They didn't see the need.

Not yet. Who would attack a bunch of cream puffs contemplating their navels? We've been visiting chapels and listening to choirs and traipsing up and down sacred hills. We've been living out our cover as a Holy Rolling group so long that we almost started to believe it ourselves. People like that don't exactly seem too dangerous.''

"What about weapons?"

"There's some, yeah," Palmer said. "But it's not like they're out in the open. They're stashed throughout the rooms. Leighton wanted to keep a low profile in case anyone came looking around."

The man nodded. "Okay, one last thing."

"What?" Palmer asked.

"While you were out cold, we wired some plastic explosives to the tree. There's a strip right by your head. One by your back. And some at your legs." He fished out a remote-control unit from one of his vest pockets and held it up in front of him. "It's timed to go off within a half hour unless I come back and disarm it."

Palmer's eyes searched the other man.

"With that in mind, is there anything else I should know about what you told me?"

Palmer shook his head. "No. Everything I said is true."

"Well, then," the man said. "We'll see you in a half hour."

"Wait! What if you don't make it back?"

"Then I guess all of us will meet our fate tonight," Bolan said as he turned to walk away.

BOLAN SCANNED the inn on the hill as Lux drove past it one more time. There were three buildings in all.

One large building where Hugh Leighton and several others were staying. Two small buildings that hadn't quite filled up yet.

It would take a massive attack to deal with all of them. The sound and fury would wake the countryside, and word would quickly spread to London, then to the world at large. Not exactly the outcome they were looking for.

This was supposed to be a containment operation that would prevent the Cohorts from getting to their destination. At the same time they wanted to find out where that destination was, without alerting the crew back in the States.

Brognola and Lux had arranged with the London station to have a backup team of special operatives ready to come in if and when all hell broke loose. They also had a team of high-level State Department spooks camping out in London and preparing to deal with British Intelligence if they found out that a little covert warfare was going on in their backyard.

It could be a messy situation for a while, Bolan realized. But when the Brits realized they had a group of subversive shock troops bottled up in one location, they'd come around. With their legendary ability to keep national-security operations secret until well after the fact, there would be little fallout in the short run.

Eventually word of the incident might reach the British public. But by then the spin machine would be in place and the Somerset ''war'' would be attributed to the same underworld struggle that wiped out many of their counterparts in Karlovy Vary.

Not many tears would be shed if the battle got out of hand.

But if Bolan worked things right, they'd be able to go in and quietly take out the key personnel. That depended on whether they encountered any resistance when they paid their visit to Hugh Leighton.

"All right," Bolan said. "Let's do it."

Lux pulled onto the shoulder of the road and managed a tight three-point turn, then drove back toward the inn.

They proceeded up the inclined driveway at a slow and easy pace, as if it were Palmer returning from his usual pub tour. Just in case anyone happened to be looking outside, Lux was driving a model similar in color and shape to the one that Palmer was driving.

After deliberating on all of the possible approaches, this seemed like the one that gave them the best chance to get inside. Instead of attacking the place, they were going to walk right in.

Lux cruised the car to a stop at the edge of the driveway near the largest building of the three structures. They were parked just several steps from the front door.

The three occupants of the car exited the vehicle and headed toward the building.

The Executioner stopped just outside the door and exhaled softly as he called in any favors the god of war might owe him. If the door was locked, they would have to go in loud. If it was unlocked, they had a chance of getting in and out without starting World War III.

Bolan turned the latch and the door opened, swinging inward into a dark alcove.

He strode inside, with his companions close behind. Directly across from them was a staircase that led to the next floor at a steep angle. Off to the right was a sitting room with a high ceiling and an unlit fireplace. To their left was a small room with a piano, and beyond was a hallway that led to the kitchen.

Two Cohorts were in the sitting room, watching something on the television. The music room was empty, but voices could be heard coming out from the kitchen.

Bolan motioned Lux to take the sitting room and for McKenna to hit the stairs, then he headed for the kitchen.

The Executioner walked at a normal pace and made no effort to disguise his approach so they would think it was one of their own who was coming to join them. The moment he stepped into the kitchen, three Cohorts turned toward him, suspended in shock at the sight of the man in black.

Here in the flesh were all of the faces Bolan had seen on the surveillance shots Brognola had shown to him.

One of the Cohorts was opening a refrigerator and his eyes peered over the door at Bolan, while another Cohort sat at the table cutting a loaf of bread with a large bread knife. There were jars of jam and cold cuts on the table. He'd interrupted their bedtime snack.

The third man was leaning against a kitchen countertop with his arms folded in front of his chest. He wore a ribbed sweater, sleeves rolled to the elbows. Of the three men he was the only one wearing a side arm.

Bolan shot him first, drilling him with a single round from the suppressed Beretta 93-R. The man slid down against the counter, arms still folded, blood streaming from the gaping entry wound in his forehead.

The man at the table leaped to his feet just as Bolan swung the thick snout of the sound suppressor toward him. It caught him in the side of the head like a hammer. The man's eyes rolled, then he sat back down in his seat. The serrated bread knife fell from his hand and clattered onto the table.

Bolan pivoted toward the remaining Cohort, who was scrambling through a kitchen drawer, either for a knife or a much deadlier weapon. The Executioner didn't wait to find out. He fired two silenced rounds, one through the rib cage, one through the neck.

The man dropped to the floor.

The soldier sensed movement behind him and cocked his elbow back into the forehead of the groggy Cohort at the table. The man had been trying to get to his feet again. His head thumped onto the wood with a deadening sound.

Bolan studied him long enough to make sure the man was no longer an immediate threat. In case they couldn't manage to take Hugh Leighton alive, this man might be able to provide intel.

He made his way back to the front of the house.

Lux backed out of the sitting room, silenced automatic in his hand. The two Cohorts who'd been watching TV had been permanently signed off. One of them was slumped in his chair, while the other was sprawled on the floor with his hand tucked into his jacket, hand clutching the handle of his holstered weapon.

THE DEAD MAN had taken her weapon from her.

McKenna had been reconning a long hallway with nooks and crannies and side corridors, searching room to room. She'd opened a door and peered inside a darkened room only to see a man sitting upright on the bed as if she'd startled him from sleep. A slice of moonlight poured through the window and illuminated his surprised face.

He immediately jumped from the bed to confront her, landing on his bare feet with a loud smack on the floor. He hesitated for a split second, glancing at the desk where his weapon lay, then looking back at her and the Heckler & Koch subgun in her hand, which loomed larger than life in front of him.

With the integral H&K sound suppressor tracking him, he realized he'd never make it to the desk in time. Instead he spun suddenly and made a grab for her weapon.

She fired one shot that doubled him over, but not before his arms flailed down on her shoulders and curled around her arm. As he fell to the floor with a thud, he took the weapon with him.

McKenna crouched to reach for the silenced pistol when she heard footsteps behind her. She whirled into a dark shadow and found herself pinned in a headlock from a man with steel-hard grip.

Her captor pressed a cold metal gun barrel into the back of her skull. "Who are you?" he demanded.

When she stayed silent, he pulled back on her hair,

tilting her face toward his as he spit out the question again. "Who are you? What have you done to him?"

"Nothing," she said. "I came back with him from the pub... We were..." She pointed toward the barrel of her Heckler & Koch, which protruded from beneath the slain Cohort. "Someone came in with that gun," she explained. "I don't know why, and then he started shooting."

The man's grip on her hair tightened, holding her still as he stepped closer to look at the corpse.

She kept on talking, feigning innocence and confusion, just saying anything at all to distract him while her hand slid under the lining of her jacket. At the same time her fingers tugged on the end of the tribladed knife pick sheathed in beneath the jacket lapel.

McKenna turned her head toward the man, giving her just enough slack to perform the maneuver. In one fluid move she pushed his gun hand away and drove the pick up under his rib cage and into his heart.

His head jerked up in fatal surprise. His teeth clenched from the pain, then he crumpled to the floor next to his slain comrade.

She recovered the Heckler & Koch suppressed machine pistol and stepped into the hall, taking deep breaths to shake off the effects of her brush with death.

Lux and Bolan quietly approached down the hallway. They took in her condition, then looked into the room and noted the dead Cohorts. Then they continued down the hall where the corridor angled in an L shape toward the last wing of the house.

McKenna followed them around the corridor and

stood in the middle of the hallway with the H&K pointed at the middle of the door.

Bolan nodded to Lux, who lashed out with his left leg with tremendous speed. The impact of the kick smashed the doorknob and lock plate free from the splintered wood. As the door shuddered inward, the Executioner charged through the opening.

The abrupt entry roused Hugh Leighton from the four-poster where he'd been sleeping. He stared at the intruder with heavy sleep-fogged eyes.

"What is this?" he said.

"This is where you get off," Bolan growled. "You can leave the tour and cooperate with us—" he nodded toward the doorway "—or you can rest in peace with your fellow Cohorts."

CHAPTER FIFTEEN

Washington, D.C.

It was shortly past 7:00 p.m. and Hal Brognola was still in his office when the call came in from Bolan.

"We're in the main house," the soldier said over the secure line, "and we're getting cooperation from the leader of the group."

"Who is...?" Brognola asked.

"Leighton," Bolan said. "Just as you figured it would be."

The big Fed nodded. Of all the known Cohorts identified from the Glastonbury recon photos, he'd seemed to be the one most capable of running the team. Fortunately he also turned out to be a realist. "What about the rest of his command?"

"Most of them have departed the house for good," Bolan said. "The rest of them have been rounded up in the other two buildings connected to the inn. Right now they're getting acquainted with their new land-lords—the group you and Lux arranged to have on standby. They'll be keeping watch over them for the next few days to see if anyone else shows up."

"So far only our people are involved, right?"

"Right," Bolan replied. "We managed to keep things fairly low key for now. No shock waves. No loud explosions when we went in. As far as we can tell, no one in the area knows that anything out of the ordinary happened here. Eventually you'll have to do some patching up with British Intelligence when this thing gets out."

"It's already in the works," Brognola replied, savoring the good news. If the Glastonbury operation had blown up in their faces, there would have been no way to contain the fallout. Not only would his British counterparts have found out about the covert action, but the Cohort organization would also get wind of it. And that would have shut down the next phase of the operation. "When we hand over a band of terrorist fugitives that were hiding in their own backyard, the British government will be more than grateful. It's been a while since they had a major victory like this. I just thank God it went down quiet, Striker."

"Yeah," Bolan said. "While you're at it, you can thank someone else, too. One of the Cohort mercs cooperated with us just before the raid. His name is Norman Palmer. His background includes SAS and some South American merc work before he got hooked up with the Cohorts."

"When did he start cooperating?" Brognola asked.

Bolan chuckled. "Shortly after Lux knocked him out. Palmer gave us all the leads we needed to go in quiet. Seems like he was ready to book on out of the group as soon as they got to the States. The timing's kind of coincidental, but I believe the guy's story. He didn't like the way things were going and he wasn't going to follow them to the bitter end. If you need someone to verify what went on in the European branch, he's ready to fill in the blanks if you deal with him.''

"Got it," Brognola said. "Back to Leighton. Is he giving us anything we can use?''

"Yeah," Bolan said. "He gave us the destination of the tour group.''

"Which is?''

"Sedona, Arizona," Bolan said. "Pretty close to Flagstaff.''

"That tracks with the intel we're getting," Brognola said. "Did he say where in Sedona? That's a lot of ground to cover. You've only got the city, then you've got the canyons, the desert...."

"I've got no specifics on this end," Bolan said. "But this is how it was supposed to play out. Leighton and his Cohorts were going to check into their hotels and a couple of bed-and-breakfasts in Sedona. Then Chandler was going to make contact with Leighton—''

"Short of a séance," Brognola cut in, "there's no way that was going to happen.''

"What do you mean?''

Brognola told Bolan about Chandler's return visit to Flagstaff and how he went out in a suicidal showdown while Bolan was casing the Glastonbury group.

"So that leaves us at a dead end," Bolan told him.

"Not at all," Brognola said. "We got a hit on the latest SIOC database search. With the input from Doreen's latest profile, the Barrows Lake briefings and the trail from the holding company, we zeroed in on an interesting operation just outside of Sedona.''

"Sedona?" Bolan said. "Why all the questions if you already knew?"

"Every bit of intelligence helps, Striker. The more details we can piece together, the more we know what we're dealing with."

"So who's our man?" Bolan asked.

Brognola turned toward his computer screen. It had timed out and gone black since the last time he worked one of the keys. With a tap of the keyboard, the screen came alive again. He was looking at a split screen that showed two very similar images. The image on the right was the fleshed-in computer sketch of the shadowy Cohort leader known as Marshal. The image on the left was Winston Grail. They were one and the same.

"The name is Winston Grail," Brognola said. "Does that mean anything to you."

"No. Should it?"

"It will in time," Brognola said. "Doreen can probably fill you in a lot more until you get a full briefing. For now, you should know that Grail is the head of a New Age outfit called THEM, which stands for the Trans Human Evolution Movement. They run seminars and retreats at a high-tech holiday camp on some pricey real estate near the canyons."

"Retreats?" Bolan said. "That's an interesting connection."

"Sure is," Brognola agreed. "You can follow the same pattern from beginning to end. He's been masquerading behind the religious angle, figuring it was the last place we'd look. And he was right. Until now."

"Winston Grail," Bolan said. "Sounds a bit too much on the money to be real. A born holy man."

"Oh, it's real enough. He had it legally changed to Winston Grail about ten years ago. Before that his last name was Knowles. That happens to be a legit identity, at least at first glance. Eventually we'll find out how they adopted it. Chandler probably had a hand in it. Documentation was one of his specialties with the original Cohorts. Hold on a second..."

Brognola worked the keyboard and brought up the vital statistics on Winston Grail.

The man who was now a celebrated New Age figure had served time in the military, went into Special Forces, then worked the South and Central American mercenary circuit for a while. He'd served with distinction, although there had been rumors about some of his links with cartel traffickers.

It was shortly after seeing a lot of mercenary action that Winston Grail supposedly saw the light and went into the enlightenment business.

"What's the plan?" Bolan asked, after Brognola filled him in on Grail's background.

"The plan is simple," Brognola said. "You and Doreen are scheduled for a visit to the Sedona complex. We've already placed a few people there. It's business as usual for another week. Then the entire complex is reserved for the special tour group that was scheduled to come in."

"We don't have a week," Bolan said. "Not if he's expecting Chandler to check in any time soon. Or if word leaks out that we canceled the tour group."

"That's why we've arranged a special flight for you," Brognola said. He could sense the urgency in the other man's voice. Bolan was still in battle mode, still pumped up from the adrenaline that saw him through the Glastonbury hit. But he was an ocean away from the next target. "The flight's waiting for you at Heathrow. Get some sleep on the way over. You're going in as soon as you land. We're working on ways to clear out the guests. Then we'll go to work on the Cohorts."

Sedona, Arizona

SEDONA WAS ALMOST a mirror site to Glastonbury. Over the past few years it had become a New Age mecca, a resort town blossoming in the middle of a desert sanctuary.

Instead of ancient castles and monasteries dotting the landscape, there were majestic red rock formations that stretched across the horizon. The mix of desert and juniper forests and rivers and canyons made Sedona and the surrounding areas a paradise for true seekers and land developers alike. Resorts and New Age centers sprang up outside the town and along the streets themselves, sitting side by side with the more established businesses. Every spiritual or material need could be met in Sedona or a short distance out of town.

One of the newest and most successful of these enterprises was the THEM complex that was less than a half hour's drive away from Sedona. It was a blend of old Southwest architecture and space-age technology, highlighted by the prismlike glass-and-steel headquarters that looked down on the rest of the complex.

The Executioner and Doreen McKenna arrived there in the middle of the afternoon, parked their rental car in the large lot by the visitors' welcome center, then toured the areas of the complex that were open to the public. They audited some of the lectures, mingled with the guests and got a close look at their targets.

Brognola's first team of "New Age" operatives who infiltrated the site earlier had been able to identify many of the Cohorts among the security staff. A few others had been spotted near the headquarters building.

Although they knew the targets, it was still too risky to move against the Cohorts. That would come soon enough.

Even now several operatives from Brognola's SIOC task force were working on ways to discreetly separate the true seeker guests from the death-seeking Cohorts. The unit was composed of veteran U.S. Marshals who were well practiced at getting their charges out of the line of fire.

There was no way the SIOC task force was going to strike until the area had been cleared of civilians.

IT WAS EARLY EVENING, a time when the guests weren't so regimented and their absences wouldn't be so noticeable.

At times like this the guests were left on their own. They could either stroll around the grounds, linger in their rooms or drive off to see the sights in the desert or in the town of Sedona.

A few of them were lingering in the open-air terrace, sipping coffee or green tea, while the desert breeze stirred their hair or clothing.

Sitting at a large round table by herself was Linda Norris, an attractive and deeply tanned brunette with a statuesque figure. According to the intel gathered by Brognola's recon crew, she was a prominent feature writer on New Age subjects.

She was in the process of transferring handwritten notes into a laptop when she looked up and saw Bolan and McKenna approaching. They'd made it a point to introduce themselves to her earlier and gain her confidence.

"Hello again," Bolan said. "Mind if we join you?"

"Not at all," she said. She clicked the save button, neatly folded her stack of pages and closed the laptop lid. "I was planning on taking a break anyway."

"You picked a good time," Bolan said.

"What do you mean?"

"After you hear what we've got to say, you might want to take a much longer break."

The reporter's light flicked on in her eyes. It was a wary but intrigued gaze. She looked at McKenna, who kept a pleasantly neutral face, then back at Bolan. "Say it, then," she said.

"First let me tell you what we know about your work," Bolan said. "You've covered the New Age scene for years. Your articles are fair, sometimes skeptical, sometimes enthusiastic, but you've always told the truth as far as you knew it."

"You've read my work?"

"No," Bolan admitted, "but some of the people I work for have. And they'd be interested in having you

do the real story about what's going on here. When
it's over we can help you fill in the details.''

''What story's that?''

Bolan paused. ''This is your third stay here, which
means you either are really thirsty for the truth, or
you already think there's a bigger story going on
here.''

She shrugged noncommittally. ''The answer's
yes,'' she said, ''on both counts. I've been digging
into some things. But before we go any further, tell
me something about your people. Who do you work
for? Magazine chain? Newspaper?''

''I sometimes work for the government,'' he said.
''That's why I'm here. Let me tell you the real story
about Winston Grail....''

IT WAS QUIET, Burne Taggart thought. Too quiet. Although things normally slowed down after hours, he
was used to having guests drift up to the headquarters
building, hoping to get a look at the man who spent
most of his time in the tower of glass and steel. Just
like the Wizard of Oz, Taggart thought. They were
all looking for a few special words of wisdom to
make their lives whole.

But tonight there hadn't been a single guest for him
to turn away. Not even Linda Norris, the woman he'd
almost developed a bit of a liking for.

He went out into the moonlight and idly patrolled
the walkway in front of the headquarters, catching his
solitary reflection in the glass walls.

''YOU READY FOR THIS?'' Bolan asked.

McKenna nodded.

"Let's pay the man a visit," Bolan said. He removed the canvas carryall from the trunk. She slung her oversize purse over her shoulder.

As they walked up the gently inclined path toward the headquarters, they noticed the other figures walking around the grounds. They were moving in ones and twos. The figures were U.S. Marshals or FBI agents, camouflaged in casual clothes. They'd gradually replaced the guests who'd all proved cooperative after seeing the IDs and having a discreet conversation. When the choice came down to making a safe exit from an imminent war zone or sticking around and debating whether it was another case of the government intruding into their private lives, they all saw the light.

Several of the agents had been planting a variety of tactical jammers around the grounds and in the buildings they had access to. The low-power barrage jammers were designed for rapid and overwhelming deployment against communication networks. Once the hit started, there would be no communications between the isolated groups. The offensive electronic-warfare units would saturate the complex with white noise, multiple tone scrambling signals and randomly generated pulses.

Bolan looked out at the rolling slopes behind the main buildings of the complex, knowing that lines of sniper-observer teams were in position. And that was only the ground force. Another airborne squadron was ready to join the assault and seal off Winston Grail's escape.

Unless he'd been practicing up on his astral projection, Grail was about to come down to earth.

Hard.

"There's Taggart," Bolan said. "Get ready to smile."

As they neared the entrance to THEM headquarters, Bolan caught a good look at Burne Taggart, Winston Grail's right-hand man since the Central American days.

The guy's face looked as if it had once been a trophy hanging on a wall before it had been reattached to him. But it wasn't the face that looked so intimidating. It was the bulldog eyes of a guard dog protecting his master.

TAGGART STUDIED the red-haired woman. She was beautiful, but then so were many of the starry-eyed seekers who came here. Almost as if they were part of a certain species, he thought.

But the guy beside her, with his canvas carryall slung over his shoulder, was definitely not one of the typical true believers, Taggart thought. There was a certain look in his eyes that he had seen before. On hard guys. On muscle. On soldiers. Someone to be taken seriously.

An alarm went off inside Taggart, but it was a split second too late.

By then the man was within striking distance and the look in his eye left no doubt that he was the enemy.

Taggart reached under his jacket for the compact ASP automatic that was tucked into the belt holster in the small of his back. He'd made a split-second lethal calculation. If he'd gone against the guy hand-to-hand, he might have a chance. But the woman was a wild card, and the fact that she was with him made it clear she wasn't on a mystic quest. He knew that if he went for the gun, he probably wouldn't have time to bring it to bear on the man. But at least he could fire a shot and warn the others. He owed his life to Grail and he was willing to pay it back.

As the gun cleared the holster, Taggart raised his left hand in front of him to divert the other man's attack.

The palm-heel strike smashed into Taggart's wrist and drove his own forearm into his throat, but he managed to pull the trigger. The loud echo of the ASP gunshot rolled across the complex, alerting everyone in hearing distance that the Cohorts were under attack.

Taggart fell backward, choking from the strike to his neck, and landing on the ASP beneath him. He craned his back and managed to pull the gun out into the open.

THE EXECUTIONER STEPPED forward, slamming his left foot hard on Taggart's gun hand.

As the stocky Cohort scrambled beneath him and clawed for the weapon, Bolan snapped his right heel forward. It connected with the underside of his chin and pushed his head back. There was a loud crack and Taggart was gone from the earth.

Bolan dropped the carryall to the ground, then lifted out the short-barreled Ultimax 100 light machine gun. He slapped a 100-round drum magazine into the weapon, then headed toward the left of the entrance.

"It's locked," McKenna said, stepping away from

the door with the suppressed Heckler & Koch in hand. She moved to the right side of the door just as a stream of automatic fire ripped through the glass from inside the lobby.

Two Cohorts stood there, spraying the area with their subguns.

Bolan opened up with the Ultimax and sent a blizzard of rounds into the lobby. The Heckler & Koch chattered away from the right. One Cohort went down. The other one ran for the stairs, covered by another gunner who crouched on the landing and raked the shattered doorway with a burst of full-auto fire.

By now the complex had turned into a shooting gallery.

The sniper teams emerged from cover and dropped every Cohort in range. Some of them were trapped in the open, while others were running into the nearest building.

During the chaos the airborne squad came in, rotors drumming, engines whining as they headed for the rooftop of Winston Grail's headquarters where his personal helicopter sat on a helipad.

Bolan sprinted toward the right side of the headquarters building, looking up at the tall glass and seeing the reflections of the helicopter squadron making its approach. There was a Sikorsky troop transport, an armed Bell scout craft and an AH-1W Whiskey Cobra combat chopper. The Cobra was in the lead, its sand-and-gray color scheme blending in with the desert terrain behind it.

The Cobra pilot launched a TOW missile that streaked across the sky, small flares trailing behind it as it homed in on Winston Grail's executive helicopter. With a loud flash and roar, the executive aircraft went briefly airborne. The explosion separated the rotor blades and sent them spinning end over end across the rooftop.

Grail appeared on the roof just in time to see the wreckage of his chopper. Like the men with him, he carried a Skorpion machine pistol, his signature weapon for all of these years.

Bolan raised the barrel of the Ultimax and sent a full-auto burst scything across the rooftop.

A group of marshals took a position near him, firing a volley of shotgun and machine-gun rounds toward the roof and into the side of the building.

While the Sikorsky hovered above the far side of the roof, the Cobra made another pass and opened up with its M-197 20 mm cannon. The cannon fire punched holes in the roof and obliterated any gunmen who were foolish enough to be standing there.

Under cover of the cannon fire, a group of marshals in paramilitary blues fast rapeled from the Sikorsky onto the rooftop. They immediately advanced toward where Grail and his few surviving Cohorts waited for them.

Bolan saw Grail standing by the edge of the roof, Skorpion raised high, aiming at the pilot of the recon helicopter as it made another pass.

Unlike the last time the government troops came for him, Grail had no room to run, nor had he any desire to do so. Instead of throwing down his weapon and surrendering, he opened up on the helicopter.

Bolan hosed the sky with the Ultimax, burning off

the rest of the drum. Several of the rounds stitched into Grail's body and hurled him to the edge.

He went over, still clutching the Skorpion, carrying it with him to his death as he sailed toward the ground, arms stretched out in a dying swan dive.

Bolan hurried over to the side of the building and saw Grail's body crumpled on the ground, then he scanned the battlefield. Doreen McKenna had joined the marshals and the FBI units who were mopping up what was left of Grail's ground team.

The Trans Human Evolution Movement had come to an end.

Winston Grail had evolved into something that made the world a better place—a dead man.

Bolan took one last look and then walked away. The Cohort phoenix had burned for good this time.

STONY MAN® 48

Conflict Imperative

In order to end a long war with internal terrorist factions, Peru agrees to hand over part of her sovereign territory to a rebel coalition. The deal is brokered by a reformed IRA terrorist, who is up for a Nobel prize for his peacemaking efforts. But the man has his own agenda, and Bolan is taken prisoner!

Available in August 2000 at your favorite retail outlet.

Take
2 explosive books
plus a
mystery bonus
FREE

James Axler

OUTLANDERS®

HELL RISING

A fierce bid for power is raging throughout new empires of what was once the British Isles. The force of the apocalypse has released an ancient city, and within its vaults lies the power of total destruction. Kane must challenge the forces who would harness the weapon of the gods to wreak final destruction.

GOUT14